MW01135056

THE YOUNGER GIRL

A dark labyrinth of family betrayal

No day shall erase you from the memory of Time.

— **Virgil,** *The Aeneid*

THE YOUNGER GIRL

A dark labyrinth of family betrayal

Georgia Jeffries

MISSION POINT PRESS

Readers are encouraged to go to www.MissionPointPress.com to contact the author or to find information on how to buy this book in bulk at a discounted rate.

Published by Mission Point Press
2554 Chandler Rd.
Traverse City, MI 49696
(231) 421-9513
www.MissionPointPress.com

ISBN:
978-1-961302-60-0 (hardcover)
978-1-961302-61-7 (softcover)
Library of Congress Control Number: 2024908934

Printed in the United States of America

For

my family

past, present, & future

~

Contents

I   JOANNA   1

II   JOANNA AND OWEN   7

III   SEEDINGS   75

IV   QUEST   105

V   GROWING SEASON   143

VI   DÉJÀ VU   163

VII   HARVEST   203

VIII   REVELATION   221

~   FAMILY PHOTOS   266

~   OBITUARIES   268

~   FAMILY TREES   269

~   AUTHOR'S STATEMENT   272

~   ACKNOWLEDGMENTS   273

~   ABOUT THE AUTHOR   275

I

JOANNA

PROLOGUE

Miss Inland Empire
of 1975

The trouble with being a beauty queen is that nothing lasts forever.

How sweet it was to stand tall and untouchable in a circle of light, looking across the church of true believers praying for their favorite. The air pulsed with electricity as the country club ballroom settled into a silent hush. Then the master of ceremonies reached for the microphone ...

"Joanna Morse!"

A dozen scarlet roses fell into her arms as last year's winner transferred the tiara to a newly crowned head. Joanna adjusted the bouquet to make sure that the stiffness in her left shoulder did not betray any damage from the accident — all imperfections must be invisible tonight — then descended the long runway toward the end of the ramp where her proud father stood cheering, whistling, and applauding with the abandon of a twelve-year-old at the World Series. What the new queen would always remember, more than the dozen roses with no thorns and the rhinestone halo that anointed her long dark hair, was when the table flipped over. China and silver and crystal tumbled off blush-colored linen into a sea of green carpet. Nobody seemed to mind. The cheering man who knocked everything to kingdom come had simply boiled over in hot joy.

Her mother waved at the staff to clean up the debris and, when they failed to move fast enough, dove in herself to rescue the centerpiece of

3

carnations and baby's breath weeping water all over the tablecloth. The woman's heart, already taxed, pumped harder as she blew kisses to her only daughter, accepted congratulations from well-wishers, and barked at a busboy to remove the wine bottles straightaway.

Joanna forced a megawatt Miss America grin. If the smile were bright enough — and wasn't hers now officially the fairest of all? — no one would notice the crimson staining her cheeks. On this special occasion nobody seemed to care that Owen Morse pounded back one too many glasses of pink champagne (it matched the carnations in the centerpiece) and shouted his child's name above the applause. When the clock struck midnight, the orchestra sashayed into "You Light Up My Life" and Owen escorted his daughter to the dance floor for a spirited spin to the last song.

By one o'clock the queen and her parents were home and still celebrating their family's finest moment. Her mother decided to scramble a dozen eggs and fry up Oscar Mayer's best because everyone was too excited to sleep. While her father whistled a catchy tune and flipped the sizzling bacon strips, Joanna arranged her thornless roses in a crystal vase then took them into her bedroom to put in front of the bulletin board papered with clippings of earlier triumphs. The cheerleader caught mid-jump with her purple pompoms raised high; the high school valedictorian delivering her commencement speech; the Girls' League president holding a framed check for her college scholarship.

"Joanna," her mother called from the dining room where she was setting the table with twenty-five-year-old wedding silver plate used only on holidays, "bring me your grandmother's antique serving fork."

Approaching the credenza where Owen had already positioned his daughter's trophy in a place of honor, Joanna opened the cutlery drawer and reached for the fork's baroque handle. Cradled underneath and securely tucked between the gravy ladle and sugar tongs, lay the carving knife she knew so well.

On this night, please God, neither her mother nor her father would threaten to use the blade — Germany's finest stainless steel — to cut each other's throat. Mrs. Morse would not scoop the knife from its hiding place and warn her husband that she would stab him if he took one more drink. Nor would Mr. Morse promise her that he would kill her first and raise his fist to strike her down. Mrs. Morse would not scream, "Try it!" the blade inches from his face, years of pain balancing on the pointed tip of a weapon that on better days sliced bread and cut onions for the family meatloaf. On this night the war of epithets would not escalate, her father and mother each outdoing the other with one vicious insult after another …

You goddamned old hag no man will take you on a bet when I leave you're not a man can't hold a job can't support your family can't even keep it up shut up your daughter needs to know the truth shut up she doesn't have a man for a father shut up just an excuse for a man shut up a broken down drunken bastard who can't do anything right shut up shut up shut up!

Joanna was the audience bearing witness to their righteous words. The sole witness they allowed to see the depth of despair that pushed each to the breaking point.

Later, she would understand that her parents' violent battles had become the only way the couple could receive the other's touch. Intimacy by wounding was still intimacy and better than none at all …

But on this night in the sweet wee hours after Joanna's coronation, the knife stayed in the drawer. The daughter did not scream at her father nor hold her sobbing mother in her arms after the poor-excuse-for-a husband staggered down the hall to the back bedroom to sleep it off. Her parents had never shared the same bedroom. "Your father snores," her mother told her when she was a little girl, "and I like to read with the light on. We're different that way." No, on this night the family ate creamy eggs and crisp bacon on Owen's mother's prized Bavarian china and passed the apricot preserves to spread on toast with love.

Throughout her reign, when all the locals oohed and aahed about how being Miss Inland Empire would surely launch her to Bigger and Better Things, she let them nurse their New York dreams. The young queen had already been blessed with a clarity of vision that saw far beyond mere career ambitions. On that magical Coachella Valley night, when breezes banished the desert heat and her parents broke bread in peace, Joanna understood her true calling. Only she could save her family from themselves. Was she not her parents' miracle child?

In less than two years her mother would be gone, her father paralyzed with grief and Joanna, newly married and pregnant with twin daughters, left to put together the broken pieces. Nothing lasts forever.

II

JOANNA
AND
OWEN

1

Independence Day 1996

Joanna swerved into a sharp right and hit the curb inches from colliding with an old RV barreling down the hill. The other driver, exiting the tired Cathedral City subdivision of dry lawns and '60s cul-de-sacs, did not bother to look back.

"Bastard!" she shouted out the window. Then she laid on her horn so long and loud that a kid on his ten-speed flipped her off. For an instant she could not make up her mind whether to chase down the driver or thrash the cyclist. By the time she decided the driver was the greater offender he had already vanished from her sight.

"Bastard." she repeated. "Goddamned bastard." And then the shame washed over her as it always did when she dared to put her rage into words. Joanna Morse had not been raised to take the Lord's name in vain nor speak in expletives. No sass, no selfishness, no troublemaking allowed. What would her mother, God rest her soul, think of her now? Mustering a semblance of self-control, Joanna straightened her wheels and snaked up the hill.

~

Owen slumped back in his Barcalounger, the one he'd picked up for a song at the Salvation Army, and glared at his old TV. *Damned picture tube, blown after only seventeen years. What in the hell was a workingman's dollar worth anymore?* He stewed in his own juices then tossed out a string of epithets at the universe that dared to black out the latest shenanigans on *All My Children*. The empty screen stared back at him.

Until it began to fill with a laughing image from long ago … a lovely young girl reaching out to him with open arms. He sucked in a sharp breath then blinked. Her arms opened wider. He blinked again. The image disappeared, but her presence still held him.

For months now, Aldine's cat eyes had been haunting him with an unholy force that rattled the old man's reason. Owen feared God, not the devil. Why he was being punished, he could not comprehend, but punished he was. Despite praying almost every night before he went to sleep, he suffered a ghost's embrace.

Over six decades had passed since he used to stand behind the doorway to his big sister's room watching her sacred Saturday night ritual. First the curves of lipstick, then powder dusting high cheekbones below pale green eyes flecked with amber. Finally, the rope of pearls and a heart-shaped spray of Evening in Paris across her shoulders.

One time, a smile teasing the corners of her perfect mouth, she caught him watching. "Junior, are you spying on your big sister?"

"Nobody's as pretty as you, Aldine."

"Honey, you're not the first boy to tell me that. Come give me some sugar."

And then she let him kiss her cheek, the lace collar on her silk dress grazing his throat.

"You're my little man. Don't forget that when you grow up and start breaking all the girls' hearts."

"I won't forget."

And then she floated out of the room, her shiny black T-straps tapping down the staircase just like Ruby Keeler.

Some nights, after his mother retired with his baby brother tucked into her big bed upstairs, Owen sneaked out of his room to wait for his sister's return. Once in a blue moon, magic happened when Aldine agreed to cuddle him to sleep. Sometimes she played with his hair, twisting one strand after another between her fingers, as reverent as a nun caressing rosary beads. Only then could he drift into reverie safe in her arms.

But one night she came in to hold him was different. Tossing and turning, she grabbed a fistful of his hair as if she were trying to pull it out by the roots. He yelped in surprise like a dog beaten by his master and pleaded with her to stop. She kept pulling, he kept screaming, until his mother came running as fast as her short fat body could manage.

"Let Junior be now, you hear me?"

His sister's lipstick-smeared mouth mumbled incoherently as she clasped her brother tight. Aldine seemed to be in a trance no one could break. He could still smell her perfume, feel her sharp pink nails digging into his scalp.

"I said 'let him go,' Aldine!"

Never one to suffer foolish behavior, his mother cracked her daughter across the mouth. All he could remember after that was Aldine being dragged away, his mother beating on her, yelling about how one drunk in the family is one drunk too many and Aldine knew better and Lord, why had she been burdened with such an ungrateful daughter. Lord, why? The next morning at breakfast his sister's torn lip was still swollen. When their mother turned her back to stir the oatmeal on the stove, Aldine winked at her younger brother. He mustered a shy smile and winked back.

Four years later she had turned up dead, abandoned roadkill on a frozen county blacktop …

The phone rang and Owen jumped, knocking over his second morning cup of instant Maxwell House.

"Goddammit!" Natasha, a loyal shepherd-lab mix rescued from the pound, padded over to place a comforting paw on the arm of the Barcalounger. Owen stroked the dog's head. Sure enough, her expression took him back to the sweet-faced collie on his mother's farm. What was her name again? Bonniedoon, that was it. Everything seemed to take him back these days. He let his shaking hand rest on Natasha's coat and closed his eyes, ignoring the phone and the spilled coffee staining the worn shag carpet.

Joanna parked in the driveway of her father's decrepit ranch house but made no move to go inside. Her hands clutched the steering wheel as the same words kept knocking back and forth inside her head: "The wine glass weary of holding the wine." Where did that come from? Some poet she had read in college, now floating in paradise or wherever it is poets go after they drain the cup dry. Not that she liked poetry the way her husband, Peter, did, not that they discussed poetry these days, or anything else since she vacated their conjugal bed. The couple lived under the same roof in the vintage craftsman they devoted a decade to restoring together, but were now divided by separate bedrooms and long silences.

The bad dreams began in March right after Easter when they were still sleeping together. In the first visitation an intolerable weight crushed her body until she was gasping for air and praying for a mercy that did not come. She awoke in the morning with the awful feeling that a weeping fat woman had been sitting on her chest, refusing to budge one ounce of her burdensome flesh unless Joanna surrendered. But what was the battle and who was the enemy?

"Why did you push me away?" Peter asked at the table the next morning, his hazel eyes dark with hurt.

"What're you talking about?"

"Last night when I tried to hold you."

She buttered a heel of toast, the dry crust breaking in two.

"You were drenched in sweat. Moaning and whimpering like —"

"Like what?"

"I don't know. Something terrible was happening. Don't you remember?"

"You know me. I never remember my dreams." She stood up to fill the teapot, the rushing water from the faucet a pleasant distraction. "Another cup?"

Her husband shook his head. "It's not the first time."

"What?"

"I've heard you crying in your sleep lately."

"Well, it is tax season," Joanna joked. "After next Friday I can breathe easy."

Peter cleared the table and began rinsing their breakfast plates. "Has your father been calling for money again?"

"No," Joanna lied.

"You run yourself ragged every time he picks up the phone —"

"Stop it, Peter."

"All I'm saying is you can't keep driving down to the desert every weekend at his beck and call."

"He's old and sick. He needs me."

"Do you ever consider what you need, babe?"

"A gallon of Earl Grey should do it."

Peter tossed her a dirty look over his shoulder. She shot one right back.

"I love you honey, but please keep the existential questions for your students." Joanna turned the burner on full force, the blue-gold flame searing the bottom of the kettle.

The space between them festered with quiet tension. Joanna was convinced Peter could never appreciate the load she carried. Her father's third mortgage to pay off, mounting bills Medicare refused to cover, and thanks to the last boozy girlfriend that bled him dry, not one dollar left from his savings Joanna had invested with such care ... it never ended. Although the good daughter knew she had surpassed her family's greatest expectations, she failed her own. Always the growing urge to do more and be more as if the smooth sands of some hourglass were disappearing, grain by precious grain. For as long as she could remember she'd lived in a burning house, yearning to escape but unable to leave before she rescued the other residents blinded by smoke and debris.

"I'm tired is all, okay?"

Peter scrubbed harder, trying to dislodge a piece of scrambled egg.

"You know what I'm going through at the office since I had to fire McNally."

"What about Lisa?"

"She's a junior accountant, Peter."

"Maybe if you delegated more responsibility —"

"Do I tell you how to teach your classes?"

"I don't understand why you refuse to hire more staff."

"I can't afford it."

"Joanna, we did the numbers, and we can afford it."

"And risk going into debt? No. Besides, that would mean more people to train and even then I can't count on them when they end up doing a half-assed job. Why do you think I let McNally go?"

Peter slammed the dishwasher door shut. "I have to get to my meeting with the dean."

The teakettle hissed as he exited the kitchen. Joanna reached for the handle without thinking.

"Shit!"

She grabbed a fistful of ice from the freezer, clenching the cold tight and hard. When Peter came in to kiss her goodbye, the last of the ice was dripping through her fingers.

"What happened?"

"A silly accident. I'm fine."

He opened her tight fingers and winced at her angry red palm.

"I'm fine," she repeated, pulling her hand away. "Tell the dean he better pony up six figures if he wants you to chair the department, Professor!"

Joanna pressed her lips against his and then waved through the open kitchen window as he backed their sensible Volvo out of the driveway. The bearded irises next to the porch were in bloom again, the beauty of the long California growing season. From December through May, lemon and lavender petals unfurled with purpose, not an ounce of struggle marring their silvery veins. Yes, it would be a lovely spring. She sucked in gulps of fresh morning air and pushed the night's strange dream out of her mind.

Two weeks later, another midnight visitation. This one from a white-haired bogeyman with bloodshot eyes. Joanna tiptoed into the guest bedroom so she wouldn't have to confront questions she couldn't answer.

"What's going on?" Peter demanded when he awoke just before dawn and found her in a different bed. "Was I snoring too loud?"

"No, it's not you … my nerves, I guess."

"Well, come back to bed," he smiled, leaning down to nibble her ear. "I'll rub your back and see if we can't get those nasty nerves to calm down."

Joanna shook her head. "I think I can rest better in here."

"Without me, you mean?"

"Just for now, okay?"

"Now" lingered through May and June as Joanna kept casting about for an acceptable source to blame. Her schedule at the office. Unpredictable hormones. Summer allergies. At first Peter teased her about being a "sensitive plant," quoting his favorite Shelley poem. But when his wife continued to retreat behind the guest bedroom door, the laughter stopped. Joanna accepted her penance. A small price to pay, she reasoned, for the privacy to wrestle her night demons into submission.

She imagined each unsettling nightmare would be banished simply by willing its demise. Surely if she stayed in the dream long enough, her subconscious could weave a different narrative. But no. The white-haired man came and went, wreaking mercurial havoc. A week or two might pass with no appearance and then he'd strike three nights in sequence. The settings changed ...

A riverbed swarmed by grinning fish ... a dirt floor under an ancient furnace crusted with cockroaches ... a row of sunflower soldiers peering through a narrow window from the garden outside. Joanna navigated each strange nocturnal scene with increasing dread, knowing that he would be waiting for her. Raging ... sobbing ... tearing out his white hair from bloody roots ...

Until she bolted upright in bed, stifling the scream that threatened to awaken her husband in their bedroom down the hall.

"Good girl," her mother used to soothe her after childhood nightmares — their terrors long forgotten — sent Joanna shivering into maternal arms. "If the bad man comes again, now you know how to get away, don't you?"

"Do I?" the little girl asked.

"Of course. Just dream yourself awake and the bogeyman will disappear!"

Joanna curled in a fetal ball around her pillow and peered into the darkness. Eyes wide open.

~~~

Owen stacked another plate on top of the week's dirty dishes lining his kitchen sink then lit up a White Owl cigarillo to compensate himself for the trouble. Natasha whined for a fresh bowl of water which she received in due time. He moved slowly since the Parkinson's had taken hold, troubled that he could not work up the energy to water the front yard rose bushes that used to fill him with such pride. The Mr. Lincolns, brilliant red blooms that he presented his wife on their last anniversary together, drooped with despair. All they needed was a daily dose to get them through the summer heat. The old man knew this, knew it as well as the back of his hand, so why was it so hard to do the right thing, the decent thing? Beer used to wash away the bad thoughts, but the last six-pack twisted his innards into such upset that he got no sleep the whole miserable night. About the same time his sister Aldine returned to afflict his mind. Since then, much to his puzzlement, he could no longer abide the taste of alcohol.

Owen tensed. Was that a knock at the door? His hearing was going to hell in a handbasket just like every other part of his body. There it was again. He hobbled to the living room, leaning on his cane like the good friend it was. Probably the damned Jehovah's Witnesses trying to save his soul again. Cracking open the door, he decided to give the do-gooders a piece of his mind.

"Happy Fourth, Dad."

Joanna put on her good daughter smile and held it as best she could. While her father fumbled with the double locks, she surveyed the bounty of food filling her arms. The summer sausage that was her father's favorite, juicy beefsteak tomatoes, hunks of smoked Gouda and pepper jack — how the farm boy loved his cheese. Such a pity people couldn't age like a wedge of cheddar, she mused, and just slice off the white speckled edge past its prime. But human beings atrophied from the inside out. The brain cells went first. Not enough stimulation. Or maybe it was the ventricles of the heart. Too much stimulation. One earthly blow after another, weakening body and spirit beyond repair.

When Joanna looked at her father now, she saw a shadow that used to be a man. A shadow wasting away, not only from the Parkinson's that assaulted his limbs, but from the bitter weight of resentment and regret. Her father's mind, so often held hostage by unhappy childhood memories, had embarked on a suicide mission. Slowly. Surely. All those years he made her mother miserable and look at him now.

"You're late!" he barked, half inclined to let her wait on the doorstep for a few minutes. "A day late and a dollar short!" Then, taking note of the groceries, he stepped aside and allowed her to enter.

"I called six times yesterday but you never pick up your phone —"

"Too many bill collectors. Can't get blood out of a turnip, I tell 'em."

Yes, his daughter had known that for years. She unloaded the groceries on the dining room table. Barbecued pork spareribs, stuffed ground beef peppers, sour cream potato chips, a dozen Hershey bars, a twelve-pack of Dr. Pepper, and all the summer sausage and cheese he could eat. Terrible for his blood pressure, but her father had his cravings and so few pleasures in his life. How could she deny him?

"Homemade?" Owen riveted on the Tupperware cake server, his taste buds already salivating.

"German chocolate," she smiled.

And without another word he shuffled into the kitchen to fetch paper plates and forks. The dirty dishes would wait another day. Remembering his manners, he emptied a carton of whole milk — the only thing left in his refrigerator — into two tall glasses. Chocolate cake without milk tasted like sacrilege. He let her serve, not only because it was a woman's place, but also because he did not trust himself to cut respectable-sized slices. So much had been lost in the twenty years since his wife died, including the discipline and sense of proportion that once structured his days. Damn, if he didn't still see her coffee cup 'round every corner he turned. Yet Owen could not bear to let go of this old house no matter how often Joanna pleaded with him to move closer to his grandkids. Of course, his daughter blamed his refusal on the drinking — she blamed everything on the drinking. But his grief was more than the overflowing garbage bags of beer bottles could ever drown.

"Is it as good as Mom's?"

"Scrumptious."

They ate in silence at the kitchen table.

She learned long ago Owen Morse would not talk before he was good and ready.

Like the time that summer after her sophomore year in college when Peter arrived to meet her parents for the first time. Her dad was "indisposed," as her mother put it. Actually, Owen was in the backyard trimming the hillside ice plant in full view, while his wife smiled her charming smile and offered homemade snickerdoodles to their guest.

"Thank you, Mrs. Morse."

"Please, call me Terry."

After Peter drove home to Pasadena without exchanging one word with his future father-in-law, Joanna went outside to confront her dad.

"You couldn't give him a chance? Why would you act that way?!"

"Why?" Owen snorted. "Why in the hell would I want to meet the boy who's going to take away my daughter?"

Then he huffed inside to turn on the TV and relax his nerves with a bottle of Miller High Life.

"Give him time," her mother said, and as so often and in so many ways, she proved to be right.

The next year on the eighth of May, Joanna's father walked his only child down the aisle and Terry and Owen danced together at the reception like their daughter imagined they had done in their courtship days at the Aragon Ballroom in Chicago. Their togetherness was the happiest memory from her own wedding.

The phone call came, one Sunday in early November, awakening the newlyweds in their darkened bedroom. Her father's voice, low and broken, choked out the news. Mom is gone … her heart, they said.

Joanna looked through the open door into the dining room, now a family mausoleum. Her mother's French Provincial dining room set had not been touched (except for Joanna's dusting) since her death. On top of the walnut credenza a three-foot tall beauty pageant trophy, tarnished with the years, still sat front and center, the same place it had occupied since the night Joanna won it. She tried to move it once, but her father made such a fuss that back it went.

"You know what I can't get off my mind?"

"What, Dad?"

She hoped that this might be the moment.

Maybe, after all these years, they would have the heart-to-heart she always wanted and he would promise to make up for lost time and remember his grandchildren at Christmas and —

"Her fried chicken. That crispy buttermilk crust melted in your mouth. I can taste it now. You?"

She served her father a second piece of cake. "Mom was a wonderful cook."

"None better."

"A wonderful woman."

Owen stiffened, sensing condemnation in her tone of voice. "Don't act like you're telling me anything I don't know." He forked a big bite of cake, stuffing his mouth full, and mumbled. "True love never did run smooth."

When his daughter said nothing, he added for good measure. "You and Pete found that out."

"We've had our ups and downs."

"Oh yeah, you have. Don't think I haven't heard the two of you going at it when I come to visit," he grimaced. "You got a temper like your mom. 'Course her being an Irish redhead, I should've known better. My sister warned me about redheads."

"Warned you? What do you mean?"

"Never mind. Point is, you favor me, and I raised my daughter to hold her temper and act like a lady, didn't I?"

"Yes, you did, Dad," Joanna bristled.

"That's right. I know you remember what you been taught." He shifted in his seat and eyed her untouched milk. "Spoiled?"

"I'm not thirsty."

"You need more meat on your bones. Getting too thin." He carved a hefty slice of cake and pushed it toward his daughter.

She let it sit unclaimed on the serving plate. "Sarah and Elisabeth send their love."

"Well, my love to them. How are my be-yoo-tee-ful granddaughters?"

"They finished their freshman year on the Dean's list."

"Time flies. Sure you don't want your milk?"

"You're welcome to it."

After a long gulp from his daughter's glass, he put the question on the table. "You still mad at me 'cause I didn't send 'em some fancy birthday present?"

"Forget the present. They wanted their grandfather at their birthday dinner."

"And I would have been there with bells on if I hadn't felt under the weather. I'll make it up to 'em. Maybe we'll go to the County Fair up in Pomona next month if I can get a few bucks ahead. They're not too big yet to enjoy the rides. I get a kick out of that Sarah, 'course Lizzie's cute too. I don't play favorites."

"The girls are in Rome all summer on the student exchange program, Dad."

"Rome, " he repeated. "Rome, Italy? By themselves?"

"They're living with a local family. Peter and I host their daughter next summer."

Owen shook his head, trying to make sense of such a thing.

"We talked about this a couple weeks ago."

"My memory's a little fuzzy these days, okay?" he growled.

"Okay, Dad."

"If you ask me — 'course you didn't — they're too young to go halfway around the world by their lonesome. Your mother and I never would've allowed you to be off on your own at that age."

"No question about that," Joanna sighed, recalling her father's refusal to allow her to travel to New York City on her senior field trip.

"Keep folks out of temptation's way and they don't get tempted," his eyes narrowed. "Pete never stepped out on you, did he?"

Joanna looked confused at the sudden turn of conversation.

"Tell me the truth now."

"No, of course not."

"Because he knew I'd take a horse whip to him if he did my daughter wrong! No question you been faithful 'cause that's how your mother and me brought you up. We had morals …"

A glob of coconut pecan frosting caught in Joanna's throat. They almost killed each other, but at least there was no adultery in the family.

"… made sure you had 'em too. See that you and your husband do the same with those little girls of yours."

"We are, Dad, don't worry —"

"Keep 'em close so's they don't get in with bad company. Your mom and me never had any trouble with you."

"You and mom raised me right," Joanna placed a gentle hand on her father's trembling wrist.

Owen took a deep breath then pulled his hand away to scoop up the last bite of cake. Joanna quickly filled his empty plate with the slice her father had cut for her a few minutes before.

"Thank you."

"You're welcome."

A quiet goodwill flowed between them for almost three minutes before the phone rang. Owen ignored it and continued polishing off his third piece of cake. After the fifth ring, Joanna jumped up. Tripping over Natasha's languid body at her father's feet, she grabbed the earpiece.

"I'm not home!" he yelled.

"Morse residence," she answered anyway.

Annoyed that she allowed outsiders to intrude, Owen speared some cake and gobbled it up.

"Yes, he's right here." She offered him the phone.

Her father glared. Turning his back, he swiped the last few sips of milk in his daughter's glass, then pulled a cigarillo from the pack in his shirt pocket. He struck a match to the tip and inhaled deeply.

"Apparently, he's unavailable. May I take a message?"

Owen eyed the feast that would fill his belly over the next few days. His daughter took care of him the way a daughter should, no denying that. And she had a good head for numbers just like her mother. Too good. It wasn't any of her business what he did with the extra money she gave him every month. So what if he liked to help out the good-looking divorcee that lived next door —

"I see … yes, of course. When are the services?"

Her father looked up, the smoke still trapped in his lungs.

"Well, I'm not sure. May we get back to you on that? I understand. Let me give you my number in case you have a problem again."

Even before she hung up, he knew. "My son-of-a-bitch brother?"

"A week ago last Thursday in Pontiac. They tried to reach you —"

"What put him in the ground?"

"Liver cancer."

"I hope he suffered. Did they say he suffered?"

"His attorney wants to know if you'll go back to Illinois for the reading of the will."

"Why should I?"

"You're his sole heir."

"A goddamn lie! What about Tazewell?"

Joanna blinked, trying to put a picture to the name.

"That no-account son of his. He kick the bucket too?"

"'Sole heir,' Dad. That's all he said."

"Bullshit."

Owen struggled to clasp the crook of his cane. Farmer's hands, born to turn the soil and seed the earth with new life, now shook with disease.

"They're messing with the wrong man, trying to make a fool out of me —"

"Dad, calm down. The attorney just wants you to have what is rightfully yours, whatever that is. Why do you think he tried so hard to reach you?"

The old man had no answer.

Joanna put her arm around her father's bowed shoulders. "Horatio is dead."

Owen started to whistle, the way he always did when speech laid too heavy a burden on his tongue, and limped outside. His daughter cleared the crumbs from the table, a cold shiver creeping down her spine.

That night the white-haired man invaded her dreams again. But this time was different. No rage, no tears, only a strange, enigmatic smile wreathing his weathered face as he stood still and silent. And then he whispered.

"Yes."

And for some reason one word was enough.

Joanna slept peacefully that night.

2

Home

Pontiac, Illinois. Population 29,000. Hub of Livingston County. Site of the magnificent Second Empire brick and marble courthouse Teddy Roosevelt once commandeered as a bully pulpit and Hollywood moviemakers later filmed for a coming-of-age comedy called *Grandview, USA*. A storybook town of hollyhock gardens and maple-lined streets where the Vermilion River carved a fertile valley from the dry back of the Midwestern prairie. Some white man tried to put a pretty gloss on the violent history of the region by naming the place in honor of a chief of the Ottawa. Celebrated for his daring bravery against European interlopers, Pontiac was butchered in 1769 by a band of his own warriors. What goes around comes around, and the tribesmen responsible for Pontiac's murder were annihilated by the chief's avengers. Once the killing fields quieted again, the wily capitalists who bribed the Indian renegades to rid the settlers of a troublesome chief grabbed the land for their own.

"Damn," Owen jerked his finger toward the rental car's air conditioner. "Can't you get that thing to go any higher?"

"I've turned it as high as it will go, Dad."

Her father heaved a sigh of disgust, the kind that always made his daughter flinch. Joanna allowed her own heavy sigh to follow his and struggled to keep sleep-deprived eyes on the road ahead. Second thoughts were distracting her focus. A whole week away from work always made Joanna uneasy, especially now with her untested junior accountant in charge. But her father needed her to sort through "the inheritance business" as he called it, so here they were.

"Might as well let the outside in," Owen grumbled, cracking the window, "least it's fresh."

A blast of furnace heat blew in from the sun-burned farmland. August on the prairie was bad enough but this one was a record-breaker. "Hotter than the devil's pitchfork," the farmers down at the Grange used to say. So hot that tender white corn withered on the stalk. He breathed in Illinois air, dank with the humidity that always hung thick just before a thunderstorm split the sky wide open.

"Rain's coming soon. I can smell it."

By the time Joanna and Owen drove into town, the new moon was rising but the asphalt still steamed. As the city limits sign retreated in the rearview mirror, the woman at the wheel felt a flutter of recognition. Not just a reminder that she had visited Pontiac as a child with her parents, but something else, something more familiar she could not name.

"Still the same," her father said soft and low.

Straight ahead a grey prison tower flashed red eyes in the twilight. Pontiac Correctional Facility was welcoming its son home. Before the family migration west for his wife's asthma, Owen had been on the fast track for warden. Appointed sergeant of the guard at the youngest age with the highest commendations of any employee in the prison's hundred-year history.

"I treated those inmates like men. They weren't used to that." His voice pitched louder now, almost defiant.

Joanna nodded, recalling the letter her father kept together with his treasured collection of pocket watch fobs. On occasional Sunday afternoons, after the glow of a few beers, he would pull out the lifer's words to read aloud to his wife and daughter. Written in precise penmanship on worn tablet paper that had been opened and folded so many times the creases had to be secured by scotch tape, the letter began: "To an officer and a gentleman ..."

The summer she turned twelve her father had trekked the family back from California to visit a good buddy on the occasion of his promotion to warden, the job Owen had coveted for himself. Old black men in white uniforms escorted the Morses up a private elevator to the new warden's quarters for supper. The trustees served roast pork and purple cabbage with silver-slotted spoons and offered second helpings of sweet potato pie for dessert. Later she found out the short friendly one with the gold-toothed smile had murdered a man on Chicago's South Side. Over a female, her dad noted. As if that explained everything.

"Turn around," Owen registered sudden alarm. "You're on the wrong road."

"The map says it's 116 —"

"The hell it is. I know this stretch like the back of my hand." He squinted beyond the crossroads of two highways, past the junction of Old Route 66.

That's where it had happened to Aldine. Across from the old Hutson place. Snow drifts more than a yard deep that night. Some folks coming back from Flanagan saw something all bloody and crumpled off the shoulder of the blacktop.

"These are the directions they gave me at O'Hare. We'll be there soon, Dad."

A brightly lit blue and yellow Comfort Inn sign beckoned beyond the darkness descending across the flatlands.

"You should've told me we'd be coming this way," he reached into his shirt pocket.

Joanna turned to see his hands were trembling again. Parkinson's or bad nerves, she never knew the cause these days. "What's wrong?"

Chewing on the white plastic tip of one of his prized cigarillos, he inhaled sharply then exhaled. A caged bull with nowhere to run, smoke streamed out of his nostrils.

"Goddammit, I should never have come! This is your fault, don't say it isn't. You just had to keep pushing me, damn it all to hell!"

"Dad, please," her throat was constricting from the tobacco, "we both agreed it would be a good idea to meet with the lawyer —"

"Pushing me the way you do, just like your mom. I wasn't ready, dammit."

"Ready to see the lawyer? I don't understand."

"Forget it. Just give me some peace."

Joanna stared straight ahead, hands gripping the wheel as if it were the last life preserver. Like his wife and his mother, his daughter was just another woman failing him. The Last Female Standing. And what good was that doing either one of them?

"… Another thing, if I need a beer to calm my nerves, I'm going to get one and you can't stop me." Owen threw his cigarillo out the window with a flick of the wrist.

"The doctor said —"

"I know what the doctor said! Just because a man's got a bunch of diplomas on his walls doesn't mean he knows everything. I'm still strong, don't think I'm not. Pull over there, right there!" His cigarillo-stained thumb gestured wild half-circles toward the "Patty's Pizz" sign, its exposed bulbs glowing naked and white.

She pulled to a quiet stop and faced her father. "No liquor."

"Hell, I can do without. Sausage and pepperoni with all the fixings, that's what I want."

Joanna helped him out of the passenger side and gave him the hand-carved birch wood cane her husband had presented to his father-in-law Christmas before last.

Owen eyed the fashionable crutch with sudden sentiment. "I like old Pete. Even if he is a dago. You're too hard on him too."

She slipped her arm through his and together they navigated a pot-holed parking lot that had seen better days.

"You paying?" The father asked.

"Don't I always?" The daughter answered.

3

Bequest

After John S. Hornbeck, Esquire finished reading the will, the anticipated response did not present itself. No words, no sounds, not even Owen Morse's nervous whistle punctured the silence.

"Mr. Morse, do you have any questions?"

Joanna looked at her father. He made no reply, so the lawyer continued talking to fill time, space, and the unpredictable recesses of their clients' minds. The house was in need of maintenance — considering his deceased brother's long illness — and the barn in some disrepair, but the eight hundred forty acres of central Illinois farmland still offered some of the county's finest yields in soybeans, alfalfa, corn —

"Gang plow."

"Excuse me?"

"Four horses in back, two in front. That's what we used to plow the land."

"Yes, sir," Hornbeck tittered, "well, times have changed."

There it was again. Dismissal of what he had done, what he had been. A man his age should be accustomed to being invisible. Owen closed his eyes, sliding into a familiar abyss that the lawyer mistook for jet lag.

"I expect you'll be renting out the place, unless you plan to leave those movie star neighbors of yours in California. When did you folks head west?"

"Thirty-three years ago this month," Joanna grimaced, the U-Haul trek across the twists and turns of the Mother Road as vivid as if they'd pulled out of their suburban driveway yesterday. The afternoon her dad left her and her mother stranded outside the locked car as he drank away his blues in a Joplin bar; the night at the crummy motel in Amarillo when a golden-hearted bouncer escorted her father back from the honky-tonk next door; the bad curve on a winding road deep in the Black Mountains north of Flagstaff when her dad, sweat seeping from every pore, froze at the wheel. Inches, mere inches, from plummeting their family over the precipice —

"No more ten-below winters, was that it, Mr. Morse? Sunshine and palm trees three hundred sixty-five days a year?"

Owen opened his eyes, trying to formulate the right words but not able to put together the vowels and consonants in proper order.

"My mother needed a warmer climate for her health," again the daughter answered for her father. Joanna, worried that her dad might be having a heart attack, cast a glance in Owen's direction. The silent killer, that's what the doctors called it when her mother collapsed three weeks before her fiftieth birthday. The silent killer.

"Well, that I certainly appreciate. Doctors do extol the virtues of dry heat, don't they? I trust your mother is in good health now." Without waiting for confirmation — why should he when he didn't give a damn — the lawyer moved on, waxing poetic about how happy they must be to find themselves back in God's country and how wonderful it will surely feel to see the family homestead again ...

~~~~~

Owen ignored Hornbeck's nonsense, focusing instead on the handsome Seth Thomas clock that clung to the top of a corner bookcase. It reminded him of the family heirloom that his mother had so cherished in his youth. Seth Thomas was the one man you could always count on to deliver a good time, his mother used to joke, a tight laugh catching in her throat. The burled walnut mantel clock with onyx columns became her most prized possession, the only family keepsake that her brother Frederick failed to confiscate after their father's untimely death.

Eight adult children in the bereaved clan, each bequeathed a generous portion of debt their land-rich patriarch had accumulated in frenzied speculation during his final days. That fateful occurrence was the bitter shot that launched the war.

Not the "Good War," when Owen enlisted to defend his country. (How could he know he'd be shamed with a medical discharge after the Coast Guard surgeon botched a simple operation and sent him back to Illinois with sinuses butchered beyond repair? That's why his mouth was always slightly open, even when no speech was forthcoming. A man had to breathe.)

No, Owen was thinking about a different war — the home front battle-field of his upbringing. The American Gothic farmhouse that this smiling shylock says now belongs to the boy who once walked its splintered floor-boards.

Owen still felt the suffocating gloom of the bedroom that froze when the small, square windowpanes iced over during the first winter frost, then sweltered in the dog days of summer. At midnight, even with the windows lashed open, he would still be awake, angry blisters of sweat marching across his brow. When the thunderstorms unleashed their furious gales, the house shook and rattled and groaned in its unrequited misery. Some-how the roof always endured its punishment and survived to see another dry dawn.

His widowed mother bundled her five children against the forces of nature and tried to teach them right from wrong. And when her middle son looked back from the vantage point of his eightieth decade, he could not fault the woman her honest effort. Still, grief and loss clogged every nook and cranny of that clapboard farmhouse. No father present for any of the children. Two were dead and gone. The last one disappeared. There was never enough money or comfort, but the biggest want was love. All the resources that ease a body's hardscrabble sojourn on earth sputtered to dangerously short supply. Hearts ached, all for lack of filling. Meager har-vests came and went, and with them the hope that happiness was possible. The good life belonged to their rich cousins down the road.

Soon after he turned ten and the Depression hit, there were more hous-es than he cared to recall. His mother was forced to lease out the family farm to bring in extra cash and moved her brood to more modest quarters in town. Three, maybe four rentals in a row, each one a cramped, piss-poor substitute for the acres left behind and all the while his mother struggling to maintain a façade of genteel poverty. Never was any gentility about being poor and never would be. Lord knows whatever happened to his mother's Seth Thomas mantel clock. Horatio probably used it for firewood.

"How'd you like to go out and inspect your property tomorrow morning, Mr. Morse?" The lawyer's smile wandered into a neighborly grin, a grin that Owen found so false and repugnant that he could no longer remain silent.

"My property, you say," Owen grunted, lurching forward in his chair. "What happened to Tazewell?"

"Excuse me?"

"Horatio's son. When did he die?"

Owen's sister Bertha and brother Absher had been gone for years. But it didn't seem right that any father, even a bastard like Horatio, had to bury his own son before he bit the dust.

"Mr. Tazewell Billingham is not yet deceased."

"Makes no sense," the old man shook his head. "If he's still alive, why did the property come to me?"

"Well, the fact is," Hornbeck cleared a plug of phlegm from his throat, "the late Mr. Billingham disinherited the younger Billingham."

Owen snorted. "You see the cold-hearted half-brother I had. What kind of a man cuts out his only child?"

"An angry man," Joanna murmured. Her father did not hear her.

"Well, Mr. Morse, I can't say that I was privy to any confidential information, all I can say is that there were rumors of bad blood between the two."

"Hell, Horatio was born with bad blood. I expect Tazewell got more than his share. That's why he was shipped off to military school in Minnesota. They figured to knock him into line." Owen cast a sharp look at the latest lawyer making money off his family calamity. "You heard the story?"

"No, that was before I was engaged."

"Oh, I could give you an earful. Kid went off his rocker a spell. Killed the family cats and fed the poor things to the dogs, can you beat that? My late wife got the lowdown in a Christmas card from my Aunt Minnie."

Owen spun around to his daughter. "I told my mother no way should Tazewell be standing up at my baby girl's baptism. You think she'd listen? No, sir. She wanted everybody to make up. Fat chance."

"Tazewell was my godfather?" Joanna asked, disbelieving.

"You know that. Remember the old picture of him holding you like some prize football?"

"No, I —"

"Yes, you do! The one with you wrapped in the christening blanket your Grandma Morse crocheted? I showed you that photo. I know I did."

Joanna nodded with a tight smile. "Now I remember, Dad."

"That's right." Owen turned back to Hornbeck. "Some two-bit godfather Tazewell turned out to be. Never sent my daughter gifts, a card, even a hello-how-are-you. Horatio and I stopped talking after my mother's funeral."

"Well then," Hornbeck cleared his phlegmy throat again, this time with more purpose. "What time shall we meet tomorrow? Nine o'clock?"

Ignoring the question, Owen looked beyond the lawyer's pained expression through a broad window that framed the old brick courthouse towering above the town square. He remembered that godforsaken courthouse too.

"We'll get back to you on that, Mr. Hornbeck." Joanna reached for her father's arm, gently helping him rise to his feet.

"Of course, of course. You let me know how long you folks will be in town and we'll work out a mutually agreeable time." He followed them to the door, his lips still moving. "Well, Mr. Morse, I'm sure your brother will rest easier knowing his land is staying in family hands —"

Owen turned on the sadly misinformed idiot who had no idea when to shut up. "The son-of-a-bitch was trying to clear his conscience, that's all. My sister Aldine told me she'd make sure the farm would come to me. Horatio stole it from under my nose. Did you know about that?"

Hornbeck appeared shocked, "No, Mr. Morse, I did not."

"Ask your boss then … F.B. Stickerling, that's his name. The one who handled my mother's business. He's got the facts. Ask him."

"Mr. Stickerling passed away some time ago, I'm afraid."

"Is that right? Well, don't expect me to cry over spilled milk. He was a good-for-nothing cheat. For all I know the same applies to you."

"Dad, please —"

He shook himself free of his daughter's grip and slammed out the door. Mr. Hornbeck assured Joanna that he was honest as the day was long and still happy to be of service then escorted her to the outside office.

"Miss Lidcombe," the attorney turned to his receptionist. "Would you kindly validate Mrs. Giordano's parking ticket from the city lot?"

The receptionist, who'd already gleaned an earful through the thin walls, cast a pitying gaze in Joanna's direction as she got down to business.

"Men." Mrs. Lidcombe tittered, her voice dropping to a conspiratorial whisper. "Can't live with them, can't live without them."

Joanna accepted the stickered ticket without comment.

"We do hope Mr. Morse enjoys his time back home. You take care now."

"Thank you," Joanna gritted her teeth and walked out.

Owen and his cane were weaving down the street like a peg-legged pirate soused on bad rum when she reached his side.

"You don't need to be rude."

"And I don't need a woman telling me my business. Your mother did enough of that."

"Mr. Hornbeck is on your side."

"How do you know? Can't trust any of 'em. Maybe I don't even want the damned property anymore."

"Then put the place up for sale."

"Like hell I will! Should have been mine when I was young enough to farm it myself. That's what Aldine wanted. Ma told me, 'Junior, before I go to the ground, this property gets put into deed for you. Aldine won't rest until —'"

"Aldine, your sister who was killed …"

"Yes, Goddammit, who else would I be talking about?"

"Don't yell at me. I'm just trying to keep things straight."

"Nothing's straight. The whole gang of them crooked as the day is long."

"Dad, please slow down. I don't understand what happened."

Out of breath now her father paused to lean on his cane. "Stroke laid her down before the legal work got done. Knowing Ma, she probably didn't want to pay a lawyer until she had to."

"So Horatio inherited everything because he was the first born," Joanna confirmed softly.

"I need a drink."

"Dad, no."

"I'm entitled to a drink and I'm going to have it."

Joanna stepped in front of her dad, blocking his path. "You want to kill yourself, do it on your own time. I'm heading back to the motel."

"And leave an old man here by his lonesome? What kind of an ungrateful daughter are you?"

Joanna was already headed in the opposite direction. Peter was right, if her father didn't get his way, she was as dispensable as the string of barflies who kept him company after his wife died.

"Joanna!"

She kept walking.

"Joanna," he tried again. "Please."

She slowed down and turned around.

"I was just kidding about the drink. Don't like the taste anymore, anyway."

"Since when?"

"None of your beeswax," he looked down, studying the scuffed toe of his cowboy boots. "You got a short fuse like your mom."

"Like you, too."

"Maybe so."

They walked in silence for a few minutes, Joanna's arm gently draped around her father's bowed back. She could feel the knobs of his spine. The man who used to be big and strong as a grizzly had shrunk to human size.

"Aldine promised me," he muttered to himself. "She died too soon, that's all. She died too soon."

As they passed the imposing entrance of the courthouse across the street, a mole-like man sat on a park bench under the elms enjoying his chicken salad sandwich and golden delicious apple, perfectly quartered. His pudgy jowls quickened with each bite. He had been watching the quarrelsome couple ever since they stepped out of the lawyer's office. Even before that, he observed them enter at half past eleven. He did not have to be in attendance to record the nature of the meeting; Miss Lidcombe, Mr. Hornbeck's receptionist, and a close personal friend from Friday night Canasta Club, had already informed him of that. One of the lovely benefits of living in a small town and why he never intended to leave again.

Tazewell watched and waited.

4

Decoration Day

Father and daughter, their graves side by side.

W. H. Younger, February 7, 1870 – October 10, 1913.

Aldine Younger, October 19, 1912 – March 1, 1933.

The sweltering summer sun bore down without mercy. Owen's knees crumpled as he placed a potted geranium on his sister's headstone. God's will, the minister said when Aldine died. A lie if he ever heard one. The old man's head hurt like hell. Stumbling up from the rocky ground, Owen pitched forward.

"Dad, be careful." Joanna rushed over to catch him.

Righting himself, he gripped his cane and pulled away. "You'll get old someday too."

Hiding his wet eyes from his daughter, he made his way toward the bench a compassionate groundsman had propped against the trunk of a lonely elm, the only tree still standing in Graceland Cemetery. Its parched leaves quivered in the prairie winds, sweeping across worn tombstones of Civil War veterans and pioneer farmers.

Owen rested his heavy limbs, looking across the horizon to the road headed back to the big brick courthouse in Pontiac.

Here on the outskirts of Fairbury, a tiny town half the size of the county seat to the north, he felt more at peace. Maybe it was the memory of the big end-of-school picnic his favorite teacher used to host here in her backyard. Homemade sugar donuts, jelly bismarcks, and all the strawberry lemonade he could drink. Mrs. Berkholder shook his hand when she presented his eighth-grade certificate three months after Aldine was killed and whispered that she knew his big sister would be proud. The next year, he left high school halfway through to hire himself out to the neighbors for spring planting. Seventy-five cents a day, but it was money in his pocket and that's all he cared about then.

Life had not changed so much in Fairbury he noted, as his daughter drove through on the way to Graceland. Once a farmer's town, always a farmer's town. He was glad to see the main drag demonstrated a certain civic pride. The bank building his Uncle Frederick used to own now sported a fresh coat of paint and polished black numerals on the clock tower. Walton's, the store where his sister once shopped, was celebrating its 100th anniversary with a ten percent discount. And the Livingston County Fairgrounds still occupied a choice piece of land a mile south of Fifth Street, home to the local country club and fine Victorians built by rich farmers like his uncle for their golden years.

A one-horse burg, his half-sister dismissed Fairbury. Aldine, abuzz with the thrill of leaving the family farm, could not wait to move into Pontiac. Sad that this is the place she came to rest in the end. A small plot next to the Younger monument that her grandfather bought for the clan a century before. Owen's other siblings were buried near his mother and the rest of the Heinemanns closer to Old Germantown where the bones of early settlers rotted in the rich central Illinois soil. His father — he had no idea. He only saw the man once after his mother dumped her last husband's suitcase on the porch with orders to never step on her property again. For years he kept a silver dollar Owen Senior had given him the day he stopped by the schoolyard at recess. "You're my namesake," his father told him, as if that meant something. Owen Junior began to whistle softly, not ready to conjure the destination to come when his days were done.

Joanna kept a proper distance, allowing her father time for private reflections. His insistence that they pay Aldine their respects came with abrupt notice just as Joanna backed out of the parking space across from Hornbeck's office. Flowers were needed, of course, so off they went to meander the aisles of Wal-Mart's Garden Center for an hour until he finally settled on the largest double geranium on display. Burgundy, the label said. Because his sister liked bright colors and said there was a place in France by the same name that she intended to visit someday — he chose that one. After they arrived at Graceland, he saturated the bloom's soft soil with water to protect it against the summer heat. Tomorrow or the next day, he told his daughter, they would return to dig a place next to his sister's stone for the roots to take hold. But not today. Today he needed to sit a spell and think. So Joanna lowered her eyes and turned away, alone with her own memories ...

~~~~~

A brand-new photo album, this one deep rose with glittering gold letters — "Our Family" — sat on the dining room table waiting to be put to good use. It was January, the month of virgin snow and fresh hope, and their last winter in Illinois.

Young Joanna, cheeks tingling from the winter winds outside, had abandoned a crusty snowman for warmer digs. Peeling off her mittens she lifted the lid from the big plastic shoebox of family photos nestled next to the album. Her frozen fingers dipped into the box and found an unexpected treasure. A manila envelope, wrinkled and soft with age, had been buried under a stack of Polaroids commemorating their last visit to Disneyland. The front of the envelope displayed an unfamiliar name written in pinched blue script:

ALDINE.

Without asking her mother's permission, she opened the envelope and turned it upside down. Yellowed clippings with bold, black headlines spilled out.

"Heiress Found Slain, Married Man Held" and "Girl in Mystery Death."

Someone had cared enough to Scotch tape the clippings on a thin sheet of cardboard to ensure the newspaper would endure long enough to be read again. Joanna's small fingertips, now warm and curious, were tracing the curled edges of the found treasure when her mother entered and broke the spell.

"What are you doing?"

"Who is Aldine?"

The cryptic answers that came only confused her. Such a sad story. A hit-and-run accident. Her father's sister, well, half-sister really. Her mother dug deeper in the shoebox and pulled out a formal family portrait of somber people in old-fashioned clothes. Joanna's father at age six, his brothers Horatio and Absher, his sister Bertha, Grandmother Morse, and in the center of the picture standing tall and lovely, a long string of pearls framing her perfectly waved hair, a fourteen-year-old girl with sad eyes.

"This is your Aunt Aldine."

Later, peering over the tiny newsprint as her mother braised the supper pot roast, Joanna tried to understand why the sheriff arrested the mayor's son, Asher Bentley, if her aunt's death was an accident. After her father came home from work, she put the question directly to the man who should know. Owen helped himself to a Miller High Life and said her mother was mistaken. No accident took his sister from him. Asher Bentley did.

"Why?" Joanna asked.

"Because she wouldn't give the S.O.B what he wanted," her dad growled, flipping on the television and raising the volume louder than usual. For years her father had no more to say on the subject, and Joanna knew better than to ask again.

Until the Christmas after her mother died.

Desperate to find some way to pull her father out of his isolation, she unpacked boxes of old family photos along with the rose photo album, its blank pages still unfilled. The next morning Joanna took the load of memories over to the house where Owen and his late wife had shared twenty-five tumultuous years, the place he vowed to stay the rest of his life in tribute to his lost spouse. "Why did my wife leave me?" the dejected widower demanded of his daughter over and over. When Joanna's futile attempts at solace fell short, Owen came to the conclusion that God must need her more than he did, so life went on. Mornings, he managed to show up for his latest job at the corner gas station. Nights and weekends, he drank himself into oblivion, demonstrating no interest in visiting his daughter and family over a home cooked meal.

Pictures of his childhood, Joanna hoped, would surely awaken her father's familial sense of belonging. She spread out the dog-eared black and white snapshots greying with age for her father's consideration. There he was, a handsome dark-haired little boy cuddling a litter of collie pups ... posing with baby brother Absher ... clutching the grade school basketball team trophy ... standing next to his mother Paulina in her Sunday best....

Owen Morse refused to be comforted. Erupting after too many years of silence, he spewed forth a Dickensian tale of indignities. The back of the hand from big brother Horatio, the birthdays and Christmases without presents (not even an orange in the child's stocking he hung on the old stone fireplace), the fifty cents his mother charged her own son to bake him a banana cream pie — can you beat that? All the neighbors, even the Schlesingers who everybody knew were poorer than church mice, read by electric lights from the new wires strung along the road next to his mother's land. But not their family, oh no. Gas lanterns, dark and smoky, that's what lit their nights. Couldn't afford electricity. And their rich cousins were living high on the hog in town. All their money and still they wanted more! His Ma said that's why Uncle Frederick bribed Asher Bentley to kill Aldine —

Joanna interrupted her father's rant. His uncle paid a man to murder his sister?

Owen bolted for the door, knocking the photos to the floor. Goddammit, he'll be late for feed time. That old Palomino mare they let him board at the racetrack stables, the one he saved from the glue factory, Goddammit all to hell, you can't let a dumb animal go hungry —

"Dad, please. What you said —"

Ignoring her pleas, Owen hightailed it into the backyard to start his pickup. The engine flooded. He gunned it, making his getaway. Joanna scooped the photos up one by one, packed them with care in the old shoebox and closed the lid.

~~~~~

After they left the cemetery and drove back in silence to Pontiac, Joanna pulled into the parking lot of the Baby Bull restaurant and asked if a pork tenderloin sandwich, the kind that used to make her dad's mouth water, might brighten his day. Owen allowed that might be the case. Inside the roadside café a daily chalkboard special advertised, "Homemade peach pie á la mode."

"Is it made with fresh peaches?" Joanna asked the pasty-faced waitress.

"Fresh enough."

"What I meant is … are the peaches canned?"

"Like I said, the pie looks fresh to me, you want some or not?"

Joanna took a leap of faith and ended up forking her way through canned peaches cradled in a sawdust crust. Or at least what she imagined sawdust would taste like if she ever ordered it for lunch.

Golden oldies blared in the background. Her father loved his Guy Lombardo but also had a weakness for the early rockers. When "Peggy Sue" came on, he started to tap his fingers in rhythm with its throbbing drumbeat. Joanna watched in wonder, the first time her father seemed to be enjoying himself in years.

"Mom used to say —"

"What?" The drumming stopped.

"Mom used to say you were the best dancer she ever met."

Her father relaxed, a shy smile lifting the corners of his mouth. Such a beautiful smile …

"And you were a real gentleman, even when she stepped on your toes." Joanna ventured, recalling the family story about her parents' first date. How nervous her mother was in the arms of a dreamboat who could put Robert Taylor to shame.

"I can't take credit for the moves coming natural. My sister Aldine taught me how to dance when I was a kid." He looked embarrassed at the vanity of confiding such a thing to his daughter.

"So you could sweep the girls off their feet when you grew up?" Joanna teased.

Owen was not amused. "Why'd you say that?"

"Excuse me?"

"What you just said. About sweeping girls off their feet."

"It's just an expression —"

"That's what she used to tell me."

"Mom?"

"Aldine." Owen went back to polishing off the pork tenderloin.

Joanna hesitated. "She was so pretty in that picture I saw. The one with the pearls."

"My sister always dressed to the nines. Nobody in this town had seen anything like her."

"But they weren't real. Were they?"

"What?"

"That long string of pearls she was wearing in the picture."

"Well, sure. Her granddad took real good care of her when he died. And that girl loved to shop," he chuckled. "I can still see Ma burn the midnight oil over her bank ledger, putting down every penny spent. Had to account to that SOB that ended up stealing all Aldine's funds for himself."

"I don't understand."

"We won't talk about that now. No use crying over spilt milk. I'll say one thing: When my sister used to get her monthly allowance, it was a good time for me. Bought me my own pair of roller skates, treats at the picture show ..." His voice drifted off, then tightened. "Yep, her dad came from money."

Owen wiped his mouth with a torn paper napkin and stared out the window at the semis sailing down the interstate.

"We had different fathers, you know."

"I know, Dad."

A full minute passed before he was ready to look back at his daughter.

"You get your cat eyes from her."

"Mom had cat eyes too."

"Not like Aldine's."

The waitress waltzed over to splash some coffee in the old man's cup. He gulped it down in two seconds.

"I need some air." Owen began to maneuver his way out of the booth then stopped to reach across the table and scoop a big forkful of his daughter's leftover peach pie into his mouth.

"Those aren't fresh peaches," he grimaced. Fumbling in his shirt pocket for another of his White Owls, her father shook his head. "I hate a liar. Only thing worse than a liar is a thief."

Then he bit down so hard on his cigar tip, it snapped in two. Spitting the plastic on his dirty plate he palmed his cane and hobbled out.

While her father smoked up a storm on the sidewalk outside, Joanna grew impatient waiting for the waitress to deliver their check. Bad pie, bad service, and bad manners from the locals. She sensed the pudgy middle-aged man in the back booth was staring at her. When she met his gaze head-on, he did not look away. Simply continued staring with flat, pale eyes.

"Something wrong?" The waitress stood with one hand on her hip and the other grasping the worn handle of a hot coffee pot.

"Excuse me?"

"You've had the check for ten minutes," she pointed to a greasy slip of paper under the plate. "You want another piece of pie?"

By the time Joanna finished with the cashier, the strange man had disappeared. So, she discovered when she walked out on the sidewalk, had her father.

5

True Love Never Did
Run Smooth

Calm down, nothing to worry about, he's fine.

Joanna hurried down one street then another, panic swelling in the pit of her stomach just as it had years ago when her three-year-old twins wandered away from her side at the supermarket.

Calm down, nothing to worry about.

She finally found her lost daughters all sticky-fingered with pudding-glazed grins, knocking back free sample cups of chocolate tapioca from a sugar-mad demonstration lady who missed her grandchildren down in Texas.

Calm down.

An old man stutter-stepping his cane along the sidewalk had vanished into the ether of this tiny town like an errant butterfly.

Damn it, where the hell has Dad gone?!

The city founders, sensible and foresighted, had laid out Pontiac on a symmetrical grid. The courthouse, befitting its architectural status, sat in the center of a perfect square. Avenues running north, south, west, and east surrounded the town jewel. Already Joanna had circled the courthouse twice and was beginning her third circuit. If he'd fallen, surely someone would have come to his aid. Curious bystanders. A paramedic called by a concerned shopkeeper. Perhaps he turned down a side street to look for his old grammar school, the one he mentioned with a wistful smile the first night at the motel. Yes, that must be it. Of course, that's where he is. But she didn't know the address.

"Hey, buddy!" her father would call to any stranger on the street whenever he needed directions. Joanna spun around in search of a kind neighborly face. Hey buddy, I need help, hey buddy, tell me where to go, hey buddy —

And then she saw him, a bent figure framed through the glass windows of Bill's Clip Joint. The old-time barber pole swirled in red, white, and blue and the front door proclaimed "Open for Business." A friendly bell jingled as Joanna entered. The shop smelled of Brilliantine and Lilac Vegetal, safe choices for gentlemen farmers with no interest in stinking up good clean prairie air with scents from a French whorehouse.

Her father, rigid and stone-faced, sat in an old Naugahyde chair. Tobacco-stained stuffing poked through one padded arm. Intently watching the barber trim the sideburns of a gray-maned man in a business suit, Owen did not notice his daughter until she stood in front of him.

"Dad, I was waiting for you inside the restaurant."

He looked for a moment as if he had just awakened from a dream.

"Is everything all right?"

He did not answer, re-directing his gaze back to the barber chair.

Joanna shifted uneasily. "You want a haircut, Dad, is that it?"

The handsome helmet of thick black hair she loved as a child had seriously thinned. Tender pink skin peeked through the center of his scalp.

"I know that sucker. Saw him down the street and followed him here so's I could be sure."

"The barber?"

Owen did not answer. Instead he propelled himself out of the phony leather chair toward the man with the gray mane. "Winston Auburn? You remember me?"

An old farmer, losing interest in the latest crop reports in the *Pontiac Daily Leader*, peered over his bifocals as Owen brushed past.

The gray mane looked up, "Have we met?"

"Oh we met all right. Your father made sure Asher Bentley got away with murder."

For the first time in twenty years Joanna heard the name her father had forbidden her to speak.

The man studied Owen for a moment then turned his back. "A little more off the sides, Bill."

Bill the Barber looked a little unsteady with all the fuss, but his hands complied. In the mirror on the wall Joanna could see her father's face turn a deep and violent red. He jabbed at the barber chair with his cane. "Junior Morse, you bastard. Now you remember?"

Winston Auburn said nothing.

Owen fisted his hands around the head of the birch cane that kept him upright. He spat, "I hope you and all your kin burn in hell." Then he limped out.

By the time Joanna got her father to the park across the street, Owen's tremors had kicked into double time. More out of breath with every shaky exhale, he sank into a bench next to the bronze soldier commemorating the fallen of the Great War.

"Maybe I should get some water —"

"I don't need any goddamned water."

"It's all right, Dad."

"No, it's not all right. It'll never be all right."

Joanna held her father's hand tighter, her own vibrating in concert with his.

"That son-of-a-bitch knew me, sure as the day is long. I may be old but I'm not dumb. God, I hated that kid. Badmouthing Aldine the way he done. He didn't care if a killer went free. Kept him and his folks in clover, all that Bentley money paying 'em off." Owen was still wheezing like a broken bellows, his gnarled fingers gripping the cane as if they would never let go.

"To hell with all of them," Joanna muttered, surprising herself with the sudden vehemence.

Her father grunted. "That's my daughter."

They sat in silence for almost a quarter of an hour, Owen's shoulders leaning into his daughter for support. Finally, Joanna put her jumbled thoughts into words.

"A long time ago, that Christmas after Mom died you told me ..." she trailed off.

"What?"

"Don't get mad at me for bringing it up, okay?"

"Jesus Christ, Joanna —"

"You said it wasn't just Bentley," she blurted. "You said ... somebody paid him to kill her."

"I told you that?"

"Yes."

Owen sighed. "That's what Ma figured. She said Uncle Frederick always wanted to get Aldine's money."

"Wasn't he your mother's brother?"

"Cain killed Abel. Just 'cause folks are family doesn't mean you can trust 'em ..."

~~~~~

Joanna inhaled sharply. In the two decades since her mother's death, she had suffered her own filial misgivings. Sometimes, in the quiet of the night when she had trouble sleeping, Joanna couldn't help but — as she delicately phrased the unimaginable in her mind — wonder. What if her mother's death was not quite as her father described it? What if he'd been drinking that afternoon? What if her mother had called for help and her father was too drunk to hear her? Even worse, what if they'd been fighting again and he deliberately ignored her dying cries?

"It was too late," Owen had sobbed when he told his daughter. The paramedics couldn't bring her back.

His eyes had pleaded for absolution but his daughter, overcome by grief, could offer none. Though she had hungered for her dad from the moment she was born, she did not trust him. Would never trust him — or anyone else — completely, she understood with jarring clarity. Nor should she. The risk loomed too large, too fraught with unanticipated consequences. To stay safe in this life, Joanna knew she must always keep her deepest self separate. She'd learned a lot at her father's knee, and Owen Morse Junior was right about not trusting. Anybody could turn on you. Anybody ...

~~~~

"… Ma went to the authorities to file charges against Bentley, but I guess she couldn't prove anything about her brother's dirty laundry …"

Owen was still talking, and Joanna realized she had no idea what he was trying to tell her. The past was past, and this was the only parent she had left. She needed to listen.

"… What could they do anyway? My uncle owned half of Fairbury. Sheriff couldn't even make the charges against Bentley stick down the line. That's what happens when you're poor."

"You said," Joanna tried to wrap her mind around the latest incongruity, "you said Aldine had money."

"Not by the time she was killed. The crook that managed her trust fund stole every last dime, and Ma found out later my uncle was in on it."

"But if the money was gone, why did your mother think her brother hired Bentley?"

"To keep Aldine from making sure my uncle got his just desserts."

"I don't understand —"

"No more, honey." Tremors were shaking his body with new force. "Please."

She hugged her father close. None of this made sense, but he was tired and upset now. There would be plenty of time to talk when he felt better.

"Do you want to go back to the motel to rest?"

"Maybe so."

He made no move to rise, just kept staring at the mashed potato clouds stuck low in the sky. A squirrel scampered over to collect his booty from the black oak that gave them shade. Up and down the trunk he raced; cheeks full to bursting. Like a fevered prospector, the animal dug a hole to hide the treasure he would reclaim later. More minutes passed.

"I miss your mother."

"So do I."

Owen fumbled in his shirt pocket for a cigarillo, looking away lest his daughter think him too sentimental. "True love never did run smooth."

The radio newscast had predicted heavy nighttime showers, but Joanna saw no hint of foul weather as she drove her father through Pontiac on his trip down memory lane. The old brick schoolhouse with the winding fire escape ... the basketball court where he played starting forward ... the library where he abandoned his grammar books to shoot marble tiger eyes behind the back alley ... and the last stop, a market where his sister treated him to bags of lemon drops and root beer chews after Saturday matinees.

"Take a right. Maybe it's down there."

And so Joanna turned right, then left again and circled the square a half dozen more times looking for the elusive market that would not be found. Waiting at the latest stop sign, her eyes drifted to the rear-view mirror. An old blue Ford idled, waiting for her to turn.

"I wanted the candy," Owen chuckled. "Aldine wanted to flirt with the butcher boy. Had a bad case on him." His smile faded. "'Til that went to hell in a handbasket too."

"What do you mean?"

"He walked out on her. That's what set the trash on fire in the end." Her father's jaw tensed. "We'll never find that place. Might as well go back to the motel."

"Over sixty years, Dad. Probably a new business now. We can check out some of the stores tomorrow."

"We'll see," he mumbled, morose again. "I might be dead by then."

"Then I'll just have a barrel of fun finding it by myself," Joanna snapped, hoping to prompt one of his prickly comebacks.

"Is that a promise to your old dad?"

"What?"

"You'll find the market for sure before we go back to California?"

"Cross my heart."

Owen rolled down the window for more air and whistled a chorus of "Yessir, That's My Baby" for a few minutes until his eyelids started to grow heavy. "There was a five and dime. A Woolworth's maybe ..."

Her father was already dozing when she spotted a 7-11 and stopped to get extra water for his medications. Also a can of salted cashews and fruit juice for a pick-me-up when he awoke. There was a long line. The dazed blonde in front of her couldn't come up with a usable credit card, and two teenagers tried to pass a phony ID for a six-pack so by the time Joanna finished, the five-minute stop had turned into almost fifteen. When she got back to the car, the passenger's side was empty.

"Dad?"

More exasperated this time than worried, Joanna returned to the 7-11 and asked the clerk if he'd seen an elderly gentleman slip into the men's room. He shrugged, too busy ringing up Snickers bars and Red Vines to notice anything but a paying customer.

"Anybody else see an elderly man with a cane?" she called out. "Plaid shirt, Levi's, cowboy boots?"

Blank faces stared back at her. A kid piped up. "Why would an old guy wear cowboy boots?"

Because he wanted his own ranch but never had the money, you little smart-ass. Bolting out of the store, Joanna's heart began to beat faster. At the end of the block she looked down both sides of the street and decided to head west on Locust.

~~~~~

The old blue Ford that had followed her from the Baby Bull was parked across from the 7-11. Tazewell sat behind the wheel, watching his younger cousin trot in the opposite direction. *Such a pretty baby. Well, a woman now.* He licked his little finger and smoothed the unruly hairs in his right eyebrow. The time to meet again was just around the corner.

~~~~~

Joanna did not want to be irritated because there was no reason to worry, none at all. Maybe her father took a fancy to a friendly dog that reminded him of his beloved lab back in California. Maybe he decided to call his next-door neighbor to make sure Natasha was getting her favorite pet chow or whatever it was big hungry dogs ate …

And there he was, leaning on his cane in front of a grand Victorian with a wrap-around latticed veranda. Joanna hurried to her father's side then blanched when she read the spring-green script on the white sign gracing a well-watered lawn:

HARTWIG MORTUARY AND FAMILY FUNERAL HOME

"That mansion is where Bentley lived."

"A funeral home?"

"Not then it wasn't. The mayor's family lived there. Him and his boy Asher, born with a silver spoon in his lying mouth."

Owen spat on the ground then reached for his daughter's arm to lean on and limped back to the car.

~~~

If he was a man, like his wife had always wanted him to be, he'd come back tonight after the moon was high and torch the goddamned place. Pick up a gallon of gas at the Shell they passed on the edge of town and set the Bentley place ablaze once and for all. Back when he was a boy, that's what he had wanted to do, promised himself he'd do soon as the time was right, but he never mustered the guts.

Until now.

Dammit, he still had a strong gait and believed there had to be some redemption in the world to compensate for its calamity and sorrow. Not that he believed in the law of man so much as he held to some notion of divine law acting through God's awakened children. And that's what he has come to be in his old age. Awake. Clear and focused, despite the botched cataract surgery that had left his right eye foggy and weak. Only fire could burn corruption clean. Took him seventy-six years to realize that fact, but better late than never.

Like it was yesterday Owen remembered the afternoon Asher Bentley had taken him for a ride in his big Packard and bought him two Snickers bars, one for each pocket. Aldine tousled his hair and made him promise to save the candy for after supper.

"My little Junior," she purred, hugging him close. And then she'd turned to Bentley with her dazzling smile, "Skinny, did you know my brother won himself a blue ribbon for being the Most Beautiful Baby at the 1920 Livingston County Fair?"

"How about that?" Bentley braked hard and dropped him at the curb. "We got business now. Your sister needs a man of property to advise her on some serious matters."

And off they sped in his Packard together.

The chubby cheeks that won the blue ribbon were sunken, the rosebud lips cracked, but Junior Morse was full-grown now. Tonight, Junior Morse would see justice done.

6

The Break

As soon as Owen and Joanna returned to the Comfort Inn, he slipped into a deep slumber. When she tried to wake him for dinner, he said he wasn't hungry then mumbled something about getting to the gas station before it closed.

"We'll do that tomorrow morning, Dad. You sleep tight now. It's been a long day."

She made sure that the amber plastic bottles of Parkinson's medications for his morning dosage were within reach on the night table then kissed her dad good night.

"Joanna?" Owen's eyelids were at half-mast now, trying to focus on his daughter's face.

"Yes?"

"I hope you live forever and I never die."

She leaned closer to tuck the blanket under his chin just as she used to do with her young daughters when they were afraid of the dark.

"I love you, Dad."

"Goodnight, honey."

She stood at her father's side a few minutes longer, waiting until his eyes closed again and his breathing softened, before closing the door between their rooms.

Feeling her own fatigue, Joanna settled in a hard-backed armchair, kicked off her shoes and flipped on the television to relax. But the chirpy weatherman's warnings about high pressure and tropical humidity held no interest. All she could focus on was his turquoise paisley tie and its uncanny resemblance to the one her father still kept in his bottom bureau drawer. A sentimental memento from the night his baby daughter was born over four decades ago. Her eyes began to mist in gratitude as she contemplated the change in their relationship since the return to Illinois, the reclaimed tenderness between them —

A clap of deafening thunder shook the room. Joanna hurried to the window and opened the drapes. The motel's neon sign cast an eerie blue gaze over fields of corn stretching as far as she could see down the highway. Dry stalks swayed in the quickening wind. But no rain.

And then the lightning struck.

A jagged knife of electricity sliced the sky in half and plunged the world into blackness. So black, Joanna could not see her hand in front of her face. A total power outage. Minutes passed. Ten? Maybe more. And still no light, inside or out …

She inched her way to the door between her father's room and her own and twisted the knob. The lock was frozen. Hearing her father's deep snores through the closed door, Joanna maneuvered her way outside into the motel corridor and turned right toward her father's room. A few steps into her blind trek she hit an immovable object. The double doors of the emergency fire exit had slammed shut. Joanna felt the cool steel bars against her belly and drove her full body weight against an exit that refused to let her through.

The Comfort Inn had transformed into a maximum-security prison on lockdown. Back in her room she managed her way to the phone and fumbled for the receiver. No dial tone. Impossible to reach anyone at the front desk. That's when she remembered she'd left her handbag and cell phone on the end table next to her father's bed. The ear-splitting thunder struck again. Rain pounded the roof like the storm that launched Noah's flood.

Joanna climbed into bed, knees huddled against her chest. She prayed her father was somehow sleeping through the deluge and waited for the lights to pop on again. When they did not, her imagination took a strange detour and ended up in the dark recesses of a Hitchcock movie seen long ago. The one with Kim Novak masquerading as some dead woman. Novak suffered an unhappy end despite the fact that Jimmy Stewart loved her. Then again maybe he only pretended to love her. There was some reason she kept trying to get away from him. That, Joanna recalled very clearly. Kim Novak at the top of some staircase trying to escape. But escape from what?

Joanna's bladder, in concert with her mood, grew heavy and despondent. More minutes crawled by. Then, it seemed, hours. She got out of bed and shuffled across the room. Start. Halt. Stop. Her steps carried no assurance of getting where she intended. Start. Halt. Stop. Start. Halt. Stop. This, she realized with chagrin, was exactly how her father walked. The only way age and infirmity allowed him to move even in the light of day. How impatient she used to be with his fearfulness, how powerless she felt now to dispel her own.

Finally she reached the bathroom. Bending down, she fingered the cold porcelain, positioned herself just so, and listened to the rush of relief pouring out of her body. Just when she was congratulating herself on being able to locate her ass in a blackout, the lights snapped on. Hallelujah.

Joanna allowed a few minutes before tapping on the door to her father's bedroom. The pitter-patter of raindrops on the roof always rocked him to sleep like a newborn. Then again this was no spring shower. Thanks to Hurricane Brenda's tantrums along the Gulf Coast, a fierce electrical storm was ripping ripe corn off the stalk across central Illinois. She hesitated before knocking again, not wanting to disturb him. Then she leaned closer to hear his heavy snoring through the door. Not a sound. The rain was pounding the windowpanes when she unlocked her dad's bedroom and found him gone. Along with the missing car keys no longer next to her handbag on the end table.

~~~~~

"Wait for me, Dad!"

Clutching her cell phone in case she needed to call for help, Joanna raced out of the motel in the middle of the thunderstorm. The same way she had been running to climb in the Buick when he was backing out of the driveway forty years before.

Her father, barefoot and pajama clad, was using his cane to push himself toward the driver's side of the rental car as fast as his creaking legs would carry him.

"Where are you going?" Trying not to let the alarm show in her voice, she smiled when she caught up with him. Even in the dark, she hoped he could see her smile.

"Lady, I don't know who you're talking to," her father glared over his shoulder. "Get out of my way now."

The rain came down harder but neither daughter nor father seemed to notice.

She grabbed his arm. "Dad, please, you don't have your license anymore, remember?"

"I'm not your father, Goddammit!" he shook himself free, knocking her so off-balance she slipped and fell to her knees on the parking lot asphalt. He hobbled into the car and sped away like a sixteen-year-old at a drag race.

By the time Joanna scrambled to her feet, he was gone. Under the headlights of a full moon, she looked down at her left knee. Skinned, bruised, blood and water trickling down her leg in crooked rivulets. Always, it was her left side that took a beating. Her cell phone lay in a dirty puddle of rainwater as the downpour dwindled into gentle raindrops. The neon letters of the Comfort Inn flashed on and off. On. Off. On.

Off.

～～～

It was just before dawn when Peter had returned her frantic call from the Comfort Inn to let her know the Pontiac ER was trying to reach the nearest relative of Owen Morse Junior. Fortunately, some orderly discovered the emergency card Joanna had slipped into her father's battered wallet next to the driver's license and Visa, both long expired.

"Are you all right?" Peter kept asking.

"I'm fine. I'll call you after I see my dad at the hospital," she promised, dumping her damaged cell phone into her bag.

"Do you need help handling this?"

"No," she said, still unsure what "this" was.

~~~~~

Police officers had found Owen Morse Junior stumbling in madness outside the Log Cabin restaurant on old Route 66. Spit dripping down his chin, he yelled to the heavens about setting the Bentley house on fire. Bentley who? Where? When? The officers demanded answers but received only rambling incoherence. They subdued him with hard steel cuffs first. Then, when they dropped him at the hospital, on came the leather restraints. Four orderlies kept him captive, each posted to one flailing limb as Haldol was injected into his wrinkled flesh. Just in case King Kong, in the body of an old man, lived.

"It was for his own good," the ER doctor on call told her.

"So he won't hurt himself or others," the nurse on duty added.

Too late for that, Joanna winced.

"When can I see him?"

They would let her know.

She asked more questions but received no answers. All Joanna could do now was comply with the rules of hospital admissions.

Sensing it was important to project a strong but measured, we're-all-adults-here demeanor, she introduced herself as Owen Morse's daughter.

The intake clerk did not bother to look up from her keyboard. "Medications?"

"Sinemet CR, 200 milligrams, three times a day for his Parkinsons; Simvastatin, 2.5 milligrams for high blood pressure; Zoloft, 100 milligrams for depression; Diltiazem, 30 milligrams for the heart. He has a weak heart."

The clerk did not appear to give a damn. Her black roots peeked out from dry red straw curling on top of her shoulders. Bad perm too.

"Any history of psychiatric hospitalizations?"

"No." Except for ... she remained silent.

Except for those couple months after the accident. When Joanna was old enough, her mother confided that Daddy once spent a little time at a rest home to settle his nerves. A hospital, actually, not really a rest home when you got right down to it. After what happened, his mind too focused on getting to work that he did not see his only child as he backed the family car out of the driveway one spring morning …

"No history of mental illness in the family?"

"None."

He lost himself. Panicked. Rushed into the middle of a busy street, screaming and wailing, zigzagging between stunned motorists, raising his daughter's body to the sky like Abraham's sacrifice so God Himself might bear witness. Of course, she was screaming too, only eighteen months old when a 2400-pound Buick sedan smashed her baby arm flatter than a pancake. (Buy American, her father advised when she saved enough to get her first car. Nothing says solid like a GM product.)

Not that she remembered anything. Not the pain nor the crushing weight nor the terror of looking into the black bowels of a machine she could not stop. Who was Joanna against its might? The mercy was that she had no memory of what came after — or even what came before. No memory whatsoever of racing out an unhinged screen door to climb into the Buick's passenger seat next to her father while her mother sat on the bathroom toilet answering nature's call.

No man has eyes in the back of his head. That's what everybody said whenever her mother recounted the dramatic details of their toddler's brush with death. An occasional ritual, especially popular around Joanna's birthdays, that seemed to inspire everyone present — save Joanna and her father — to titter and laugh and shake their heads with genuine amazement. The Goodyear tire marks were imprinted in her baby fat for over two weeks! Nothing broken because her bones weren't fully formed yet! Only a month older, the doctors said, and her left clavicle would have been crushed! (No need to reference the painful scar tissue that reared its ugly head with the passing of the years.) Thank heavens their little girl was not damaged.

"Our pride and joy," her mother would smile, eyes glistening with relief, "what would we do without her?"

"Ma'am, did you hear what I asked?" the clerk stopped typing and looked up at Joanna. "Substance abuse?"

"Well, he drinks. He used to, I mean. He's been sober over three months now."

Dad deserves some credit for that. Although Joanna had no comprehension of how or why he stopped his nightly binges. Some mysterious thing louder than his daughter's voice scared him straight.

The clerk resumed tap-tap-tapping away on her keyboard like a rabid woodpecker assaulting a defenseless old elm.

"Any previous episodes of delusional behavior?"

"Delusional?"

The clerk looked up, more bored than exasperated. "Does he know who he is? Where he is? It's not a trick question. Is the man in touch with reality?"

The muscles in Joanna's jaw jackknifed. "I don't think it's necessary to take that tone —"

"What do I need to do to get a complete answer here, ma'am?"

Joanna glared at the rude woman in front her. Who in the hell was she to pass judgment?

"My father is not well —"

"Does he know who *he* is?"

"Yes, yes he does."

Liar. The clerk's watery eyes narrow. Liar, they say.

The problem, Joanna wanted to tell her — if only the bitch had one crumb of compassion which clearly she did not — the problem is that her father does not know who *she* is.

7

Cause and Effect

The sight of her father's naked buttocks made her want to cry. Joanna looked away and cleared her throat to announce her presence. Once. Twice. Thrice. But his bare bottom stayed visible. Exposed. His pasty skin whiter than the skimpy hospital gown failing to cover his private parts. Mustering dignity for both of them, she walked in and lifted the sheet at the foot of the bed to cover him. He did not seem to notice.

Over thirty hours had passed since her father arrived at the hospital. When the staff insisted that his condition must be stabilized before visitors were allowed, Joanna occupied herself with necessary business. First, she had to claim the Corolla ditched on the front lawn of Hartwig's Mortuary & Family Funeral Home just before Owen Morse had wound his way to what was left of Old Route 66. Once the Mother Road, now a ghost road of weed-infested broken blacktop, it split into pieces after Illinois built Interstate 116 back in the seventies. Thankfully, the rental car was not damaged, the sergeant on duty said as he handed her the ignition keys. More than could be said of her father. Then there was the call to Hornbeck's office that she had to return. When they offered different times to visit the family farm, she said that could wait for another day.

"Would you like to schedule later in the week?" Mr. Hornbeck's secretary inquired.

Joanna's voice cracked when her father's health became an unexpected topic of conversation. A dizzy spell, she lied. Tests at the hospital to make sure he didn't suffer a stroke.

Mr. Hornbeck's secretary promised that Mr. Morse would be in her prayers. Joanna thanked her, hung up the phone, and finally fell into a deep dreamless sleep. Awaking after thirteen hours with a drug-like hangover, she still wore yesterday's clothes. Determined to see her father no matter what the doctors said, she pummeled her face with a dozen splashes of cold water and headed to the hospital.

Owen lay on his left side staring out a dirty window that faced the rooftop parking lot. A Technicolor sea of late-model Toyotas were lined up side by side next to their brother Hondas and sister Nissans, all those damned Japanese cars that put his beloved GM on the ropes. Today he stayed silent on the subject of American manufacturing's demise, his fingers busy twisting grey strands of hair into circles of tactile comfort.

It was a small inhospitable room with only one chair. The same soulless Swedish Modern that had been in the reception area of the mortuary where she had gone to make arrangements for her mother's burial. Her father did not accompany her that morning. He had already done what he could. Called the paramedics when her mother collapsed. Followed the ambulance to the emergency room where she was pronounced dead. No man should be expected to do more, not after his own heart cracked open along with his wife's.

"How are you, Owen?"

The doctor had advised her not to identify him as her father. The patient was, apparently, still not ready to remember he had a daughter. He stopped twisting his hair and looked at Joanna for a long moment then laughed. A little boy's laugh of recognition.

"Don't call me OWEN! You know I hate that name."

Joanna smiled in relief. This was true. He'd never liked the foreign name given by his Welsh-born father. Hope softened the fear lodged in her throat. He *did* know her. Yes, they were both in on the joke now. It was all a silly game that had gotten out of hand. The Game of Pretend they used to play when she was a little girl, before they moved to California, before her mother and father started hating each other. She would pretend to be the beautiful princess in the dark watchtower, he the ogre climbing to capture her in his big, burly arms. Her fate was always the same. Being tickled to death on the living room carpet. Sometimes she laughed so hard she peed her pants.

"Help me, Mommy!" Joanna screamed.

That was the cue for her mother to stride in from the kitchen — "You two monkeys at it again?" — and attack one hairy male armpit while Joanna's small fingers strained to reach the other. Her dad rose to the occasion, summoning an ear-blasting ogre roar to terrify his tormenters. The three of them rolled and wrestled and laughed until the Game of Pretend ended with her mother rushing back to stir the pot of spaghetti sauce on the stove. The ogre vanished and her beloved father reappeared, hoisting the princess on top of his broad shoulders and escorting her to supper in the family castle.

"What do you want me to call you?" Joanna asked her father, ready to keep playing the game if that's what he wanted.

"What you always call me," he chuckled, still twisting his hair, "Junior!"

"Junior." Joanna repeated without expression. Her father studied her face, sensing her disapproval.

"Are you still mad at me?" he pouted, the hair twisting fast and furious now.

"I'm not mad at you."

"Then why can't we go back to the fair like you said?"

"Where?"

"The Fairbury Fair! You promised you'd take me back last Saturday. After I finished hauling hay at the Deckers."

Joanna nodded dumbly.

"But you didn't. Why not? Were you out with the butcher boy again? The one you're sweet on? Or is that old bald guy still bothering you? I can beat him up if you want."

She attempted to formulate the exact words that would bring him back to his senses. "I'm sorry ... I'm not sure who we're talking about ... Junior."

"Is it because of what the gypsy said?" he pressed. "Is that it? Is it?"

She didn't answer. There were no answers. Only his questions coming at her again and again.

"Why won't you talk to me?"

Her father opened his hand and reached for the woman at his bedside. "Aldine?"

～～～

Owen Morse's doctor had just finished rounds and was heading to the elevator when Joanna ambushed him with her latest barrage of questions.

"How can you be sure it wasn't a stroke?"

"The MRI showed no evidence of significant stenosis, branch vessel occlusion, vascular malformation, or aneurysm."

"A concussion? Maybe he fell, a brain hemorrhage —"

"Again, this would have been indicated on the MRI."

"I'm afraid to ask." Joanna's voice grew softer. "Alzheimer's?"

"According to the nursing staff his short-term memory appears to be excellent. Mr. Morse not only remembers the exact breakfast, lunch, and dinner menu items he'd ordered," the doctor chuckled, "he even regaled orderlies with the latest exploits of Susan Lucci after he watched his favorite soap opera."

Joanna did not find the doctor's lighthearted approach to a very serious matter at all helpful. "Dementia, it must be dementia."

"A man of your father's advanced years and history of alcohol consumption would be a prime candidate, no question. But dementia is not a sudden onset condition."

"Never? How can you be sure?"

"Actually, your father is doing very well since we stabilized him with medication. Maybe his earlier episode was a simple panic attack or temporary psychosis —"

"Temporary, yes."

"— because the only time your father demonstrates any confusion at all now is …" The doctor stopped, looking too bemused for Joanna's taste.

"What?"

"… when you come to visit. Odd, isn't it?"

Odd? Odd was when two even numbers did not add up. And numbers, she understood. Numbers were her business. Joanna had devoted her entire professional life to balancing the ledgers of the most successful, and she was proud to say, upstanding families in Pasadena, California. A CPA above reproach, she provided the certitude of equations that did not lie. Four and four equaled eight. Three and three equaled six, only six, always six, six into infinity. There was no question that could not be answered through rigorous computation. Her mind raced to find a logical explanation for this so-called medical expert's argument that her father suffered from a peculiar form of delusion only in his daughter's presence. Every effect is preceded by a cause, this she knew as surely as she knew that her name was not Aldine Younger.

Perhaps she had asked too many questions about his dead sister when they were eating that lousy peach pie and that's why he drove off in the middle of the night and abandoned the rental car and ended up wandering down a deserted stretch of old highway — all to communicate that it was a sensitive subject best left untouched. Of course, she knew that even as a child. But it was not her idea to spend two hours lost in melancholic reverie next to the wind-swept grave of a woman buried sixty-three years ago!

Mourning the past never served a purpose as far as she could see. The only thing that made sense in life was to do your duty today, whatever that may be. Which was the exact reason that she dragged her father halfway across the country to get a proper accounting of the family legacy that he was due. How else would he ever find the peace that had eluded him all these years? Any loving daughter would have done the same.

"According to the psychiatrist who spoke with Mr. Morse," the doctor squinted at a jumble of illegible notes on the clipboard, "his wife is dead ..."

"Yes."

"... and he had a daughter who died in a car accident when she was a baby ..."

Joanna's stomach heaved. "There was a car accident but obviously I did not die."

"You're his only daughter?"

"Yes, I'm his only daughter. Am I on trial here?"

"Excuse me?"

"Never mind. What else did my father tell you?"

"Let's see ... he's in town to settle some business about a family home-stead that his half-brother left him in a will?"

"Yes, that part is accurate."

"Apparently he's planning to move into this homestead with his sister Aldine?"

"Impossible. She died in 1933."

"And this is the woman you say he is confusing you with?"

"Yes." Yes, yes, yes, how many times did she have to repeat this?

"The mind is a funny animal," he shrugged, closing his clipboard with another maddening half-smile as he ambled back toward the elevator. "There's no statute of limitations on grief, is there?"

He was the doctor — why was he asking her questions? Would she require him to be conversant with tax codes that enabled physicians to avoid paying undue penalties on their six figure incomes? No. All she expected — wanted, needed — was for somebody with the brain, heart, and vision to tell her what to do next.

"Excuse me ... excuse me!" her heels clicked down the corridor in hot pursuit.

The doctor turned, not even trying to hide his exasperation at her persistence.

"Please," Joanna stopped, out of breath. "Just tell me what you're do-ing — what I should do — to bring him back to reality?"

"We'll observe him through the end of the week. If he still doesn't recognize you then we'll transfer him to the psychiatric hospital in Peoria for further evaluation."

"At his age? No. I don't think that's a good idea at all."

"When the time comes, Mrs. Giordano," the doctor stepped into the open elevator, "that decision will not be your responsibility."

Joanna stood frozen and alone in the hospital corridor. Not her responsibility? Ridiculous! No matter what the damned doctor said, somebody needed to shake her father out of fantasyland. Maybe if she showed him pictures of his grandchildren? Yes, ground him in the present, that's what needed to be done. She charged back to her father's room and arrived in a dead heat with the nurse's aide carrying a big bouquet of long-stemmed white roses.

"Flowers!" Owen beamed. "You're not mad at me anymore, are you, Aldine?"

His daughter's cheeks flushed hot and angry, but her words were steady. "I already told you I wasn't mad, remember?"

"I hope my redheaded girlfriend is pretty like the gypsy told me."

Joanna's head pounded. What in the hell was he talking about?

"And love me even when I'm bad? Will she, Aldine? Will she?"

"Of course," Joanna said, determined to bring her father back to reason. But when she displayed wallet photos of her daughters from their 12th birthday party and Owen asked if they could all go roller-skating together after the fair, she knew it was time to leave.

"We'll talk about that tomorrow." She tucked the photos back in her purse and stood up to leave.

"Wait! Some sugar before you go," he pursed his lips into loud smacking sounds like a little kid.

Joanna carried Owen's goodbye gift — a white rose in her right hand — as she walked out.

"Because you're pretty as a rose, Aldine."

She waited until arriving at the reception desk downstairs before handing off the long-stemmed beauty to an overworked clerk who acted like Valentine's Day just came early. No card had been attached to the roses. Although she wished her family would have ordered a flower with some color, Joanna called Peter from the lobby pay phone to thank him for his thoughtfulness. Her husband had no idea what she was talking about.

"Well then, I guess you must have told the girls?"

"Not yet, not with the time difference."

That's right. Their daughters were in Rome half a world away.

"What does the doctor say?"

"He says …" Joanna hesitated, "… it looks like Dad will be under observation for a few days."

"So he's all right then?"

"Yes. A little confused."

"You're sure you don't need me?"

She answered his question with her own. "So you haven't heard from Sarah or Elizabeth since I left?"

"They're on that side trip to Lake Como, remember?"

"Still?"

"They'll be away for a week. You've only been gone two days, Joanna."

"Of course," she laughed, covering her anxiety with small talk before she hung up.

Still muddled about the roses, she decided to phone the local florist shop to get the name of the Good Samaritan who made her father's day. But they had no record because the sender paid in cash. All the clerk remembered was an older gentleman with a soft voice, so soft she had to ask him to repeat the name of the intended recipient twice.

"Maybe an old friend," the clerk offered. "News travels fast in Pontiac. And you know how some folks are. They don't like to draw attention to themselves."

"Well, thank you anyway." Joanna exited the phone booth and walked to the parking lot.

Fifteen minutes later, overwhelmed with the recent onslaught of unsolvable mysteries in her life, Joanna sat in her parked car with nowhere to go. She turned the ignition key, then switched it off, unsure what to do next. She closed her eyes against the sun's glare on the windshield. Her temples pulsed, her throat tightened, and she found it difficult to take a complete breath.

"Please, God," she whispered. "Please ..."

Inexperienced in prayer despite occasional holiday church attendance, she decided less was more; if God were truly listening, the great being would know what to do. Provide guidance. Give her a sign, for crying out loud. Isn't that how the Almighty communicated with people? He showed them signs. She sat in silence, waiting. Still, no lightning bolt of illumination on demand.

Damn it.

She lifted her eyelids, flipped the visor to shut out the merciless afternoon light, and started the car to head back to the motel. At the edge of the hospital parking lot, a green and white billboard with a latticed border greeted drivers as they exited:

**"HARTWIG MORTUARY & FAMILY FUNERAL HOME
FOR YOUR EVERY NEED"**

8

Locust & Main

Such a cheery looking fellow for an undertaker. Toothy grin, ruddy cheeks, pink polo shirt tucked into pleated khakis. Charles "call me Charlie" Hartwig pumped Joanna's hand and introduced himself as the good citizen who called police to report an elderly man disturbing the peace shortly before midnight on Thursday.

"I'm generally a sound sleeper," Charlie volunteered, ushering her into his Victorian sitting room decorated in tasteful floral damask.

"At least that's what the wife says. But she was down in Springfield visiting her cousin's new baby when your father came pounding at the door, so it ended up being me who answered. Raining cats and dogs and this elderly gentleman in his PJs, sopping wet, wanted to speak to somebody named Bennighan."

"Bentley? Could he have been saying Bentley?"

"Well, you might be right there. I considered that possibility the next morning. Sure I can't interest you in a cup of coffee? Fresh brewed, still on the stove."

She shook her head, unsure how the happy-faced Mr. Hartwig could share a home with cadavers awaiting his personal touch in the basement downstairs. This grand house, as much as the business conducted here, unsettled her.

"You know the name then?"

"Sure, Grandpa George bought this place from the Bentleys for a song at the end of the Depression. A beauty, isn't it?" Charlie gazed upon the interior of his home with pride. The Italian marble fireplace, high gloss mahogany banisters, leaded glass windows with the view of the park across the street.

"Lovely." Joanna managed a polite nod.

"Death has been good to our family," Charlie chuckled then added an aside. "Humor of the trade."

"Yes ... about my father?"

"In sorry straits, I'm afraid. Thought I was the housekeeper's husband and told me that as soon as he found a gas station open he'd be back to ... how'd he put it? Oh yes, 'settle affairs,' that's what he said. And then off he went back into the rain. He gets on pretty well with that cane of his, doesn't he?"

"Yes, he does."

"That's when I saw the car parked in the front yard right next to the hydrangea bushes. Well, he gets in, puts it in reverse, knocks our sign down then gets stuck in the mud. I grabbed the umbrella to go help him but he steps out, yelling and shaking his fist to stay back, then heads down the street toward the turn-off to old Route 66."

"I'm sorry for your trouble. If there are costs to reimburse —"

"Just some skid marks. Grass grows back, and my handyman's coming to fix the sign tomorrow. It's the ash tree next to the old garage that could be bad for business. What's left of it."

"He hit the tree too?"

"Lord no. The darned lightning set it on fire. Burned all the leaves and charred the trunk something awful. Even seared the paint off the garage doors."

"The lightning started it?"

"That's what we figure."

Joanna remembered the police report, her father's words that *he burned* the Bentley place down. Did he see the burning tree and think he set the fire?

"Thank goodness it was storming buckets that night and put the sucker out."

"Yes, thank goodness."

"Enough about my problems." Charlie leaned forward with a look of practiced concern. "How is your poor father? A small stroke or something, was it?"

What do you care, Joanna wanted to scream. *Looking for a new customer to fill with formaldehyde?*

"He's recovering," she lied. "I hope to take him home to California next week."

"Glad to hear it," he lied right back.

She could tell Charlie didn't believe her. Why should he? She didn't believe herself. "Do you know anything about the family that lived here before? The Bentleys?"

"No, I'm afraid that was before my time." He stood up, signaling he had places to go, people to see. Joanna stood also. And kept talking.

"And you never heard any stories handed down from your parents or grandfather?"

"None of that drinking in the rusty water trough of the past for my folks," Charlie smiled, walking her to the door. "Progress, that's our motto. Keep moving forward. Three generations in the undertaking profession, you got to keep up with the times, all the industry developments and such. Gives customers confidence."

"No history of the house and its former owners then?"

"Like I said —"

"The reason I ask is because," Joanna pushed on, "when we bought our home in Pasadena —"

Opening the door, Charlie turned to his guest with new interest. "Pasadena? Pasadena, California?"

"Yes. It's an older home like yours. Built in 1924. The real estate agent gave us this whole file, kind of a house biography ..." Joanna realized she was babbling now but Charlie was listening hard with a hint of — what? Curiosity? Compassion?

"... that had been accumulated from city records and newspaper archives. Interesting family stories, that sort of thing. Our first owner was a newspaper editor from Indiana, the first to publish the poetry of James Whitcomb Riley —"

Charlie interrupted. "I bet you get front row seats on New Year's Day."

"Excuse me?"

"The Rose Parade. Bet you never miss it."

Not exactly. Her husband had grown tired of the pre-dawn risings soon after they moved to town. And now their children were more interested in partying the night away on New Year's Eve than waving at animated fantasy creatures and princesses perched on flowered thrones. The last time Joanna went, she went alone. Standing at the corner of Colorado and Orange Grove, she could not believe her good luck in moving to the city of roses after all those years in a desert burg where only cactus bloomed. Electricity still danced down her spine every time another band of high-steppers swung into action, blowing their joyful noise all the way down the boulevard. "Throw away your cares, get happy," her father used to whistle when a favorite band marched by on the TV screen. "Throw away your cares ..."

"I was thinking about taking the missus out to see it in person. Do some reconnaissance for our big Frontier Days Parade here," Charlie winked. "Maybe you could twist a few arms to get us some good seats?"

"Of course, whatever I can do to help."

He plucked one of his conveniently placed "two-for-one" business cards from the hallway table. On the front: Hartwig Mortuary, Charles Hartwig, Proprietor. On the back: Chamber of Commerce, Charles Hartwig, President. Then he presented his credentials to Joanna and waited for her to do the same.

Which she did. Quid pro quo.

"A CPA?" he noted, lifting his eyebrows in respect.

"Yes."

"Smart. Folks always need a tax man." He quickly amended the offending noun. "Or gal, as the case may be." Appreciating their common brilliance in career choices, Charlie decided to be more generous. "There is someone who might know about the Bentley family. Old Marcus Washington. Must be pushing ninety by now."

Joanna pulled out her Day-Timer, pen at the ready. "Can you give me his number?"

"Nope. Mr. Washington doesn't believe in phone service. Disconnected his years ago."

"His address then —"

"Who knows? He pulled down the numbers on his porch too. Just head down St. John Street. The last house on the north side. With the peeling shutters. Can't miss it."

"It doesn't sound like he wants visitors."

"Tell him Charlie Hartwig sent you. Mr. Washington's nephew got killed in a head-on collision back in '77. I put him back together for the family visitation, one of my finest preservations, if I do say so myself."

Joanna expressed her gratitude and promised to return the favor which Charlie had no doubt she would. He watched her drive away then stepped off the porch to go take a closer look at his damaged property.

"A sad sight, that is." The man in the blue Ford rolled down the window to offer his condolences.

Charlie, still surveying the remains of his prize ash tree, smiled at his right-hand man from the Chamber's Board of Directors. "You keeping banker's hours now?"

"Had business to attend to in Bloomington this morning. I told them I'd be back by noon. You should've heard the fuss. They can't keep the place operating without me."

"That's the truth."

"Taking the tree down, Charlie?"

"Not sure yet. You want to hear something funny?"

"I could use a laugh."

"They say lightning doesn't strike in the same place twice. But three times this old tree's been hit by lightning since Easter! What're the odds?"

"Time to cut out its roots, I'd say."

"Maybe so." Regret tinged Charlie's voice as he admired the thickness of the blackened trunk. "Over a hundred years this has been here. Planted when the house was built, we figure."

"A man has to protect his property," Tazewell pointed out. "That's all a man has."

9

Marcus Washington

Joanna knocked on the carved oak door of the two-story clapboard house again. Louder. A lace curtain, touched by an invisible hand, lifted.

"Mr. Washington?"

She leaned on the doorbell once, twice, then a third time, hoping the irksome jangle would do its job.

Still nothing.

"Charlie Hartwig sent me!" she announced, rapping on the door again until it finally cracked open.

"For what purpose?" a reedy voice demanded. No human being showed himself.

"I ... I thought you could give me some information about the Asher Bentley family who used to reside in Pontiac."

A full minute passed without a response.

"Mr. Washington, are you still there?"

The door widened a sliver more.

"Who are you?"

"Joanna Giordano. I'm in town on family business with my father, Owen Morse."

Another long pause.

"Junior Morse?"

"Yes."

A gentleman, bent with the years, inched the door wider until he and Joanna were face to face. He wore a frayed silk dressing gown, topped by a paisley ascot knotted in the wrinkled folds of his neck.

"I'm sorry to disturb you. My father's in the hospital ..."

She felt his watery eyes, hard and suspicious, taking her measure.

"... and his mind is not quite clear I'm afraid, so I thought —"

"What?" His voice sounded gruffer.

What indeed. "Maybe you could help ..." she drifted off. "... in some way."

"You think talking about the man who killed his sister will clear his mind?"

"You remember what happened then. Did you know Aldine Younger?"

His face tightened as he started to close the door.

"Please, Mr. Washington."

"No."

"I'll pay for your time."

"It's not always about money, Mrs. Giordano. Something your family never understood."

"I don't know what you mean."

"Kindly leave before I call the police."

"You can't call the police. Charlie Hartwig told me your phone is disconnected," Joanna blurted. "Please, this is for my father. If you used to know him ... and my aunt ... I would be so grateful."

Marcus looked away. "I'm not dressed to receive visitors."

"Maybe I could come back later. A more convenient day?"

Another interminable pause.

"All right then."

"Oh, thank you so much." Joanna swallowed in relief.

"What would be a good —"

"Not today."

And he shut the door.

"When?" Joanna called out, banging on the wooden barrier between them.

Marcus gave no answer.

Joanna stood on the porch a full minute before resigning herself to the unpleasant fact she had been dismissed. There would be no audience with the inscrutable Mr. Washington this afternoon.

"Rude bastard," she muttered to herself, slinking back to the car. Then again, he didn't know her from Adam. What if some stranger showed up on her father's front step without warning? He'd send the interloper on his way too. Yes, she would come back and Mr. Washington *would* help her. "No" was a word Joanna had long ago refused to accept.

Behind the closed door, Marcus waited, his temple pressed against the unyielding oak. Not until he heard the car engine accelerating down the street did he move. Instead of returning to the kitchen where he had been brewing his daily constitutional cup of tea, he walked in a different direction to a different destination. Toward a precious legacy that had never left his possession.

"I trust you," Aldine had said. "You will keep it safe for me."

His gait surer now, he advanced toward the back bedroom where he kept prized family possessions. He stood for a short while in front of yet another closed door. Preparing for the choice he was about to make. His gnarled fingers turned the brass knob, and he entered the place that had long since been sealed against human disturbance.

Across from the old bed a walnut Victorian secretary stood nine feet tall, only a few inches from grazing the ceiling above it. Marcus, his worn joints straining at the effort, bent down to open the bottom drawer. Under the folds of his mother's embroidered linens lay a leather diary clasped with a brass-plated lock and tarnished key. Held in confidence, as he had pledged to Aldine. He lifted the keepsake out of its hiding place with trembling hands and began to read the secret long-ago words of a girl who had died before her time ...

III

SEEDINGS

Private Musings & Verse by Miss A. Younger

JULY 6, 1925

Tea Party

Aunt Libby sipped from a china cup
Nibbled stale bread
Oozing with deviled ham
And sat on her throne like a queen
In a circle of crones under big hats

Say how do you do Aldine
Pass the plates
To the good pastor's wife
Strawberries red-faced and plump
Such a happy crop this year

I did as I was told
Laughing
Too loud
Much too loud
For ladies with stapled lips

My aunt's mouth turned upside down
Her forehead puckered and frowned
I could not stop laughing
She did not know
I spied a curly gray hair
Peeking out of her pretty little nose

I will never grow old

Ma made me go. Like always. July 1st every year, rain or shine, my
Aunt Libby welcomes her bosom buddies from the Daughters of the

American Revolution for her Summer Soiree, as she calls it. O let freedom ring and spare me their silly chatter!

With pretense of attending to feminine necessity I excused myself
from the tea table to take a gander at the family portraits lining the
back hallway. What a handsome couple my aunt and uncle looked on
their wedding day, him with his dashing dark Valentino eyes, though
I've never heard them exchange a sweet word. Ma says they deserve
each other whatever that means.

"Thick as thieves, the two of them."

"That's a funny thing to say, Ma."

"What's funny about it?"

"Because Aunt Libby is kin to the famous Younger outlaw gang."

"Who told you that?"

"Horatio."

Ma kind of smiled, which doesn't happen often, but when I asked
if my dead papa and I were Younger outlaws too, she shushed me.

All of a sudden I heard some sharp steps and turned around to
see Uncle Frederick hauling down the stairs lickety-split, no doubt off
to the hills until the hen party was over. When I was little he used to
always have a pocketful of wintergreens for me when our family gath-
ered for the Threshermen's Parade, but on this occasion he did not
even cast a friendly smile my way.

"Hello Uncle Frederick, how are you on this fine summer day?"

"As well as can be expected."

He pulled himself up stiff and business-like.

"What is that behind you, Uncle?" I nodded to a framed needle-
point on the wall behind him. There was a fierce-eyed dragon smack
dab in the center, all done up in threads of gold and silver and purple
and green.

"Ah, that is the Heinemann coat of arms your late grandmother
embroidered with her own dear hands after coming to America."

"From the city of Kassel," I said, showing off my smarts. "Ma says
we come from a long line of burgermeisters accustomed to breaking
bread with important folk. No wonder the dragon is so grand. Does he
breathe fire?"

"It's heraldry, Aldine," he said, his mouth curling at the corners like I didn't know anything.

"There are lots of stories about dragons in the Brothers Grimm. Do you remember the one about —"

"I don't have time to read fairy tales, child."

"Ma said the Brothers were neighbors back in Germany and that's why we have so many of their old books. Pretty pictures but the covers are terrible worn —"

"The ladies must be missing you in the parlor. If I were you I dare not keep them waiting one minute longer."

All right then, I can take a hint. After my uncle grumped his way out the door, I braced for another cup of bitter tea at the hen party. Soon as I walked in Ma nodded for me to sit down straightaway next to my sister, Bertha, boring as can be. I helped myself to the last egg salad sandwich and did my honest best to pay attention but the Pastor's wife was in the middle of a long loud conniption fit about her poor husband and how he works himself to death among his sinful flock trying to be helpful so I said —

"Why not leave the work to Jesus?"

One of the other ladies laughed. My aunt quickly poured the Pastor's wife another cup of tea and passed the cookies but nobody answered my question.

"Watch your tongue," Bertha whispered real low, so's my cousin couldn't hear, "what do you know about the Son of God at your age?"

Plenty, I wanted to say but knew better. Ma gave me one of her hard looks.

Fact is, I've been on speaking terms with Jesus ever since I started Sunday school. Not the sad-eyed dying thing on the cross but the wild and mighty Jesus who turned the tables and told the crooked priests to go to hell. Jesus always knew he was born to fight the Philistines. We have that in common. But alas, only Mrs. Tilstrom who always gives me the highest marks in class seems to appreciate my special nature. Papa Morse too, when he's not in the dumps weighed down with big feelings.

I am thankful he mostly saves his harsh words for Horatio, though he can show his short fuse with Ma too when she nags him bad. Last week after supper when Ma was busy in the kitchen washing the boys, Papa Morse brightened up and told me about his adventures traveling the world — I swear his Welsh brogue sounds as pretty as a harp — and he said that I have the makings of an adventuress myself! I confided my dream to sail to the Greek Islands some day and dive in the deep blue Aegean Sea and he promised to teach me how to swim down in the creek so that I will have no fear when the time comes.

"You got to be brave-hearted," he said. "That's the only way to make your way in the world."

As brave as an Amazon warrioress I'll be, braver than any girl before or since! *Ay*

OCTOBER 1, 1925

Junior and Absher were wailing to beat the band when I came home from choir practice and Papa Morse was nowhere to be seen. Bertha said good riddance because he and Ma had a terrible row on account he was a lazy good-for-nothing living off Ma's kindly nature instead of providing for his family like any decent husband. You heard him yelling and stomping around when Ma told him to go around town and look for more milk delivery accounts. He's evil mean, I don't care what you say.

I kept my thoughts to myself like usual. Bertha says whatever Ma says but I know different. Just because Papa Morse has big feelings doesn't mean he's all bad. I don't care if he isn't my own blood! Who will teach me to swim now?

MARCH 22, 1926

In our house animals get fed first. Every morning my big brother sees to the livestock, slopping the sow, pitching alfalfa for the horses, grinding soybeans for those dumb white-faced Herefords, but to heck with the rest of us. Horatio struts around like he's king of the hill since Ma dumped the Welshman's clothes on the front porch and sent him packing. The sad thing is I swear Old Lou the Guernsey kicked Horatio in the head when he pinched one of her teats sometime a while back. Ma, being Ma, pretends his mean streak only showed itself after my stepfather moved in. Truth is, Horatio has been disturbed longer than I care to remember.

Nobody knows that better than Owen Junior! I feel a world full of pity for the boy. His looks favor the stallion that spawned him. Black hair, brown eyes, complexion dark as a Spaniard. Just as fearsomely handsome too. No wonder ugly Horatio hates the little tyke, what with his pretty face and Junior's daddy laying the leather strap on Horatio in the back of the barn when Ma went into town. Now that my step-father's left us — Ma says the Welshman went to sell his milk to another widow — Horatio's got Junior in his clutches good and hard.

At Friday dinner my big brother sat at the head of the table like the Emperor of China. Sure enough he carved the breast of roast chicken for his own plate. Junior, his big eyes all round, fixed on that old hen carcass like it was the Last Supper and Pilate's soldiers were coming at dawn. Absher too, but being as he's the baby, Ma cut him a special portion to fit his size.

"Can I please have the drumstick?" Junior begged.

"Wait your turn!" Horatio ordered.

Junior, slow with the tutoring of his table etiquette, reached for the drumstick anyway. Horatio roared like the beast he is and slapped little Junior's hand away. Hard. Things went quiet as a graveyard. Ma stood up, sighed deep and loud like she does, then ordered everybody to mind their manners and spooned an extra helping of snap beans on Junior's plate along with the darned drumstick. Horatio never sasses Ma, he knows better.

But the worst was yet to come for Junior. Soon as the table got cleared, Horatio pushed Junior outside to finish off hog butchering. The poor boy started crying while Horatio mocked him awful. Ham hock, Tenderloin, Pork Chop — each pig had a name, courtesy of Horatio. Cutting tender pink throats is all in a day's business for him. No matter, Junior loves those pigs same as Bonniedoon's collie pups. Not that Horatio gives a good g___ d____ about the pigs, the pups, Bonniedoon, or anybody else. In my smart new womanhood I can now see how he's like my stepfather that way.

Down by South Creek where the Vermilion River pools at the end of Ma's property is where Papa Morse used to fish. I can see him now, his big head of silver-white hair shining like King Neptune himself, spinning his grand tales like each one was meant just for you. It was a wonder how he slipped his strong man hands below the surface of the water and called forth the carp that swam there. First one then another, he tickled their soft bellies until they went into a trance, gently herding them into the narrow part of the creek under the sycamores. Then he suddenly threw 'em way up on the bank too far from the water for them to flop back in and escape.

Like a snake charmer he is. No wonder Ma fell for his glad handing when he was the main delivery man in these parts, picking up the freshest cream to sell to the markets in town. He was high and mighty in the good old days! But not a whisper from Papa Morse since Ma sent him on his way. If he can't even pen a letter to his own blood sons, who am I to expect an affectionate nod? He is not my Papa anymore no matter how much his honeyed tongue said otherwise.

One day I too will be off to greener pastures just like the Welshman. Only I'll have a bag of gold in my pocketbook so's I can stand tall and rich and above all the rest the way they said my Grandpa Younger did.

I will never look back.

Never!

MAY 3, 1926

During one of my sad spells of late, Miss Parrish the librarian acquainted me with the brilliant poetess, Edna St. Vincent Millay! I read — *no, devoured* — *A Few Figs from Thistles* over and over, time falling away until Miss Parrish dimmed the lights and sent me off with the precious book tucked under my arm. I could not sleep and rose at early dawn emboldened with a sure sense of destiny. Dear Edna loved and lost but she was not defeated. No! Instead, she melted into a magic phoenix and sought her muse. Truly she is a goddess for is this not immortality on God's green earth? To give your words to the miserable and starving? She will feed my soul forever more! So, I dedicate my very first proper poem — humble and poor as it is — to the *Goddess Edna St. Vincent Millay*. We mere mortals worship at her feet.

Do I Know You?
by
Miss Aldine Younger

Even Morning Glories tell lies
That cannot be set right
By Eventide's light.

Forever true blue, they promise,
False trumpets swooning
In the cold glow of a silvered moon.

JANUARY 12, 1927

Midnight the cat is blacker than black. Not even a sliver of moon above her eye or below her pink mouth. Black as witches brew, but she smiled at me when I offered her warm milk from old Lou's udder. It made no matter to me the pitiful cat was full of burrs so sharp they could prick blood from the hired man's big old calloused thumb. With great care I picked them out one by one until her fur ran smooth again. We have become true friends.

She possesses a superior sense above most creatures hence her arrival in the barn a full week before the plague descended. It was Sunday night, the 5th of December after we came back from the wake for our dear choirmaster Mrs. Lawson. The sweet lady has gone to her reward and I miss her so. Full of melody, she called my singing when I stepped in for my friend, Ruthie, abed with a bad case of chicken pox. "Your daughter has a gift," she told Ma. A gift!

Eternity and a half passed before my mother could be prevailed upon to let Mrs. Lawson give me voice lessons and I don't know why because all my private tutors get paid out of my trust fund from Grandpa Younger but finally — *finally* — the happy occasion of my first private lesson came. I shall remember it to the day I die! Mrs. Lawson's perfect soprano guiding my lowly first alto with such grace and so it went for three whole months every Wednesday after school before the flu laid her low and pneumonia set in. Now she is singing in God's Choir of Angels and I am surrounded by a passel of four-legged demons.

Sunday night after Mrs. Lawson's wake the scratching began in the wall behind my bed. When I called out to Ma, she said the house was settling. Whatever that means. Come morning light I hear tapping on the roof, like some bogeyman rattling the shutter to get inside to cheat the cold wind. Horatio heard it too. It was the damned squirrels again, he said, and went to get the pitchfork. Sometimes when his nerves get unsettled, that's how he slides into a calm state. Spearing squirrels. Afterwards he chops up the dead creatures and feeds them to the hogs for supper. Nothing goes unused in our house, a point of pride with Ma.

But no squirrels were to be found. Then I see Midnight sniffing around the kitchen door at a long skinny tail under the doorstep.

"Lord Almighty!" Horatio cried. "Is that a Norwegian Blue?" The worst kind of rat, he told me. Ten pounds full grown, more than two feet long from their noses to their tails. "They're worse than mean," he said. "They're *smart*."

D— that Horatio! He was right! Just before suppertime two days later, I opened the oven to pull out Ma's gooseberry pie like she ordered and that's when I saw him. Creeping slow and quiet on all fours behind the stove, his long slimy tongue licking up the fresh berry juices still warm and bubbling.

We'd been invaded. The whole house was full of his kind. I stood real still, staring so I wouldn't forget what he looked like. The color of filth, that's what he was. I started shaking and crying and screaming bloody murder. The rats are in the rafters, on the roof, crawling in the kitchen, stealing our food!

"Get hold of yourself, Aldine, you're almost a grown girl." Ma took no pity on me. "What would your poor dead father in heaven say to see you in such a state?"

"If my dead father were here instead of heaven, this awful old farmhouse wouldn't be crawling with rats," I told her, but she did not appreciate my reasoning.

"The cat will take care of the rats."

"How can that be, they're bigger than Midnight and what if they eat her then come after us?"

"Aldine, Aldine," she kept saying my name over and over like I could not hear her but I was hearing just fine.

"Daughter, you must put it out of your mind," she said. Then she looked me straight in the eye the way she did after Junior came down the cellar to look for Bonniedoon's lost pup and saw me crying and hiccuping and trying to catch my breath, and he got scared and called for Ma but I don't remember crying. Not then. Only now.

"Put it out of your mind," she said again. Louder. Real loud. "What do you think I had to do after we buried your father in the cold ground and you not even a year old yet? And before that, little Horatio only a toddler and Bertha still in my belly when their poor daddy got killed? Me widowed twice before I turned 35?! I had to put it all out of my mind, you understand me?"

I never saw Ma go on like that before, so I nodded yes, and she calmed down and said to get back to my chores, and I did. After supper, I came upstairs and got down on my knees to pray to my wild and mighty Jesus for deliverance from the Norwegian Blues. But afterwards, when I lay on my bed, I could hear the rats gnawing inside the wall behind my bed.

Were they eating their young for supper?

I plugged my ears and sang all five verses of "Onward Christian Soldiers" just like Mrs. Lawson taught me and drifted off for many an hour into a deep sleep.

SEPTEMBER 19, 1927

Pontiac is the bees' knees! Kohlinger's Drugstore has its own soda fountain so I can order butterscotch sundaes whenever I want and the counter boy gives me extra chocolate sprinkles every time and right next door there's a ladies shoppe that sells fashions all the way from Paris — even fur coats which will fill my own closet someday soon — and down the street a movie palace plays the latest pictures on double bills!

Ruthie and I saw "It" with glorious Clara Bow three times and would've gone a fourth except Ma says enough is enough and I'm wasting my nickels on silly shows. But I so love Clara's clothes and think she is surely the most talented thespian I have ever seen on the silver screen! If not for the misfortune of arriving too late for our fall play auditions on account Ma needed me to help with unpacking, I feel assured I could have followed in the footsteps of my idol Clara. But who knows what dramatic opportunity Destiny will present me by the time our spring play casting call rolls around?

With the bounty of such present and future happiness I sometimes feel sorry for Horatio having to stay out on the farm to tend to the livestock for the new tenants but Ma says hard work will keep him out of trouble. Junior and Absher smile more now and that's a pleasant sight for Ma's tired eyes. Our new house sports a fine little porch just like the fashionable homes north of the Courthouse Square. Ma finagled a good lease from the owner due to her widowhood and large brood, so things are looking up money-wise too what with the rental fees from her farm tenants. She is a miracle worker when it comes to pinching pennies, a talent I cannot claim. So many pretty things to buy! Thank heavens Ma can charge off my school frocks to my income from Grandpa Younger.

My friend Ruthie says she thinks I am the best dressed girl in the sophomore class and that everybody else thinks so too. When I wore a sailor chemise with matching white stockings the first day of school, Sarah Haddington and Lucy Mae Gibson made their mothers buy lookalike dresses the very next week. Not every girl can be both popular and sweet-tempered but I do my best. No wonder so many of the boys are vying for the privilege of being my beau.

Even older rich gentlemen like Asher Bentley.

Ruthie saw him following us in his big shiny Packard as we walked home from school last Friday and almost had a conniption fit. Mayor Bentley's son is giving us the eye! She is my dearest friend and bright as a button but knows nothing of the ways of men. "For goodness sake, don't look back," I told her, "that will only encourage him." But she looked back anyway and I was glad.

Mr. Bentley, being a take-charge Man of the World, tooted his horn and pulled up right next to us.

"Hello, ladies, haven't we met before?"

"Oh, no, I'd remember," she giggled. "I'm Ruthie Kessler and this is my friend Aldine Younger."

"William Younger's granddaughter?"

"Yes sir," I said.

"Pleased to meet you, ladies," he tipped his hat. "Need a ride home?"

Ruthie started to nod yes but I elbowed her, so she straightened up and said, "No thank you, Mr. Bentley."

"Next time," he said, fixing his big blue eyes on me so hard and fast I thought I'd melt. Then he winked, "My pals call me Skinny ..."

Five days later

I feel his gaze upon me wherever I go now. When I came out of the market with a box of flour for Ma, he was driving by in his big Packard and slowed down to wave and toot that horn of his. Nobody else on the street seemed to notice and why should they? He intended his greeting for me and me alone.

On the eighth day

My joyful fate unfolds! Every minute shimmers like a sonnet in Miss Millay's tome of poems. As in all great romance the eventful day began in an ordinary manner when Ma announced I needed to sign some papers at the bank for my trust. Though Mr. Powell is a stuffed shirt and such boring appointments leave me fit to be tied, I wore my new lemon yellow georgette with the lace collar and pretended I was going to visit my personal gold vault à la old King Midas.

Well! Who should be chatting away with Mr. Powell and my Uncle Frederick when Ma and I walked in but Asher Bentley, looking handsome in a Sunday suit that perfectly matched the sea-blue depth of his soulful eyes!

My mother and uncle were frosty polite to one another as is their usual practice. (If he can afford to buy a bank and the land it sits on, why won't he lend his poor struggling sister a few funds to navigate the hard times? Ma says, I'll tell you why, because he's the meanest, cheapest man I ever met.) Today though, Ma kept her sentiments to herself and said the proper how-do's. Uncle Frederick introduced Asher Bentley by his Christian name and let Ma know how his father, the former but still Honorable Mayor Bentley, is a big supporter of local business and the son himself is a bright local light with his University of Illinois law degree.

Mr. Bentley — I do not yet feel right calling him Skinny — spoke most refined to Ma and me, never letting on we had made each other's acquaintance, though he gave me a look sealing the truth of our secret. Just as Ma was pulling me away — I could've stayed forever — a homely matron waltzed over like the Queen of Sheba. The only thing pleasing about her appearance was a velvet hat that surely came special delivery from Marshall Field's in Chicago.

"Have you met Mrs. Asher Bentley?" Uncle Frederick asked. Ma said yes, on the occasion of Aunt Libby's tea party some years back.

"That would have been before my time," I smiled sweetly, and I could tell Mr. Bentley was tickled by my spunk. Small wonder he can't take his eyes off me with an ugly wife like her. Snooty too, like the socialite Adela Van Norman that Clara Bow bested in my favorite picture. In time men always see through that kind of female. On the way home after Ma ran out of breath complaining about Uncle Frederick's greedy, high-handed ways, I casually inquired if she didn't think

Mr. Bentley was a fine figure of a man with his true-blue eyes and high forehead.

"Mark my words, he'll be bald like his father in five years. I've never been able to tolerate a man without hair. The Welshman had a fine head on him even if it did turn white before his time."

Ma got all sudden quiet then. She wished she hadn't opened that can of peas and neither one of us whispered another word until we got home. Then Ma allowed it was all right for me to take Junior and Absher outside to play because I was a good big sister and watched the boys close.

And on the 10th day of the 10th month

I looked a terrible fright, my new short bob dripping wet from gym class (Miss Brandon insists I show up for the synchronized swim trials next week as my strong stroke is sure to secure me a place on the team!) when who should appear by my side as I turned the corner on Oakdale?

"Hello there Aldine, did you fall into the duck pond?"

Asher Bentley himself crossing my path again! Only this time he stepped out of his Packard and walked right up to me big as day. I was tempted to sink into the dumps because of my unsightly appearance but no man fancies a Dreary Dorothy so I played the cool cucumber.

"Oh no, I just swam the British Channel with my pal Gertrude Ederle. Great fun it was too."

He kind of chuckled and came closer. "How old are you, Aldine?"

"Fifteen. Well, almost. In eleven days actually but who's counting? October 19th to be exact." *Oh Lord,* I thought, *stop blithering like a little fool.*

"Well, that'll be a special day. How about I take you dancing to celebrate?"

"Dancing? With you?" (I thought my heart would stop.)

"Sure, I'll pick you up right here and we'll head over to a little road-house I know."

Asher Bentley to be my birthday escort? I wanted to pinch myself in case I was dreaming! But I knew it was important to display the poise and sophistication that would reassure my beau he'd made the right choice. Mrs. Lawson used to say I possessed a maturity beyond my years, bless her soul.

"Roadhouses are such the rage now. I can't think of a more delightful place to go."

"Been to quite a few, have you?"

Not wanting to tell an outright lie I simply smiled. A mysterious cat-caught-the-canary smile like Clara Bow does with her rosebud mouth. Hopefully, my mouth looked like a rosebud too.

"Bet you haven't been to the Wilmington Gun Club yet. Best fried oysters and near beer in the county. And if your pretty little feet get tired of dancing, I'll take you outside for some skeet-shooting under the harvest moon."

"Well, I sure hope I don't shoot you instead of one of those pheasants, Mr. Bentley."

He seemed tickled at my moxie and said he'd take his chances.

"Me too."

"Well, it's a date then. See you right here at 6:00 after supper on your big day, Birthday Girl, and your Ma doesn't need to know. None of her business, is it?"

He had a point. I'm almost a woman now.

"You just tell her you're going to visit one of your girlfriends for a couple hours and I'll have you back by ten."

"My mother expects me home by nine."

"Nine it is."

"Truly, nine on the dot. If I'm late she'll bawl me out something awful."

"Don't you worry, honey, you can count on me."

He came closer still, his voice sweet and tender. "I know you're a real good dancer too. A modern girl like you, swimming across the Channel with Miss Ederle, needs to kick up her heels now and then."

I laughed and he laughed too.

"Don't ever get serious, Aldine. Life's too short to get serious."

"If you say so, Mr. Bentley."

"Skinny, remember?"

"Skinny," I said real low and ladylike, so he wouldn't get the wrong idea.

"That's my girl," he said and drove off.

That's my girl!

NOVEMBER 24, 1927

A heartbeat away is too far for S and me but circumstance dictates otherwise. And so we must endure absence forced on our kindred spirits with the fortitude known only by great amour. As my words cannot do justice to our eternal bond, I will entrust sentiment to the Voice of the Goddess, Edna St. Vincent Millay.

A man was starving in Capri,
He moved his eyes and looked at me,
I felt his gaze, I heard his moans,
And knew his hunger as my own

.

My own … my own … my own new and only love!

JANUARY 10, 1928

We all have our crosses to bear, even the strong and rich of this earth. Poor S and his trials! How terrible to live under the same roof where his dear mother died and no comfort whatsoever from his cold wife and hardly none from a father up to his neck in town business day after day. How glad I am to be the single ray of sunshine that brightens this dark winter for my amour and how dearly I cherish his soft gentleman's hands.

Never could I tolerate a farmer's rough mean touch upon me; prairie dust caked under homely nails so deep even lye soap is defeated by the prospect of soaking them clean — never! Being a property owner of means, S has no interest in working the land himself, but instead supervises laborers hired by his father. Once, just once, after he returned from important business at one of the family farms, I noticed a smell that brought unpleasant associations to mind. My sweetheart sensed my discomfort and now always sprinkles on a goodly measure of toilet water before we rendezvous.

Sad to say, our precious times together are fewer and farther between since Ruthie abandoned me. Such a coward about telling a little fib now and then — all in the high service of true love!

"What if our mothers found out you were with S instead of me and you know, Aldine, he's twice your age and married too!" I fear my ex-friend Ruthie has been bitten by the green-eyed monster and it pains me deeply to see this flaw in a once sweet and sterling character.

Though she swore she would not betray our sacred pact, I suspect some hint might have been dropped as Ma has been watching me like a hawk ever since I saw her and Mrs. Kessler talking up a storm at the church Christmas Bazaar. Now my skirts are too short — it's 1928 for God's sake — and nothing I do seems to please my mother anymore. *Lord, Aldine, be sensible.* I laugh too much, I shop too much, I even read too much. Poetry is a waste of time and trashy novels put ideas in my head that will surely lure me into bad company. Maybe, Ma, I had ideas about how to jazz up my boring life long before I broke the spine of my first romance on Kohlinger's paperback rack!

Deep down, I suppose Ma knows that. She knows everything. Just ask her.

"Look at Conley Delicath, now that's the kind of beau a girl should have. Hasn't your sister done right well for herself?"

Sure, he's a nice enough boy, but no college man like S and all Conley ever hopes to do is open up some little shop in town. He's never danced in St. Louis, sailed on the Great Lakes, or visited the Statue of Liberty in New York City. S has done all this and some day, he says, we'll go shopping in Paris so I can be draped in furs and jewels — the belle of Livingston County! Bertha is welcome to her shopkeeper. I have myself a man of the world and I mean to keep him.

FEBRUARY 28, 1928

My French teacher Mademoiselle Borame says it's très important to keep the mind occupied *at all times* — preferably with worthy artistic pursuit. Thanks to her advice and the favor of the Fates during my Tuesday afternoon try-outs, I am honored to walk hand in hand with my dramatic Muse. In April I will grace the Pontiac High School stage in our spring play, The Girl — non, en francais, s'il vous plaît. La Jeune Fille Avec Les Yeux Vert — c'est moi!

Despite this great success, I have been feeling low of late so Mademoiselle B lent me her splendid books by Madame Sand and Monsieur Flaubert to direct my thoughts to a loftier plain. When I arrive in Paris someday soon, I will no doubt converse in high culture and conjugate my verbs as well as any French-born. Pondering the sage thoughts of the Great Authors I have been struck over and over by the fearsomely wondrous powers of the mind. After much study, my body — so often a rapscallion creature if ever there was one — is now able to follow my mind's will.

At last I have broken free of the tyranny of The Curse!

Two years of that nonsense is more than enough. Hurting and cramping 'til I cry myself to sleep and for what? No smelly blood for a good while now and I don't expect it ever to return. Of course, Ma being a worrywart, grilled me like a center cut pork chop on that wood-burning stove of hers and dragged me down to Doc Symington's office. He made noises about examining my private parts but there was no way I would tolerate that familiarity. I wailed so long and loud his pickle-faced nurse peeked in. The old geezer put those cold, dry hands back where they belonged and changed his tune. Maybe I was ailing from pleurisy in my feminine organs or low resistance from the bad flu that went round after the first winter frost. How long would it last, my mother wanted to know, and what could be done?

"Build her up with malt," Doc Symington prescribed. Everybody knows malt is a bona fide cure-all. Bad back? Sore feet? Weak lungs? Sprinkle a tablespoon or two in the morning cream of wheat and you'll have a new lease on life. That's what the weekly ad in the *Pontiac Daily*

Leader says. So Ma bought a tall can of Prairie Farms Miracle Malted and settled in to wait for a miracle. (Not appreciating the great powers of my mind no matter how hard I try to set her straight!)

Fine by me as I've taken a liking to that thick yellow powder and find I cannot get my fill at home or in town. Kohlinger's serves the best frozen custard malt, more delicious even than their butterscotch sundaes and thank the Lord. My sweet tooth aches to beat the band since I've had to bear the absence of loving arms to comfort me these past three weeks. To my great distress Valentine's Day came and went without a word from my amour. I saw him outside the library for a fleeting moment yesterday but all he rattled on about was how busy he is with farm affairs and time is running him ragged something awful.

"I know you understand, Aldine. You're my little pal, right, honey?"

I hope he's hurting terrible without me, especially tonight with the snowfall so heavy it could freeze a blind man's nose. But I *will not* dwell on the dreary! The sweet smell of spring is just around the corner and as soon as Grandpa Younger's check arrives in two days I can go shopping for a stylish new blouson to match the periwinkle blue hyacinth that will be in bloom by Easter. How pretty I'll look when S finishes his stupid chores and comes 'round courting. So pretty I might not give him the time of day considering the loads of attention I've been getting from all the boys in my class. Eddie Schrieber asked me to the Winter Wonderland dance and I do believe I'll say yes and to heck with Mr. Fancy Pants. Who does S think he is to ignore our precious love and pretend it makes no matter? A girl needs a beau to treat her true …

Windowpains

The old poets say
Eyes are the Window of the Soul.
I beg to differ.
Eyes are the Window of the Double-Dealing Lover.
Pull the shades,
Smear the sky with night

No stars in sight
Only black diamonds
And crushed sapphires.
In the glare of the morning sun
I lean on my splintered windowsill,
White paint peeling,
And see through you.

APRIL 4, 1928

When Ma told me we'd be voyaging to the Great North Upstate, I was beside myself with nervous excitement, despite the fact that the purpose of our travels is for my repairs. That's how she put it down in her expense ledger:

Travel to Chicago, two tickets - $25

Hotel, two nights - $37.50

Aldine's repairs - $122.00

My mother is honest as the day is long. Not one penny gets taken from my interest account without just cause. I am a fortunate daughter.

The train crept past one tall tenement after another as we came into town. A great Big-Shouldered metropolis just as Mr. Sandberg, a poet of impressive moxie, wrote. Ma says he's a godforsaken Socialist but I don't care. His words are strong and fierce with feeling. I could not wait to get into the city proper! Then what a disappointment to see the old fly-trap Ma booked us. She fell on the bed in a snoring slumber soon as we unpacked so I just slipped out to take some air.

My first visit to this grand place and how dearly I wished it might have been under kinder circumstances. Still, I wore my smartest cloche to help ease my mind for the business ahead and determined to carry my head high. The men passing by lifted their hats, bold in giving me the eye. They could look all they wanted, I was not in fear of any of them. My pace quickened with a strange anticipation I could not name. When I rounded the corner of Michigan and Adams, the air changed with the neighborhood. Across the street the big old Art Institute of Chicago said hello and I said hello right back.

Night was falling, and the folks inside the cafés looked as if they were having a gay time. Live, drink, and be merry for tomorrow you may die no matter what Ma says. I waltzed into a pretty little French bistro — that's what it said on the window in gold and black letters, Cheval Blanc Bistro — and acted like I belonged. The waiter wore a crisp shirt and black bow tie and knew his manners.

"Table for one, mademoiselle?"

"Mais oui," I said, knowing that Mademoiselle Borame would be pleased with my accent. *Une Naturelle*, she wrote on my last exam, *Une Jeune Naturelle!* I opened the menu — also gold and black with the picture of a magnifique white horse on its cover — and ordered a croque monsieur avec pommes frites.

A glass of champagne sure would hit the spot right now I smiled, just to see what the waiter would say. He acted a cool cucumber considering Prohibition and all.

"May I offer mademoiselle a café au laît instead?"

"Merci, non. Do you have orange pop?"

They did not, so we settled on iced tea instead. I folded my gloves as a young lady should and waited to be served. Outside the window next to my table all of Chicago walked by. The streetlights twinkled like diamonds just as they do on the Champs-Élysees where I will be living in high style as soon as I reach my majority and Grandpa Younger's legacy comes due. London, Rome, Vienna. Anywhere but Pontiac —

"Miss?"

A gentleman of about thirty — I know he was a gentleman because of the cut of his navy serge suit — presented a piece of paper with my likeness upon it.

"I thought you might enjoy this. My apologies for taking the liberty but you reminded me of my sister and I ... well ... if I'm not intruding, may I join you?"

I held his gift in my hand, recognizing the same kind of graph paper we used for sums in algebra, all crisscrossed with fine vertical and horizontal lines. Etched in blue ink, my face looked out the bistro window toward what I'm not sure, but I appreciated the way he drew my expression all the same. Soft and thoughtful, exactly like the photograph of Miss Edna St. Vincent Millay in my favorite book of poems.

"Yes, please. Join me."

And that is how I made the acquaintance of the distinguished architect, Mr. Thornton Herr. When he mentioned that his sister, Miss Charlotte Brontë Herr, was a published authoress, I confided my hope of embarking on a life in the literary arts myself. He advised traveling west to Occidental College where his sister studied. I asked him to write the name on my portrait and he kindly obliged. Then he told me that his father, a newspaper editor of repute in Indianapolis before retiring to a resort town in California, happened to be the very first to publish the poetry of James Whitcomb Riley!

I pinched myself at the good fortune of Destiny.

"Have you seen the Great Hall at Union Station?" Mr. Herr asked.

"Oh yes, my mother and I were very taken with the sight when we arrived."

I did not see fit to disclose that Ma complained all bitter about what a fortune it must have cost, a waste of taxpayers' hard-earned dollars. Corinthian columns don't come cheap, I had said, proud to know such particulars from my history class.

"Who needs 'em," Ma snapped back, "who needs 'em anyway?"

Mr. Herr regaled me with story after story about his adventures working for Louis Sullivan and his gang of Prairie School architects. And when I finished my croque monsieur, Mr. Herr ordered us some delicious gâteau au chocolat for dessert. His treat. As much as he seemed all bright-eyed about Chicago, I could tell he was terrible lonely for his family out west. Will I miss my folks after I leave for greener pastures? *Qui peut dire?*

"California irises bloom in December," Mr. Herr told me, "and the seasons follow their own drummer." On the street where he built his parents' home in California, magnificent camphor trees came by boat all the way from China to line the sidewalks. Unlike our ordinary Illinois trees they lose their leaves in spring instead of fall — but only after new green leaves have already sprouted! So these creatures that nature blessed can never be sad and empty. He said the mighty camphor leaves looked like bronze and gold medallions, drifting down from heaven whenever the slightest breeze stirred. A person could not believe such beauty existed unless you saw it up close to bear witness.

"As you must do, Miss Younger!"

Before Mr. Herr excused himself to attend an evening

appointment, he offered his business card and extended a cordial invitation to look him up should I happen to travel west at some point in the future.

"Nothing would give me greater pleasure, sir."

He tipped his hat and I nodded farewell. In that moment a revelation struck my soul in assurance that our paths would somehow cross again. I floated back to the boarding house imagining myself to be an old-time Spanish galleon on peaceful seas. A New World lay ahead ...

Until Ma ripped the wind out of my sails soon as I walked in. She was fit to be tied when she woke and found me gone.

"Why is it, Aldine, you do not have the sense the good Lord gave you? Capone's gangsters on every corner — the streets of Chicago are not safe for a young girl at night!"

"Safe, Ma? Tell me, where is safe?"

For once my mother did not answer. Just looked all scared and mad at the same time like the night she walked into the bathroom when I was getting out of the bathtub and she saw my belly.

Good Friday

Romans 8:13–16 — _If by the spirit you put to death the misdeeds of the body, you will live. The spirit himself testifies with our spirit that we are God's children. Now, if we are children, then we are heirs of God and co-heirs with Christ, if indeed we share in his sufferings in order that we may also share his glory._

My mother instructed me to reflect upon the Lord's wisdom as I regain my strength. Our family must make a respectable appearance at church on this coming Easter Sunday though Ma refuses to let me speak my part in the spring play Saturday night because I look peaked and not yet myself and who knows what folks might think. This is terrible unfair and I cried and carried on at such injustice but Ma shushed me and told me to be grateful for my blessings.

She says I lost so much blood when the doctor cut into me he saw fit to fix me against future family calamity and afterwards she had to nurse my raging fever and bring me back to health. I do not remember any of this. All I remember is walking on a beautiful street where golden Chinese Camphor leaves fell like pennies from heaven and melted into a giant chariot that carried me to the moon.

Nobody will ever know, Ma promised.

Funny. I've heard these words before.

Nobody will ever know.

IV

QUEST

10

The Girl with the Green Eyes

Marcus Washington be damned, she fumed, driving in circles around the courthouse square. Waiting did not come naturally to Joanna. A wife and mother by twenty-two, graduate degree at twenty-three and her own professional practice before her thirtieth birthday, urgency stalked her days like a hungry wolf. She had even pushed her daughters to skip kindergarten and sail through first grade because, well, there was no time to waste. Her mother's early death, Joanna supposed, was the reason she sometimes viewed life as a ticking bomb. Move. Move fast, move sure, move now — before everything blows to smithereens.

She darted into a parking place on the south side of the street, the head-in kind with no annoying meter ready to expire. In urban LA drivers had to master parallel parking to pay five quarters for thirty minutes on a broken meter that swallowed each coin only to raise a red flag: "FAIL." As Joanna stepped out of the car, the historic courthouse straight ahead obstructed her line of vision. She felt oddly unsettled by its dominating presence but had no idea why.

Turning her head, she focused instead on the Law Offices of Hornbeck & Hornbeck across the street where her father had heard the reading of his brother's will only two days before. Soon her father will collect what he is owed — Joanna would see to that — but for now she needed a strong cup of tea to clear her head. In search of the nearest café, she walked down the street toward the Pontiac Library. According to the quaint homemade banner, "August Book Days" was in full celebration.

"Give one, take one," chirped a Ladies Auxiliary volunteer behind a card table of old paperbacks.

A teenage babysitter, hand-in-hand with two antsy children on summer vacation, trotted into the library's air-conditioned sanctuary. For no reason Joanna could consciously articulate, she forgot the cup of tea and followed. When she was fifteen, Joanna had to beg her father for permission to babysit for their neighbors' bratty boys. He never wanted her to hold any job until she finished her college education. But she was desperate to earn her own money. By sixteen she'd already salted away over $500 and stacked more bills when she went to work after school at L' Express. Other girls bought jeans at discount; she made deposits in her savings account.

"What kind of man am I if I can't support my family?" her father used to complain to his wife. "She doesn't need to be hiring herself out to do other folks' work."

True, she didn't. A man of modest means, Owen nonetheless lavished his only child with her own pony as soon as she could ride, the latest portable stereo, fancy party dresses and a blue-flowered canopy bed designed to float any young girl into dreamland. Apart from a sober home, he denied her nothing. Until his work and heart dried up in equal proportions.

"May I help you?" the librarian asked the woman standing at the circulation desk.

Joanna did not hear the question, enthralled as she was with the babysitter's antics at a nearby table. Giggling and teasing her young playmates, she provoked disapproving glares from a couple of patrons. Undaunted, the teenager beamed at her surly judges and blew them kisses. Joanna almost laughed out loud. What brave assertiveness, as if no one else's opinion mattered but her own. Joanna had been a different kind of teenager, serious and well behaved, who in her father's apt tribute, "never gave us any trouble."

"Ma'am?" the librarian ventured again. "Did you need something?"

"Yearbooks," Joanna blurted, her intensity surprising both women.

"High school, I presume?"

"Yes, here in Pontiac."

"Go Indians." The librarian grinned and spread her two fingers in a "V" sign behind her head. "What year?"

Joanna quickly did the math. "I think 1927–1931. Yes, that's right."

"Oh, my, I don't know if we have issues going back that far. We'll have to get our research archivist to do some hunting in the stacks. Might be in our Pontiac Sesquicentennial City Pride section. Anything else I can help you with while you're waiting?"

Joanna hesitated, the assurance from a moment ago ebbing now. Her eyes darted back to the fresh-faced teenager holding court with her young readers. But they were gone. In their place at the table a bi-focaled retiree squinted over a stack of *Christian Science Monitors*.

"Your local paper —"

"*The Pontiac Daily Leader.*"

"Do you have editions going back to 1933?"

"On microfiche. We have two machines in our periodicals section. What months do you need?"

"Let's start with March."

While Joanna waited, the librarian stepped into the archivist's office to deliver the special request. He looked through the glass to observe the patron with such an unusual request and nodded. Ten minutes later the librarian returned, a messenger of disappointing news.

"I'm sorry, but most of 1933 seems to be missing. All I could find was November through December." She plopped the boxed microfilm on the library table where Joanna was sitting. "We'll keep looking."

Joanna picked up the dirty white box and wondered if this would be a waste of time. But the librarian was a nice lady and the yearbook search might take a while longer so Joanna threaded the film. Peering into the viewfinder, her hand guided the black dial, until she saw a bold-faced headline:

"BENTLEY TRIAL DATE SET FOR NOV. 13"
Judge Clyde H. Thompson, in the Circuit Court this afternoon, definitely set for a hearing at 1:30 o'clock on the

afternoon of Monday, November 13, the trial of the case of The People against Asher Earl Bentley. Bentley was charged with murder in connection with the mysterious death of Aldine Younger of this city who was found dead on the pavement of State Highway Number 116 near the Thomas Hutson farm on Wednesday morning, March 1, of this year ...

Dizzying clusters of dark text and white space jumped out as Joanna wheeled faster ...

"BENTLEY CASE EXHAUSTS
PANEL OF 50 JURYMEN"

Today's efforts to obtain a jury to hear the evidence to be presented in the case of The People against Asher Earl Bentley, charged with murder in connection with the death of Miss Aldine Younger on March 1 of this year, had failed up to 2 o'clock this afternoon. Following three days of examining prospective jurors, only four had been found who satisfied both the state and the defense.

... on the next page a cartoon suddenly popped up between paragraphs: a grinning ear of corn peeking out of its husk. Joanna peered closer and realized the cartoon was actually an illustration for a gossip column entitled "The Daily Ear." Underneath, more farmland humor — "The Ear Knows" — and next to it, a profile of an aquiline nose. In big bold type the headline trumpeted:

"THE TRAGEDY OF MISS ALDINE YOUNGER"

Our hometown heartache will perhaps one day be a song of lament performed by the great balladeers of Old Appalachia! As with the haunting "Barbara Allen," the short life of Aldine Younger is a cautionary tale for today's flaming youth and their families.

Only a year ago the late Miss Younger testified against **Herbert Powell,** the executor of her trust fund and longtime pillar of our community. Alas, as the girl's testimony revealed, Mr. Powell had fallen from his lofty perch into temptation's false embrace. The jury, moved by Miss Younger's passionate pleas for the return of her fortune, convicted Mr. Powell of embezzlement and sentenced him to incarceration in the penitentiary for one to ten years.

And now the tragic young woman has lost more than her fortune! Her broken body was found in the frigid darkness near Rooks Creek Bridge the early morning of March 1. **Mrs. Paulina Morse**, her aggrieved mother, has spoken out with pleas for murder charges against Mr. Asher Bentley, the 40-year-old son of **William H. Bentley**, thrice Mayor of Pontiac.

The Bentley trial promises to be highly attended. Witnesses scheduled to take the stand for the prosecution include **Sheriff Pemberton** and **Will Haskell**, the hired man at the Hutson farm overlooking Rooks Creek Bridge on that fateful night. Her uncle, **Frederick Heinemann**, is expected to speak on behalf of the family as her mother is too aggrieved to take the stand. (Word has it that Mrs. Morse has confided the difficulty of raising her high-spirited heiress daughter to many a sympathetic shoulder collecting her bitter tears…)

For the defense, the senior Mr. Bentley will be the prime character witness on behalf of his son. It is believed that the junior Mr. Bentley — University of Illinois Law School graduate that he is — will take the stand. We have heard rumors that prominent forensics specialists from Chicago will appear on behalf of the defense as well.

We presume that Mrs. Asher Bentley will also be in attendance. Shortly after her spouse's arrest she declared her wifely loyalty to the *Chicago Daily Times*: "Regardless of what happens, I'll stick by my husband and help him all I can."

On a final shocking note, *The Ear* has learned that **Mr. F.B. Stickerling**, Miss Younger's former family attorney, and **Mr. Benjamin Washington**, the Negro attorney whom Miss Younger engaged to press her case against Mr. Powell, have both met behind closed doors with at least one barrister on Mr. Bentley's defense team. Why, we can't surmise ...

Joanna sat upright in the hard-backed chair. "Negro attorney Benjamin Washington." Could Marcus Washington be related?

"You requested these, I believe?"

The voice was masculine. A pair of pudgy hands presented her with a rainbow-colored stack of old yearbook annuals. Half-tucked in the pocket of his short-sleeved shirt, a badge introduced the archivist by name: "Tazewell."

"Oh, thank you." Too distracted to look up, Joanna did not notice the helpful archivist's badge. "I appreciate your time."

Tazewell was taken aback by her unexpected courtesy. Not that he deserved one whit less. How very young she looked. And she must be at least forty now. Older in fact. He had just turned fifteen a week before her christening, the only time they ever actually met. She did not recognize him yet. That would come in due order.

"We don't get many requests for these precious gems."

"I'm researching some family history."

"How fascinating. I'm here every Thursday and Friday if I can be of further help."

"I was lucky today then."

Tazewell had no faith in luck, but he did believe in timing. Timing and preparation.

Joanna was sliding her finger down the alphabetical directory of the 1927 Pontiac yearbook when she sensed the archivist move closer.

"Our librarian informed me you were also looking for some issues of the 1933 *Daily Leader*?"

"She said they're missing?" Joanna finally turned to look at the archivist.

"Oh, not necessarily. Perhaps they've just gone into hiding," he smiled at his small joke. "Check with me tomorrow night about a half hour before closing, I won't be so busy serving other patrons then."

"That's very nice of you."

"The pleasure will be mine."

Such old-school manners, Joanna mused. She watched him return to his glassed-in cubicle, feeling she had seen him somewhere before.

Once again focused on the well-worn annual, she realized she had already opened the yearbook without looking while she and the archivist chatted away. Now, in a whimsical touch of bibliomancy, she found herself face-to-face with a family ghost on page 36.

"A. Younger, Swimming Club."

The girl athlete faced the camera head-on with a broad smile and short curly bob à la Amelia Earhart. How brave she looked at fifteen — so young and brave. And there she was a few pages later in the cast of "The Girl with the Green Eyes," prancing across the stage with a fluffy boa twisted around her shoulders. And again, in the front row of the Edna St. Vincent Millay Poets' Society, dressed to the nines in leather cage T-straps and a long-waisted sailor dress. Her young aunt sported style with confidence, the confidence born to one blessed with natural gifts and a naïve blindness to the obstacles of the world.

Aldine's niece sat for a long time trying to fathom how such a blithe, bold spirit came to such a sad end. What a waste. What a terrible waste of promise and possibility. She turned the pages of the annuals of 1928 and 1929, hungry for more, but the campus "IT girl of 1927" had disappeared without a trace. Had she dropped out of school? Failed to show up on photo day? Not likely. Especially the way she performed for the camera. Aldine at fifteen shimmered with delight in herself. Aldine at sixteen, and seventeen, and eighteen was absent and unaccounted for. Two years after she should have graduated, Aldine Younger re-emerged in the local limelight. The yellowed newspaper clipping taped to a cardboard frame with the headline Joanna had never forgotten: "Heiress Slain, Married Man Held."

Joanna pressed her forehead back into the viewer of the noisy microfilm machine, groaning and limping on its last legs. But the more she poured over the old newspaper articles, struggling to glean the secrets between the lines, the more lost she became. Squeezing the wheel forward, backward, forward again, her hand cramped, her eyes ached, and the tiny newsprint wriggled like earthworms. Suddenly nauseous, Joanna finally snapped off the machine. Lunch was what she needed. A light vegetable broth with salted crackers to soothe her unsettled stomach. She jumped up, knocking the stack of yearbooks into disarray as she rushed to the exit.

11

The Buttercup Pantry

"Is something wrong?" the young waitress in gingham arched her neck, following Joanna's eyes upward. A Victorian ceiling, its ornate plaster molding soiled with the soot of the last century, stood sixteen feet high.

"No," Joanna redirected her gaze. The café had seemed welcoming enough when she walked in. "Homemade" vegetable soup and a BLT with a touch of mayo on thick slices of whole wheat seemed to settle her queasy stomach at first. Yet the longer she sat at the table with the cheery yellow gingham cloth and matching napkins, the more agitated she became. "I'll take the check now, please."

"Are you sure? Our specially prepared cobbler of the day is blueberry-rhubarb served warm à la mode."

Both the girl and the onslaught of gingham were getting on her nerves now. "Just the check."

"Maybe next time for dessert then."

Maybe not, Joanna thought, relieved when the server moved on to attend an elderly regular at a nearby table. Staring at the old man's straight back, she concluded he must be younger than her father. A head of hair still thick and wavy, probably quite something in his youth. Owen's hair thinned before he turned 50. Annoyance at life's losses, small and large, further darkened her mood despite the sunlight slicing through the slats of the front window shade.

Joanna tried to calm herself with the deep breathing she learned at yoga class but her sharp inhales slammed up against each other like a long line of train cars falling off the tracks into a bottomless canyon. Her father, Joanna reasoned, might be taking a turn for the worse. She must get back to the hospital. But still no check. Rising from the table she caught sight of a majestic old brass radiator in the corner. It seemed familiar somehow. As if she'd warmed her hands over the moribund heater just yesterday. She walked over to trace its solid heavy ridges with her fingertips.

"Can I help you?" the empty-handed waitress was hovering again.

"Yes, you can bring my check," Joanna barked. "I've been waiting ten minutes."

"Please pay at the register, ma'am." The girl forked over a slip of paper from her apron pocket and scurried off.

Waiting for her change at the exit, Joanna stole one last look at the ancient radiator.

The owner grinned as he counted out her bills. "Great old building, isn't it?"

"A market."

"Excuse me?"

"This used to be some kind of market," Joanna announced with conviction.

"The first Kroger's in Pontiac, 1923," his jaw jutted with civic pride. "Usually only the old timers remember."

Her dad will remember as soon as she can bring him for a visit. Joanna's eyes glistened. How happy he'll be to know she found what she'd promised.

"How'd you know?"

She searched for some answer that made sense. Finding none, she thrust a couple dollars toward this pleasant man who, as far as she could tell, meant no harm.

"For the waitress."

Joanna turned to leave and collided with a young couple too busy melting into each other's eyes to see anybody else. Struggling to get her breath again, she pushed her way through the door.

A block down the street her temples began to throb. Taking a detour into the corner drugstore, she hurried toward the display of yellow-labeled aspirin. The plastic bottle felt reassuring in her hand. Soon the pain would go away. But then she reached inside her handbag for her wallet and found only a fistful of air. Realizing she must have left her money in the café, she tossed the aspirin on the counter in front of the startled clerk and raced out the door.

Half running now, Joanna could not understand her rising panic. What's the worst that could happen? No more than five minutes had passed since she left the café. Surely she must have left it on the counter when she paid her bill. What other explanation could there be? There was a new cashier unwrapping rolls of quarters when she returned. One roll, then another, spilling into the metal pockets of the vintage cash register. No, the cashier hadn't seen a black wallet with a gold clasp. Yes, she would check with the owner as soon as he finished in the kitchen —

"Is this yours?" The old man standing in line stooped to pick up a black wallet half hidden underneath the counter.

Joanna grabbed the wallet from his hand, relief flooding her body. Quickly checking to see that cash and credit cards were still intact, she slipped it into her shoulder bag and secured the strap. She loved the wallet from the moment she saw it at Nordstrom's After Christmas sale. So solid and sensible. The finest quality crocodile embossed calf leather, smooth to the touch, with every compartment she could possibly need. It made her feel safe.

"Mr. Holloway doesn't miss a thing," the cashier chortled.

"Thank you," Joanna managed, focusing on the elderly gentleman in front of her. He sported a dapper bow tie and a button-down tweed vest that complemented his grey eyes. Eyes that, she realized now, were as milky and hard as marbles. Glazed with cataracts, she presumed.

"Thank you very much, Mr. Holloway," she repeated, using his name in respect.

As he counted out the precise dollars and coins to pay his luncheon check, she realized he was the wavy-haired man she had noticed, the one she had thought so young. Older than her father by at least a decade, she surmised now. When he finished, Joanna stood aside to open the door for him, the least she could do for a man of his years.

"After you." His veined hands took ownership of the door.

"Thank you again." She hurried out.

"Money doesn't grow on trees," he admonished, following her.

"No."

"You'd best be more careful next time."

"I will."

He peered at her a long moment and she at him; for some reason, neither inclined to move on.

"My father came here as a boy, when it used to be a market," she volunteered.

"A lot of folks did. Best cuts of meat in town," he smiled. "I can testify to that."

"Junior Morse is my dad."

His smile faded.

"I thought perhaps —"

"I left when I was young." His eyes seemed to recede into their sockets now. Opaque. Unreadable.

"But then you returned."

"No more reason to stay away."

And still neither one of them turned to leave. Until another female voice intruded.

"Grandpa!" a middle-aged woman in clunky espadrilles vaulted toward them.

The old man pursed his lips. "Hello, Barbara."

"You told me you'd come over for supper." The woman swung her arms through her grandfather's, rambling on a mile-a-minute. "You know the boys were expecting you and then you don't answer your phone. What am I to think for heaven's sake! Don't make me worry like that, you hear me?"

"No," he answered, flipping off his hearing aid and removing his arms from hers. He looked once again at Joanna then nodded in farewell.

As Joanna turned to go, she caught sight of a young man's reflection in the café window. Tall and broad-shouldered, he wore a white shirt and long blood-spattered butcher boy's apron. In the instant the image appeared, it vanished. She looked over her shoulder. No one was there.

Unnerved, she strapped her bag across her body as she'd learned to do on a business trip to New York City. Marching toward the car she breathed easier and gave thanks for a decent end to a day with a bad beginning. Good for her, discovering that the Buttercup Café might be — no, surely was — the market her father had hoped to find. As soon as he's back to his senses they'll come in for a couple slices of blueberry-rhubarb cobbler.

Then again, more trips down memory lane could confuse him. Joanna's mind raced; perhaps that was a bad idea. Better to get him out of the hospital and on a plane to California as soon as possible. If he has to see the old homestead, she and the lawyer will be there to keep him fixed in the present. Clearly her father needed to sell the property, along with his dilapidated house in Cathedral City. How many times had she picked out a nearby condo for him in an effort to bring him closer to his family? Starting now, Joanna determined, she would not take no for an answer. A father needed his daughter nearby. They'd find him a new home together, a place that would make him feel happy and healthy. Together: that was the key.

More rain? Joanna looked to the sky but saw no clouds. Still, she felt a drop of wetness on her cheek. There, another one. It took a moment before she tasted the salt of her own tears grazing her upper lip. By then she had already traveled two blocks beyond where she parked her car and was finding her way back. Still wondering why the reflection of a strange young man in the window of the Buttercup Café unsettled her.

And then it came to her. The young man was no stranger. Simply the unlined face of the elderly Mr. Holloway before the years had advanced, his gait slowed and arteries hardened. A lost visage from another time.

12

Comfort Inn

No sleep came, only flashing images of murder, mayhem, con artists, and criminals. Joanna clutched the TV remote to her breast, punching one channel after another in search of electronic oblivion. Titles screamed across the screen. Throbbing synthesizers one minute, cool jazzy ballads the next. She had hoped to lose herself in a landscape of illusion where all the pretty faces would still be smiling when the end credits rolled. Instead, one hard-nosed detective after another risked life and limb in spasms of violence to bring the guilty under the iron fist of justice. How brave. But they knew what they were doing. They knew the crime. They knew the suspects they wanted to put behind bars.

All Joanna knew was that a dead woman took her father captive and she had no idea how to bring him back to her side where he belonged. She pummeled a pair of synthetic foam pillows to give better support to her aching head — no goose down in this place — suddenly aching for the baby-faced doll that used to share her childhood bed. She had first seen the chubby playmate smiling at her from a brightly lit storefront the week before her sixth Christmas.

"I like that one," she had told her father, small mittened hand safe in his firm grasp.

Five days later Sharon — Joanna had always wanted a little sister with a pretty name — straddled the seat of a red tricycle underneath a tall evergreen draped with shiny tinsel and Technicolor ornaments in the family living room. Her father's secure arms still wrapped her in love then. Before the downward spiral of drink, depression, and withdrawal. Forget the current spasm of memory loss, Owen Morse had gone missing decades ago. But to be perfectly fair — and she wanted so much to be both perfect and fair as all good daughters do — she and her father had managed spurts of happiness in their time together. Those moments were the only reason she still believed in the possibility of miracles.

The ringing phone jarred her consciousness.

The hospital? Some emergency? Joanna grabbed for the receiver, knocking the cradle to the floor.

"I'm sorry ... hello?" Her heart pounded against her chest. "Can you hear me?"

"Joanna?"

Struggling to acclimate herself to her husband's voice, she said nothing.

"It's Peter."

"Peter," she repeated. "It's late."

"I know. I'm sorry. I just wanted —"

"Can I call you in the morning? Before you leave for class?"

She could hear his hesitation in the silence.

"Please. I'm so tired."

"If tomorrow would be better —"

"Yes." Then she added a quick "love you" and hung up.

Joanna stumbled out of bed and began rummaging through her father's stack of medications for the bottle of Ambien. She had never taken a sleeping pill in her life. Such an idea challenged her worldview of sobriety. No liquor, no drugs, no mind-altering substance of any kind, not even an experimental joint during her college days. Only one glass of champagne at her own wedding. But tonight, she unscrewed the cap on the Ambien bottle with uncharacteristic abandon and popped two small white pills in her mouth without thinking. No more feeling, that's all she wanted. No more ...

At ten o'clock the next morning she awoke, sluggish and numb, her sheet plastered with the slick, clammy feel of nightmare sweat. More bad dreams. But this time, thanks to the Ambien, they vanished with the day's light. Her pillowcase was saturated with saliva. Tears. Sweat. Saliva. Lately her pores dispersed bodily juices at an unprecedented pace. Joanna Giordano still appeared concrete and sure to undiscerning strangers. But inside, the woman she thought she was had started to crumble into jagged pieces under the deluge of her father's crisis and an ancient family tragedy she did not know how to assimilate.

Pushing herself into an awkward sitting position, she slumped against the headboard and stared at the silent images of some local news show. The anchorwoman's mouth moved but no words came. Joanna reached for the remote control, studying the mute button as if it were a foreign symbol she'd never seen before. Her left shoulder hurt like hell, pain slicing deep inside inflamed muscle. The old childhood accident she assumed. Why was it acting up now? She crawled out of bed and twisted her protesting body into a series of therapeutic yoga asanas. Nothing helped.

Joanna uncoiled her limbs and wondered when the Comfort Inn would live up to its name. Morning light exposed fading flowers on the bedspread then danced feeble pirouettes across the worn carpet. Through the sliding glass window crows played hide and seek among the green stalks of summer corn. Seduced by nature's relentless resilience, she sucked in a dozen ragged breaths. Then she stumbled over to the coffee maker to brew herself a wake-up call.

Last night's dream knocked on the door of her consciousness. Not the white-haired man but two wraithlike figures bleeding into columns of color. Midnight blue shadows hovering between spirit and earth. Mirages. Some unreachable communion slipping closer and then suddenly gone. But maybe — she grasped this thought with all her might — the dream had never occurred at all. Just her imagination. Funny how nothing seemed certain anymore.

The phone jangled. Her breath caught in her throat. Her father. The hospital. She scrambled to pick up the earpiece before another ring.

"Hello?"

"You said you'd call."

"Peter."

"You remembered my name. I guess that's a good sign."

"I ... I overslept," she mumbled. "I'm sorry."

"Are you sick?"

"Of course not. Is everything okay? The girls —"

"I'm not calling about the girls." And then more softly, he said, "You don't sound like yourself, honey."

"Of course, I'm myself. Who else would I be?"

She caught sight of herself in the faux maple dresser mirror. The disheveled hair and taut jaw, eyelids swollen and smudged with yesterday's mascara. Jerking away she glanced at the black liquid collecting in steady drips and hurried to pour herself a cup.

"Dammit."

"What?"

"I just burned my hand on this stupid coffee pot."

A long pause. "When did you start drinking coffee?"

"They don't have any tea. This isn't exactly the Four Seasons."

"I thought coffee gave you headaches."

"Not anymore. I need caffeine, that's all. There's no mystery here."

"Do you want me to come back there? I can get a red-eye out of LAX tomorrow night."

"No."

"Why not?"

"It's not your responsibility."

"My God, Joanna, does everything in life have to be your sole and complete responsibility? Your father finally cracks up —"

"He's not cracking up!"

"The way he's been drinking all these years, I'm surprised it didn't happen before."

"There you go again, kicking the poor guy when he's down."

"You can't save a man who doesn't want to be saved."

She slammed the phone into its cradle. When Peter immediately rang back, she did not answer. Instead, she studied her reflection in the dresser mirror. Someone stared back, someone she could not yet fathom. Only much later would she accept the presence of a voice she was still trying to deny.

13

Jackrabbits and Roses

Why white roses? In a hospital room already bleached of color, except for vomit green uniforms the staff wore, why not a splash of red or yellow or tangerine pink? Healing colors that could do a body good. White roses seemed — Joanna did not even want to say the word — funereal. As distressed by the color as the anonymity of the sender, she turned away from the offending vase of flowers and kissed her father's forehead. Still sedated after a bad morning, he slumbered on.

"Ripped the IV right out of his arm," the head nurse reported when Joanna arrived. None of the medical professionals in charge of her father's recovery could provide any reason for his agitation or explain why he attacked the orderly in the corridor, knocked over a cart of empty breakfast trays, or started shouting for somebody named Alan Dean. Or perhaps it was James Dean, the dead actor? Another patient had been watching *Rebel Without a Cause* on an old movie channel and it was so easy for the elderly to get confused.

So now Owen Morse lay snoring, pumped full of enough Haldol to keep him from disturbing anyone for quite some time. Joanna reached for her father's hand, the palm dry and cuticles so torn and tough the nail beds were disappearing. Once he played basketball with a boy's strong grip and expected more from life than rough edges and hard times. All those years of working "an honest day's labor" as he called it, but not one spent bringing his deepest dream to life: working his own land. The Standard Oil station he managed in Peoria was only a temporary stop before buying a couple hundred acres of farmland to call his own once they saved enough money. He was a good provider who took care of his family first.

Then California happened. The doctor said her mother needed a drier climate for her worsening asthma and their Anaheim relatives — only blocks from Disneyland — were happy to host the young family while they got their bearings in the promised land. Hazy images of Alice's spinning teacups and her parents' hushed arguments behind a guest bedroom door were all Joanna carried with her when they left the shadows of Sleeping Beauty's Castle for their new desert home.

"After the wife's health takes a turn for the better ..." Owen's tale used to begin. He had entertained his regular customers at the local gas station with dreams of heading north to the green fields of Fresno's Central Valley. Tomatoes, corn, maybe even winter wheat when he moved on to bigger cash crops. Time passed. Any extra dollars were put aside for their daughter's college education. Owen's dream became smaller and more distant. An acreage would do, somewhere up the road closer to Riverside. A place to raise a few chickens and sell fresh eggs to folks who wanted home-grown food with flavor.

After the Chevron closed to make way for the new interstate, his wife went to work at the local library to meet their mortgage payments, and Owen resigned himself to one menial job after another and nursed six packs in front of a flickering TV screen to get to sleep at night. His aspirations had been embalmed in regret, like a family of dead flies stuck in amber. His handsome face, dulled by the bloat of alcohol, lost its expression.

At Joanna's Berkeley graduation her father wore a twelve-year old suit and forgot the camera. Her mother would have remembered, he sighed, but she was gone. Then he wiped the wetness from his eyes, and after apologizing to Joanna's husband and in-laws for being unable to join them for dinner, instead headed to a local pub to soothe his sorrows. His little girl understood. She always understood.

The dark flush of guilt that washed over her on commencement day was back again here at his bedside. Owen quit school at fourteen because his mother needed financial support. Joanna earned multiple degrees because her parents provided for her first. The daughter squeezed her father's hand tighter. In the place her hard-knotted pain occupied, other feelings took up residence. Gratitude. Compassion. Love, above all. But there was something more. Bigger, deeper, holier …

Forgiveness.

Her father stirred, snoring louder. Maybe *All My Children* would bring him back to a safe space of familiarity. Joanna flipped on the overhead TV and tried one channel after another, searching in vain for Erica's smirk. Finally she settled on the soothing monotone of a Discovery Channel documentary. As intrepid biologists tramped into the bush to locate a generation of missing jackrabbits, Joanna began to doze. In and out of a sleepy twilight zone, she caught the hazy image of a scientist training his binoculars on an empty field where thousands of jackrabbits used to roam.

"It's difficult to construct the species' history of loss," he droned. "Predators began to multiply …"

A nurse tapped Joanna on the shoulder. Visiting hours were over. As she leaned over to tell her father goodbye, a sickeningly sweet smell distracted her. The damned flowers, she thought. How could one bouquet suck the oxygen out of the air like that? But it wasn't one. Now there were two glass vases overflowing with white. Dozens and dozens of white roses.

"Where did these come from?" Joanna demanded. But she already knew the answer before it came. A ghost who left no trace.

14

Legatum

Joanna rang Marcus Washington's doorbell but heard only silence. She knocked on the door. Deaf or cantankerous, he still refused to answer. Despite the August heat wave, she began to shiver in the shade of the stately elms framing the front porch. She knocked again, louder, without reprieve.

"Enough!" The old man bellowed from inside. He cracked open the door, his face obscured by the shadows of the dark entryway. "I expected you'd show up."

"May I come in?"

He led his unwelcome guest into a book-lined parlor. He patted a beautifully woven cane rocking chair then stood aside to watch her lower tense shoulders against its strong back.

"You look poorly," he sniffed, peering at her damp forehead. He disappeared into a small pantry off the kitchen.

"Mr. Washington?"

No answer.

Through a bay window Joanna spied rows of hollyhocks choking the backyard. Someone should prune them, she thought. Cut the spindly suckers back so the rest of the garden could breathe. Tick-tock, tick-tock, tick-tock … the pendulum of the grandfather clock in the corner of the room pierced the silence with relentless time keeping. As the hands struck one, a booming chime jolted every cell of her body. She jumped to her feet with a sudden urge to run away. Run from this house and this town bringing her nothing but misery. It wasn't only her father's condition. The town itself felt intolerable. Suffocating.

Eyes closed, mouth open, she sucked in oxygen and wondered why the charm of the heartland she loved as a child had worn thin. Thinner than the pages of the old leather-bound Bible her father hid away next to a treasured collection of pipes. Unlike his cigars, the pipes were "too good to use." Every now and then he packed a pinch of Prince Albert into a carved bowl to inhale its smoky vanilla fragrance. Then he tapped out the tobacco to save for another day that never came.

The family Bible, once the cherished possession of her Grandmother Morse, stayed locked up with the precious tobacco. Occasionally her father would allow her to thumb through the pages, dry as cornhusks from a century-old harvest. Not that he brought the family Bible out from its hiding place often. It seemed enough to know some divine comfort existed if a body grew desperate enough.

Like her parents, Joanna was an Easter Sunday Protestant who seldom attended church. But last spring, when a client invited her to vespers at All Saints Church — the grand old Gothic across from Pasadena City Hall — she found the prayers moved her to tears. Afterwards she lingered in the church garden's stone labyrinth. A full moon had transformed the concentric circles of stepping stones into an inviting platinum path. But when she ventured forward, determined to reach the center, she lost her way —

Joanna spun around to see Marcus, precariously balancing a bamboo tray with teapot and cups as he entered.

"Excuse me, what did you say?"

"I was inquiring whether your father's health had improved?"

He lowered the tray to the library table. Steam spiraled from the spout of the chipped teapot.

"I thought ... no, not yet. Thank you for asking."

"Sugar or honey?"

"Plain is fine."

"Your aunt preferred a teaspoon of clover honey in her tea, though I think she enjoyed coffee most of all."

His stooped back bent low as he poured. Not one drop spilled as he handed her the cup of tea. "Peppermint. A clarifying herb."

Joanna looked at him, her eyes watering as the hot brew burned her lips. "You did know my aunt then?"

Settling into his favorite armchair, Marcus collected himself before answering.

"Our legal practice represented her when she filed embezzlement charges against Herbert Powell. I assisted my father with the case. The jury returned a verdict for our side."

"Well," Joanna began, her mouth still stinging. "I suppose our family owes you a debt of thanks."

"You suppose incorrectly." As he poured his own cup, his hand became unsteady.

"I don't understand —"

"I'm afraid Miss Younger was unable to take much comfort from the verdict."

"But you won the case."

"Powell's legal team filed an appeal. February 23, 1933. After I informed Miss Younger, I understood she planned to travel to Indiana to seek counsel from a friend. That was the last time we spoke. On March 1st ..."

He left the sentence unfinished.

"She was killed."

"Yes." The old man sank back into his chair.

"March 1st," he mused, "the same date the annual interest from her grandfather's trust used to be deposited in her bank account. The promise of the legacy due when she reached eighteen."

He sipped his tea slowly, so slowly, as if he wanted to parse every drop, and then decided that Junior Morse's daughter had a right to know.

"She once told me ..."

"Yes?"

"... March 1st was her true birthday because that was the only day of the year she knew hope."

Both voices went silent. The only sound, the old grandfather clock's tick-tock, tick-tock, tick-tock.

"To confide something so personal she must have ..." Joanna struggled to find the right words. "Placed a great deal of trust in you."

"I believe Miss Younger always knew that I was true to her best interests."

He closed his eyes for a moment, steeped in the memory of the winter's day they first walked into his father's office ...

Mrs. Morse had trudged in first, her spine straight and stiff. Aldine followed with a dancer's smooth grace. The mother was a short little thing but substantial all the same. Five feet tall and almost as wide. Not the daughter. Tall, slender, an elegance about her with that fox coat she wore so proud. Different from other young ladies, the way she met his eyes direct and steady.

He offered each a chair and politely explained that his father had unexpectedly been called into court on another client matter. The mother sighed and sat down. Not the daughter. She stood by the window holding herself apart. The mother fiddled with her purse. Their family had a matter of concern and needed to engage legal assistance.

"How can we be of help?"

The daughter challenged his question with one of her own.

"Aren't you curious why we came to you?"

The mother looked embarrassed. "Aldine, I don't think it's necessary to get into that."

"Well, I think everybody here is entitled to know what our situation is. The rich white lawyers around here won't touch my case. They think I'm trouble. Might stir up a hornet's nest and nobody in this damned town wants to do that. It could be trouble for you too, Mr. Washington, in case you want to keep that in mind."

"My daughter speaks plain," her mother said.

"An admirable trait," he assured her. "Shall we proceed?"

Aldine smiled, moving closer, and extended her hand to his ...

"Mr. Washington?" Joanna leaned forward. "Are you all right?"

He lifted his eyelids and refocused on Aldine's niece, noting a family resemblance he had not seen before. He found it disconcerting.

"Yes. Yes." Marcus placed his cup on the table. "As I was saying, it took over a year before we could get Powell served and the trial scheduled. Miss

Younger lost patience with the repeated delays. So one day she decided to drive to her uncle's residence to demand his assistance in recovering her money. Apparently, she'd appealed to him before since he and Powell were in the banking business together. She didn't get any better results this time."

"What happened?"

"Herbert Powell was leaving her uncle's just as she arrived. The two men denied any collusion, of course, but there was an unfortunate scene. Her uncle escorted her off the premises, so she went to the neighbor's house next door where she called my father and insisted that he confront 'the lying cheats,' as she called them, who took her property. Well ..." he shook his head. "Mr. Benjamin Washington did not respond kindly to a young woman's orders. He instructed her to go home. She refused. I felt called upon to go to her aid myself. There she was on the sidewalk sharing her tale of woe with every passerby whether they wanted to hear or not."

"I don't blame her."

"Nor do I. But Miss Younger could have jeopardized her own case. I calmed her. Took her for a walk near the river. The view of the water used to soothe her ... mercurial nature."

"Mercurial? That's an unusual word."

"Surely your father has talked about his sister?"

"He was very attached to her, I know that." Too attached, she thought, but did not say.

"Indeed. She was a young lady capable of inspiring great devotion." His face softened for a moment. "Unfortunately, her choice of companions ..."

"Asher Bentley?"

"Certain individuals do not merit discussion." Marcus lowered his gaze and picked up his cup again. "There are limits to what one can do to protect a client."

"I understand."

"Do you?" His dark, watery eyes fastened on Joanna.

"Yes, I think so" she stammered. "At least you made sure Herbert Powell paid for his crime."

"Your father didn't tell you?"

Joanna's stomach began to spasm.

"Powell won his appeal. The Illinois Supreme Court reversed his conviction six months after Miss Younger's death."

Why? Joanna wanted to scream but the answer came before the question.

"A temporary court appointed executor was judged to have served papers on Powell in an untimely fashion," the old man's mouth twisted. "We supposed the money that paid for Powell's appeal came from Frederick Heinemann."

"My great uncle," Joanna lowered her eyes.

"Sometimes, Mrs. Giordano, I'm embarrassed for my former profession." He looked out the bay window at his hollyhock garden.

"According to my dad, Asher Bentley's conviction was overturned too."

"The Springfield justices again," he sighed. "They questioned the veracity of a witness that swore he overheard Bentley threaten your aunt shortly before she was found dead."

"Did you believe the witness?"

"I did not attend the trial, unlike some of the gossip mongers in this town who dined out on salacious rumors."

"But you have an opinion."

"My opinion is that justice seldom comes in this world. The next world perhaps. I'll know soon enough."

"The transcripts from the Bentley trial ... do you have them?"

"No. Why would I?"

"But, I read ... " Joanna hesitated.

"Yes?"

"In the library I was reading the Pontiac paper's coverage of his trial. One article mentioned that my aunt's former attorney, Benjamin Washington, your father I presume, was asked to be a consultant for Bentley's defense team."

Marcus stiffened. "Cases were few and far between for men of color in 1933, Mrs. Giordano."

"May I ask how your father assisted Bentley's lawyers?"

"My understanding is," Marcus cleared his throat, "he reported his observations about his former client's character."

"Meaning?"

"Miss Younger was a modern woman who wanted to chart her own course. I admired her independent spirit, but my father did not approve. Unfortunately, he neither solicited nor desired my opinion. I left the practice of law shortly thereafter. Cane-making," he gestured to the Lincoln rocker in which she sat, "proved a more honest livelihood."

"This is your workmanship."

"Yes. And no shame in it."

A quiet moment passed between them.

"It seems to me you and my aunt were kindred souls."

The old man's eyes narrowed. "What do you mean?"

"Well, each of you seeking your own path in spite of others' opinions."

"You believe that to be brave, Mrs. Giordano?"

"Yes, I do."

"Ah, well, my father thought such behavior foolish and reckless and made no bones about it. He warned me that in the fullness of time we all live with the consequences of our choices. But your dear aunt —" his voice caught, "— for all her brave intentions, did not see how she was putting herself in harm's way …"

Marcus shook his head, trying to cast off a past that could not be undone.

"Why did you come back to Pontiac? After what happened? After all these years?"

"My dad received an inheritance from his brother. He didn't want to return alone."

Marcus studied her a long moment.

"The Bentley trial transcripts and witness depositions are in our local courthouse. You need to read everything to understand what happened."

"But there's nothing that can be done now. Legally, I mean. Both cases —"

"— are dead and buried, yes. There are other considerations."

Confused, Joanna made no response.

"Legatum, Mrs. Giordano, legatum."

"I'm sorry. I never studied Latin."

"Bequest is the English translation. Incomplete, but we work with what we have."

"My aunt left no bequest. It was all lost, you said."

Marcus bent toward her. "But not the memory of who she was ... that is what you should know."

He slowly rose to his feet. Their meeting was over.

"I appreciate your seeing me." She put down her cup, a hairline crack she could now see spoiling the smooth porcelain.

He nodded, leading her back to the entryway. "Junior Morse is fortunate to have such a caring daughter at his side."

"Do you have children, Mr. Washington?"

"No."

She put her hand on the tarnished brass doorknob to let herself out but could not budge it.

"Rusty hinges," he apologized, placing his wizened fingers over hers to give the knob an extra twist.

Needles ricocheted down Joana's spine. Static electricity, she assumed, jerking away. Her host took no offense, at least none that he showed.

"I hope you find what you're seeking," he said, wrenching the door open.

"You said you've seldom seen justice in this world."

"That is the truth."

"What if this is the only world we have?"

The old man glanced outside at the tall elms shading the heat of the day, their leaves stirring in an unexpected breeze. "That possibility did not seem to disturb your aunt."

"What do you mean?"

He said nothing, lost in reverie so long Joanna wondered if he had heard her. Then he offered a small smile, the first she'd seen crease his face.

"The last time I saw Miss Younger — there were important papers she wanted me to secure for her — there was a moment ..."

He hesitated.

"Yes?"

"... she told me she intended to live forever."

Startled, Joanna laughed out loud.

"Please," the old man leaned closer, his warm peppermint breath delicate as a hummingbird's wing. "Stay safe."

The laughter caught in Joanna's throat. Before she could speak, Marcus Washington shut the door.

15

Courthouse

Joanna drove in circles around the courthouse square. Avoiding the inevitable. Marcus Washington had advised her to read the Bentley trial transcripts, but she felt a deep compulsion to do the opposite. Instead, she sucked on a raspberry Slurpee from the 7-11 where she had bought her father his nighttime snacks then flipped the radio dial from one local country western station to another. White blues lamentations plunged her mood further into the toilet and the day's shadows lengthened. Joanna goosed her car into an open parking place in front of the courthouse entrance, glaring at the brick behemoth in her path. What in the hell would she possibly find in there that could help her father? Preoccupied as she was, no internal radar alerted her to the driver who had followed her at a comfortable distance from the hospital parking lot earlier in the day.

~~~~~

Tazewell found the object of his attention conveniently predictable. Of course, she made the pilgrimage to her father's bedside first thing. He wondered if she appreciated the long-stemmed white roses selected with such precision. Expensive, but he had no doubt his reward would be delivered in due time. The trip to Marcus Washington's house, however, surprised him. Curious. What could she possibly want with that old fossil? Annoyed at her change of pattern, he parked down the street at a discreet spot under the shade trees and watched her walk toward the courthouse. Patience surmounted life's every obstacle. Patience and cunning.

~~~~~

With each step Joanna took toward the courthouse doors, loneliness seeped through every pore. *Alone, so godawful alone.* Exhaling a deep breath, she pushed through heavy oak doors and entered. The high-ceil-inged Victorian corridor had suffered a number of twentieth century indignities, the major being an ugly security turnstile to enable the guard to execute an effective weapons check. But it was late in the day and no security personnel appeared to be in attendance. Although the mosaic floor tiles were chipped and worn with age, the mahogany staircase was still grand. She followed the winding steps to a horseshoe circle of rooms, each foreboding in its emptiness. Uneven afternoon sunlight slivering its way through dirty windows did nothing to lift her spirits.

A small courtroom was deserted, the judge's desk shut down for busi-ness. The neighboring room housed a long table with vacant chairs and on the wall a gathering of dignitaries. Pontiac's former mayors looked down from framed photographs, their countenances unwaveringly male. She fol-lowed the brass nameplates around the room until she came to the one honoring William Bentley. Father of Asher, the older Bentley's icy eyes seemed to chastise any unwelcome observer audacious enough to gaze upon him. Joanna stood her ground anyway, so mesmerized by the old patriarch's face that she did not hear the footsteps behind her.

"Visitors aren't allowed in here."

Joanna jumped, her nerves raw and naked. The security guard smirked. Burly, his cheeks pitted with deep acne scars, he ushered her out with un-ceremonial speed. She didn't like his face any more than she cared for William Bentley's. Downstairs she wandered through another maze of rooms before discovering the County Records office. Scratched oak bench-es were stuffed with sweaty, unsmiling bodies. The more enterprising cooled themselves with free cardboard fans, courtesy of Hartwig Mortuary & Funeral Home, that had been stacked on a side table. The ancient room's air conditioner had sputtered its last breath before noon.

"Take a number," the sign ordered. Not even a please. Joanna grabbed 44 and squeezed into a corner seat before another latecomer could slip in. Hard looks, hard benches. She hated the place. Joanna closed her eyes and prayed that her father, despite all evidence to the contrary, would be well enough to fly back to California by Monday.

"44!"

By the time the woman in a pink-flowered shirt called her number it was almost 3:30. Joanna approached the counter, doing her best to avoid looking at the pancake-sized stains under the clerk's armpits.

"Form?"

"Excuse me?"

The lady pointed to a half dozen stacks next to the "take a number" sign: "Birth certificate? Marriage? Death? You need to complete a request form."

"I'm looking for trial transcripts. Oh yes, witness depositions as well."

"Here you go." The lady pulled an official looking piece of paper from one of the stacks and eyed the clock. "Let's get this puppy done right now. Name?"

"Well, there are two actually. The first would be Aldine Younger vs. Herbert Powell."

"Year?"

"1932, I think."

"My lands. The second?"

"State of Illinois vs. Asher Bentley, 1933."

"Those dockets are going to be packed away to kingdom come. I'm afraid you'll have to come back next week."

"What? That's impossible. I may not be here."

"Well, we're not going to be here after noon tomorrow. Not until Tuesday. County employees got a long Labor Day weekend coming up, ma'am."

Labor Day? Joanna shook her head, feeling like she was in some kind of time warp. The lady pointed again, not to a stack of bureaucratic forms, but to a wall calendar sporting a four-color shot of a handsome green and yellow John Deere parked in front of a blood red barn. The calendar stated with no uncertainty that today was Thursday, August 29.

Or was it March 1? The color photo above the calendar page morphed into a black-and-white etching of a 1933 Lawson 20-40 tractor next to a vintage silo.

"No," Joanna blinked.

"Well, I'm sorry you feel that way."

"No, I mean — can't I go back there and look for the files myself?" An hour before Joanna had resisted even walking in here and now these god-damned documents were the most important thing in her life.

"That is not our usual procedure —"

A male voice interrupted. "May I be of some assistance?"

Joanna turned to see the archivist from the Pontiac Library standing behind her.

"Oh, what a nice surprise to see you again," he smiled at Joanna, explaining that he had clearance to access county records for a research project at the library. As a professional archivist, he would be happy to assist the busy staff in finding documents for one of his patrons …

"Authorized Personnel Only," the lettering on the door warned. Joanna and the helpful archivist entered a dark room choked with heat, dust, and thousands of court dockets bound in black binders. A staffer perched at a precarious angle on top of a wheeled ladder as it crept from one row of files to another. Half-dozing, he looked like he had not seen the sun in a dozen years.

"Looks like it was a late night for old Jack Finley. Let's not disturb the poor man," Tazewell whispered, leaning closer. "What are we looking for?"

Joanna displayed the request form for his edification. "Aldine Younger vs. Herbert Powell and —"

"Did you say Aldine Younger?"

"Yes. She was my father's half-sister."

"Mine too!"

The two cousins stared at one another. She, in confusion. He, in feigned surprise. "Are you … Joanna Morse?"

"Yes." Joanna sucked in her breath searching for a name that eluded her. "And you … you must be … Horatio's son?"

"Please. Call me Tazewell."

She stammered about their recent arrival from California, ending with the delicate subject of Horatio's will.

"Yes, Dad took my advice," Tazewell lied. "Junior deserved that farm. And my life is in town. Has been for years."

What a reasonable, understanding man. Our lawyer must have been misinformed.

"Well, we have work to do before closing. If you don't mind my asking, why all this research into our dead aunt's sad past?"

Joanna hesitated.

"Not that it's any of my affair —"

"It's for my father."

"I understand. May I?"

He pulled the request form out of Joanna's fingers into his own. Delivering a sharp kick to the ladder, he jostled the staffer awake.

"Rise and shine, Finley. We have a lady waiting!"

Over an hour passed. And still the transcripts and depositions remained un-viewable, buried deep in the bowels of the courthouse, hiding in some unforgiving corner that refused to surrender old secrets. Tazewell finished a perfunctory search of the bottom shelves as his cousin combed through all the middle sections back and forth lest she miss something.

"Are you sure there's nothing in the bottom files?" Joanna pressed.

"We'll keep looking," he assured her, turning away and going through the motions.

"Aldine Younger vs. Herbert Powell, you said?" Finley squeaked, rolling on his creaky ladder from one upper shelf to the next.

"And the State of Illinois vs. Asher Bentley," Joanna repeated. "Two separate dockets."

"Ah, both cases," Tazewell nodded, seeming to validate her search. Now he knew why the old Pontiac newspapers had been so important to her when they met in the library.

"Ten minutes 'til closing!" the lady announced at the door, dimming the lights off and on for good measure.

"Please, not yet," said Joanna, her eyes blurred by the blizzard of court dockets.

"You're welcome to return tomorrow ma'am, but we close early. Twelve noon sharp."

"No worries," Tazewell moved closer to his cousin. "We can come back together tomorrow."

"Nine minutes!" the lady barked. Just as she shut the door, Finley announced his discovery.

"A. Younger," he croaked, pulling out a binder from the topmost shelf. As he stumbled down the ladder, a yellowed file spilled out of the binder. Tazewell stretched to catch it, like a bridesmaid reaching for the tossed wedding bouquet before another's hand touched it first. But it wasn't a thick bible of transcripts that came tumbling down. Two short pages only, signed in Aldine Younger's scrawling script, and dated February 24, 1931:

LAST WILL AND TESTAMENT OF ALDINE YOUNGER

Joanna scooped the file from her cousin's hands.

"Without asking my permission first?" Tazewell smiled.

Ignoring her cousin's "joke," she read quickly, fearing that at any moment they would be forced to leave.

"… all the rest and residue of my personal estate I may now own — or hereafter acquire — to my mother, Paulina Morse. In addition I bequeath my real property, Lot 4, Section 2 north, 320 acres and the farmhouse upon it to my younger brother, Owen Morse, after our mother's death, provided he has reached his majority at age eighteen …"

"Our aunt, rest her soul, would be so happy to know Uncle Owen finally received what she intended, don't you think?"

Fifty-eight years too late is all. Joanna stared at the old, mimeographed pages, not yet ready to look at her cousin or offer a polite response.

Clickety-clack, clickety-clack, the stepladder rolled closer.

"I found this," Finley lurched off the ladder, clutching a folded blue document. "Must've fallen behind the binder."

Tazewell opened his fist to grab Finley's latest treasure, its bent spine swathed in one long dust bunny. Wiping off the paper with his handkerchief, he read to himself.

"Oh my, this is quite something."

"What is it?" Joanna asked.

"A legal petition requesting that Aldine Younger be held in conservatorship."

"I don't understand."

"Well," Tazewell wore a dutiful look of chagrin, "it seems her mother wanted to lock her up."

"Lock her up, lock her up. Take the keys and lock her up, my fair lady."

And then the room went dark.

V

GROWING SEASON

Private Musings & Verse by Miss A. Younger

AUGUST 31, 1928

The school bell rings tomorrow but I am deaf to its call.

My mind is made up no matter how bad Ma nags and needles. This summer long my books kept me more than occupied. In the months to come I am sure not to miss school one whit — not even a little bit! Since Mademoiselle Borame abandoned us at the end of spring term for some snooty private lycée in Springfield there seems no point in returning. The other teachers are boring, silly, and strait-laced. My classmates even worse — childish as can be. Always gossiping over this boy and that girl with my former friend Ruthie the worst among them. I have outgrown them all and am far better for it. My every waking hour shall now be devoted to drowning myself in the nectar of great poetry and literature so I am prepared for college stud-ies out West when I collect my inheritance.

Of course, I must keep my grand plan secret! No one in my family will be sympathetic to such worthy ambition. Ma has gone completely a-dither with Bertha's engagement and all the dreary details of the nuptials to be. Thick as thieves they are and nosy tyrants to boot. If I wish to renew my acquaintance with S, that is my business. 'Tis true Ma made me swear never to see him again but the oath was not of my free will so I feel no obligation to honor it.

When I saw S waiting for me at our special place on the last day of school I confess my heart turned cartwheels at such a sight. He told me he missed me terrible, making many apologies for not being in touch, and begged that we take pleasure in each other's company as before. After giving his invitation deep thought, I agreed on the condi-tion that S promise to treat me right from here on out and he agreed without hesitation. I do pray S keeps his word though I am learning not to second guess the Fates. He will or he won't. Maybe no amour is ever true and that's the way of the world. I shared nothing of my mis-adventure in Chicago. No man likes to have a girl cry on his shoulder. Thanks to the mess the doctor made there will be no chance of future calamities so why not kick up my heels until I leave this stupid town?

Looking forward to a little fun after my trials, I could hardly wait until S arranged to slip away and pick me up on Friday night. Sure enough, we went dancing at the Wilmington Gun Club just like the good old days of our courtship. I tried to teach S some Charleston jaybird steps but he said you can't teach an old dog new tricks so I let him bounce around his old-fashioned way. We took long swallows from his fancy silver flask and had a high time 'til the cows came home.

Like before I sneaked inside the house through Junior's window — he was sleeping like the cherub he is — so I lay beside him to cuddle and warm my toes but some bad dream took hold and there was Ma screaming in my ear and Bertha at her side, dragging me out of Junior's room. My mother and sister had no right to lay their hands on me. I tried to push them away, but there they were! Yanking me to the stairwell and lashing my wrists to the banister with Ma's old dishtowels. I can still see those ugly linen chains, dirty white from too many washings, all the bright color bleached to a memory of what was. Ma was panting hard, big belly pumping up and down, mouth moving so fast that, try as I might, I never did understand the words tumbling out. Bertha stayed silent as a stone, her head twitching back and forth between Ma and me like she had no sense of her own. And all the while their fists bore blows down upon me with a fever's fury!

Then and there my floating time came upon me. I pretended the sass was knocked out of me then closed my ears to Ma's wailing and just lifted up. Above that drafty old jail, above all the folks that cause me grief, above the cornstalks under the prairie stars, higher and higher and higher until I was a cloud on God's midnight face. A powerful feeling rose forth from deep inside my chest, wide and vast and strong until it came near to bursting my very heart. I sensed I might burn up from the pure fire of it before I was through. The wind began singing my name, not in any language somebody else could understand, but in Nature's special tongue just for me.

In recent days I have come to converse with the lilies of the valley blooming in front of the First Methodist Church where Mrs. Lawson, bless her soul, used to sing God's graces. Once upon a time I felt myself to be only a speck of dust. But I have learned to fool my tormenters and spin their cruel blanket of fog round and round until I glisten hard and beautiful. A Pearl of Great Price that nobody will ever be able to touch again ...

Spring Blooms at Night

On a distant golden street
A giant Chinese Camphor
Waits to shelter me.

Black bark shadows
Old roots pushed above ground.
Draped as tenderly as
A maiden's lost organza gown.

December Irises bloom next door,
Stretching rouged throats,
Beseeching a wayward wind to
Caress lonely petals.

Come closer, they say,
See how I will shimmer and shine
Drinking the honey-sweet rays
Of the Occidental sun to come.

JUNE 17, 1929

The years of lovely lace are long behind me now. Sweet life fell out of a hole in my pocket and I can't figure how I lost it. Even a bad penny rolling all alone down the sidewalk is picked up sooner or later and gets spent for a fun time. Every day I waste away behind the dungeon counters of Bertha and Conley's Confectionery Shop is another nail in my coffin. A half-pound of divinity fudge lickety-split, Aldine! Did you wrap the almond nougat proper, Aldine? The customer is always right, Aldine, you know better than to contradict your elders! Do this, do that, stand up, sit down, turn around — I'm sick of it. Idle hands are the Devil's playground says Ma. A writer's hands are not idle, say I in my heart of hearts, but why talk aloud to my mother about anything? She never listens anyway.

S is no better. Always in his cups and full of one angry woe after another, he ruins every occasion we sneak out together. No more will I be trotted about like a prize Shetland in her feathered harness just so he can play the big man to impress his roadhouse cronies. All those sweet apple butter promises of his will never be kept. My gentleman amour is no gentleman and hardly my amour these dark days. Sometimes I can barely climb out of bed …

Junior is my one salvation, teasing my funny bone with his lispy voice until I float out of my deep blue doldrums into the world again. Such a tender flower! I fear for his future with no proper father to raise him to manhood. Ma is awful bonded with little Absher and distracted by money troubles so Junior gets nothing but hind tit (to use one of Horatio's uncouth expressions). Naturally it came down to me to buy my precious brother a pair of skates when Ma refused to scrape together the dimes to do so. I taught him how to right himself after a bad spill and his tears dried as soon as I told him the story of a brave little boy with derring-do just like him. He wanted more stories after supper but my brain was too vexed battling the Muse. I showed Junior some of my pitiful effort — shamed though I was to expose such failure even to a child — and he seemed to appreciate my fatigue. We hugged close and off he went to chase fireflies until Ma yelled to come in for bedtime. The next day, much to my surprise, what does Junior present in his finest penmanship? This dear little rhyme I will treasure always!

A Poem to Aldine from Junior

Once upon a time
A princess in her castle hi
Called brave nights far and ni
One stronger and better than the rest
Slade the dragons big and small
His princess laft with glee
Stay with me she said
Her cat eyes brite and glad
And they lived happy ever after
In the land of two.

JULY 14, 1929

Never trust a gypsy. They'll lie with no shame and rob you blind.

That's what the old ladies at my aunt's Daughters of the American Revolution tea said, but what do they know? They still wear flowered hats and long polka dot dresses. All day long flapping their jaws about paprika and potato salad and proper ladies like Mrs. Coolidge vs. that hussy Mrs. Wilson, being so forward the way she took over her poor husband's business. Old Ice Bucket Coolidge in the White House makes 'em proud to be American again, don't you know? Take those biddies to the county line and they'd think they'd gone to New York City, that's how ignorant they are.

But the gypsy at the fair on Saturday had a way about her. Not like the carny freaks and roustabouts. I consider it terrible manners to stare at the Bearded Lady who has enough problems without folks poking fun at her long face so I sat Junior down for a fried chicken lunch. My brother was chewing on his third helping when I directed his gaze to a tall woman at the edge of the tent.

The purple scarf was what caught my eye, a big silky thing draped around her hips all swirly and full. In the newsstand magazines Vogue models wear scarves on their hips too. She stood under a sign with a big black hand that said: "Palmist. Love. Money. Health. Happiness. Madame Giselle tells your future." I walked over to see what she charged but as I got closer a strange scent near to knocked me over. Not that she was dirty. Her skin shone clean enough. Still, her perfumes were unlike any I ever smelled before. Junior didn't mind, being too busy feeding his face with the last drumstick from some dead hen. Madame Giselle grabbed my hand and peered at my palm like it might offer up the secrets of Solomon's mines.

"So what do you see? Will I move to Paris and marry a prince?"

She lifted up her face to meet mine but didn't say a word. Just stared deep into me with eyes blacker than a crow's until I decided to keep my business private. I pulled away from her smelly grasp and turned to leave.

"Never mind. I prefer that my good fortune be a surprise."

"Wait," she said, touching my arm, her voice soft as creamed butter.

"Maybe the boy would like me to read his palm? For him, a nickel."

She knelt down to take Junior's hand, still sticky with chicken grease, into her own. Rings, lots of rings, silver and gold, graced her fingers.

"Would you like to look into the future and see what a big man you will be?"

"Can I, Aldine?"

"Sure, why not."

"Will you come in with me?"

"Not today, I'm going to have myself a cigarette. Don't you worry. I'll stay close."

Madame Giselle scooped up the nickel as soon as it touched her palm, then took Junior behind a gauze curtain, the kind you can only see through part way. I lit up my Old Gold with the fancy lighter from S and blew smoke circles the way he taught me. One after another, like the Apache war signals they show in the Tom Mix talkies my little brothers like so much. Maybe I'll see some Indian chiefs on the way West I was thinking when all of a sudden Junior came out and grabbed my hand.

"You done peeking into the future already?"

He nodded and dragged me over to the carousel with the pictures of brave knights and fair ladies from olden times.

"Let's ride together, okay, Aldine?"

"You think I'm going to let you have a swell time all by yourself?"

Junior picked the palomino the way he does every year and I climbed sidesaddle on the while stallion, a proud steed that looked like it galloped out of the German fairy tales Ma used to read to me when I was little. While we waited for the carny music to crank up, I crossed my knees to show off my silk stockings and black patent T-straps. I didn't care who got an eyeful and plenty did.

"So Junior, I bet the gypsy said you'd get a lot of girlfriends when you grow up."

"She said I'm going to meet a lady with red hair and ask her to marry me."

"I don't know if your big sister approves. Redheads have redhead tempers. You know the Monahan girl that hangs out at the soda fountain? She's always getting mad at somebody for no reason at all."

"Like Horatio."

"Just as bad."

"But Horatio doesn't have red hair."

"No, thank God. He's a big enough sourpuss as it is."

"Do you think the gypsy lady just makes up stories, Aldine? To scare people?"

"Getting married isn't scary." (Unless you pick the wrong man like Ma did but I kept my feelings to myself.) "What else did the gypsy say?"

The carny music was playing so loud I couldn't hear Junior's words. He started to look a little green around the gills, the carousel spinning as fast as it was. All of a sudden he upchucked all over his town pants that Ma ironed before we left. I tried to flag down the carny man to let us off, but he was too busy sneaking sips from the gin bottle in his jacket pocket to pay us any mind. All I could do was rub Junior's back while he retched some more, his shoulder blades so delicate they felt like they might snap in two. By the time the carousel came to a stop Junior was mortified. The other kids poking fun, the carny man yelling about the paint on his damned palomino, the couple behind us complaining loud and rude. I got my brother to a latrine and cleaned him with my linen hankie the best I could. He bit his bottom lip so hard to keep from being a crybaby a drop of blood smeared his front tooth.

"It's all right, Junior, that carny man was driving the merry-go-round too fast —"

"Aldine, the gypsy told me a bad end will come to you if you're not careful — a terrible bad end!"

"Oh for heaven's sake, that's the silliest thing I ever heard. And you believed her?"

"Don't laugh, Aldine! You promise you'll be careful like she said?"

I wiped his nose with the edge of the lace chemise under my skirt.

My hankie was already soaked with his retching, no use to anybody anymore.

"Aldine?"

"Don't you worry, honey." I held him close a spell and tried to put his child's mind at ease.

"You can't trust a gypsy, don't you know that?" He shook his head. "Well, now you do. Don't forget it."

After supper Junior followed Ma into the kitchen and told her what the gypsy woman said. Putting no store in such things, she shushed Junior then bawled me out.

"What kind of a big sister are you, Aldine? Letting your brother talk to un-Christian riff-raff?"

If that gypsy woman is right, my mother will be sorry for treating me so mean.

MAY 11, 1930

A mean drunk is the worst kind of drunk, Ma always says and now I too know the affliction of such unhappiness. I hate S and his silly jealousy.

If one of his pals so much as asks me to dance, it's my fault for flirting — when I was only being friendly like I always am — and he grabs my hand rough and says it's time to leave just when the band's warming up to my favorite tunes. Darn him for spoiling a girl's innocent fun!

Enough is enough. I pray daily to my wild 'n mighty Jesus that I link arms with a new amour to lift my spirits. A fine young beau not weighed down with a bushel of misery and bald headed regrets. Some-one strong and funny and Samson haired like the new butcher boy at the market! He told a swell joke yesterday while he was wrapping up the suet for my mother's cabbage soup. Even little Junior at my side laughed out loud like he was in the front row at the picture show. If not for Mr. O'Brien's eagle eye from the back of the store, I feel sure the butcher boy and I could have chatted up a high time.

"Eldon," he bellowed loud enough to wake the dead, "customers are waiting."

"Yes, sir, Mr. O'Brien," he answered right back, "well, I'll be seeing you, Miss —"

"My name is Aldine," I said flashing my sweetest smile. "See you next time, Eldon."

"Hap," he said, "Hap Holloway. Nobody calls me Eldon but my boss and my mom, okay?"

"Okay, Hap!" I gave my hips some extra swing on the way out.

Life is a wondrous thing. One day the cellar of despair, the next a bowl of cherries with Chantilly cream on top. Even Bertha has been all aglow thanks to Ma gifting her and Conley with the Heinemann high boy. Ever since I can remember Bertha's oohed and aahed over Grandma Heinemann's wedding chest and now she has her heart's desire gloating in a place of honor against the parlor wall. The way my sister runs her hands over that old piece of wood it might as well be a pet dog.

"Honduran flame mahogany, Aldine, *flame* mahogany from the finest trees halfway around the world and over a hundred years old!"

I thank goodness Ma did not unload any decrepit hand-me-downs on me with my travels to California less than a year away. Soon I'll be able to rouge my knees and sleep 'til noon and write poetry to my heart's content. After I'm gone I expect S will be burning in Hades together with the rest of his drunken cronies ...

OCTOBER 25, 1930

Almost a whole week as A Woman of 18 and still I await my gift from Grandpa Younger! Patience, patience, my mother says. Maybe Mr. Powell caught the bad flu going around and surely all funds will be deposited by tomorrow. Ma acts the flibberty-gibbit these days, her head a-swim with nonsense about moving back to the farm because poor Horatio — a grown man of 23 — cannot manage harvest time on his own since the tenants up and left.

And what is to become of me? What is my unfortunate fate in Ma's grand plan? I'm supposed to live with Bertha and Conley! Surely Sister cooked this up to keep my nose stuck to the grindstone at her stupid shop. If such terrible hardship comes to pass I beg Jesus that my purgatory last no more than a month. I could not survive any longer.

Thank goodness for Hap, my sweetheart, and loving pea pot. On Independence Day — an omen for my new womanhood — we sealed our passion in Starved Rock Park. God's most glorious cathedral in our neck of the woods and home of the great prairie drama when the good Indian tribes avenged Chief Pontiac's murder by the evil Illiniwek on the Bluff of Death. As Hap and I lay in the sun-dappled meadow, I could hear the voices of the ancients ringing from every tree and flower —

Live Now!

Darling Hap is much impressed with my secret plans. "Let's go west, young man," I said, "my trust fund will support us in high style." I know he's tempted, and if not for concerns about his mother's failing health, would surely hop on a train with me this minute. California, here we come! How we laugh together!

You'd think Ma might appreciate a sweet man who makes her daughter smile but no, all I hear is what a mama's boy he is and why doesn't he get a haircut and court me proper instead of meeting me down at the picture show on Saturday nights. 'Tis a heartache that my mother will never understand the ways of the young though I know her many sorrows have taken a toll and now her vision is weakening too. Before Hap and I leave for our western adventure, I will buy Ma a lapel broach in pure gold to pin her spectacles close at hand. Never again will she have to hunt in vain for her second eyes.

JANUARY 15, 1931

Spendthrift?! How dare my mother make such a cruel claim? Herbert Powell should be locked up, not me. But no, Ma makes excuses for that old two-faced crook and punishes her innocent daughter with threat of jail under Sister's roof. I could not believe the ugly legal papers my own parent thrust in front of my weeping eyes.

"See here, Aldine, if you will not mend your foolish ways, Bertha must be made Conservator to keep you in line."

Such heartless vindictiveness just because I put a matching grey fox hat and coat on a layaway account to keep hopeful as I await my missing inheritance! Mr. Cabaleri had just raised the morning shades at the Antoinette Shoppe. The minute I entered, what did I see? A grand silver fox coat right up on the prettiest mannequin in the store. Mr. Cabaleri made no protest when he saw me petting its soft fur like it was already my own. Clara Bow has her leopard. I will have my fox.

Why is it a crime to stay warm on these freezing days anyway?

Ma did not seem to comprehend my question so we railed and went round and round but I could not apologize and she would not waver. Finally my pride gave way and I begged with no shame —

"Please don't put me under Bertha's hold, Ma. Please!"

She sighed, her face pinched in such fearsome judgment that I worried no mercy would be coming.

"Will you promise to be a good daughter, Aldine?"

"Yes, Ma."

"Trust your elders?"

"Yes, Ma."

"I think it's time to make your will."

I said nothing at first, not sure what she was driving at.

"You need to protect your family in case God shoots another thunderbolt our way. I'm no stranger to hard times, as you know."

"Yes, Ma."

"So it's fine with you that we go to Mr. Stickerling to draw up the will next week?"

"Will you make him tear up the conservatorship papers?"

"If you do what I say."

"All right then." (Though I have not yet seen those papers torn to bits like she promised.)

After I signed the will in Mr. Stickerling's office with dear Sister bearing witness, a fit of laughing came over me so terrible bad I started hiccupping the way I do. Ma looked mortified and Mr. Stickerling rushed to hand me a glass of water. I said thank you and took deep gulps.

You think I'll be flying off to heaven sometime soon, Ma? Or maybe Hell is the proper destination for a daughter like me. Tell me, where am I headed?

"The Lord knows," my mother gritted through her teeth, and pulled me out the door before I could say another word. In the middle of the night when Ma was full asleep, I huddled safe under the covers to commune with my goddess Edna. Only she could soothe me now ...

Recuerdo
by
Edna St. Vincent Millay

We were very tired, we were very merry —
We had gone back and forth all night on the ferry.
It was bare and bright, and smelled like a stable —
But we looked into a fire, we leaned across a table,
We lay on a hill-top underneath the moon;
And the whistles kept blowing, and the dawn came soon.

We were very tired, we were very merry —
We had gone back and forth all night on the ferry;
And you ate an apple, and I ate a pear,
From a dozen of each we had bought somewhere;
And the sky went wan, and the wind came cold,
And the sun rose dripping, a bucketful of gold.

We were very tired, we were very merry,
We had gone back and forth all night on the ferry.
We hailed, "Good morrow, mother!" to a shawl-covered head,
And bought a morning paper, which neither of us read;
And she wept, "God bless you!" for the apples and pears,
And we gave her all our money but our subway fares.

MARCH 2, 1931 — The Spring from Hell

Ma thinks her shyster lawyer will get justice with his polite high-toned letters — oh dear Mr. Powell I'm sure there's been some confusion, oh dear Mr. Powell we're awaiting your kind response, oh, dear Mr. Powell what pleasure it would give me to wring your wrinkled turkey neck and dump you in the Vermilion River on a moonless night!

Take the bull by the horns I decided and went straight away to the bank to collect my rightful inheritance and sure enough that old skin-flint Powell was nowhere to be seen and who comes over to shush me quiet but Uncle Frederick.

"Stop making a scene, Aldine!" My uncle steered me to a back office and closed the door. "Propriety, dear girl, propriety."

"Mr. Powell is trying to cheat me —"

"Mr. Powell who has protected your fortune with his own life since your grandfather died? Mr. Powell who toiled day and night to make wise investments so you could receive your trust fund interest like clockwork on March 1st every single spring without fail, Aldine? Have you no appreciation at all?"

"I have reached my majority, I deserve my full share —"

"Of course you do and you shall have it."

"When?!"

"As soon as Mr. Powell recovers. He's been ill for some months now but wants no one to know. Some folks are not as loyal as we are to our family friends, Aldine. In these hard times bank customers might leave if they got wind of Mr. Powell's health decline."

"Then why can't you help him catch up on his duties, Uncle Frederick? Ma says you're a man of influence here at the bank."

"I'm afraid your mother overestimates my authority. How is she, by the way? I hear there've been problems out at the farm with Horatio."

No way she would want Uncle Frederick to gossip about Horatio's fits and starts so I played it down. "Ma's fine, busy as ever."

"A good Christian woman, nobody works harder to take care of her family. Think of your mother now, Aldine. Would she want you here putting your business in a sorry light in front of the whole town?"

He had a point there. And if old Powell was bad off, I didn't want to make such a fuss that he'd kick the bucket before he could settle my affairs. So I went on my way.

All through the night I tossed and turned trying to sort through the mess. The next morning I went to see Stickerling despite his terrible rudeness to me on my last visit. He was too busy kissing another client's behind to give me any mind so he sent me off to a corner with the box of my legal files and ordered me to study up because if I bothered him with more questions they better make sense.

I poured over a bunch of boredom 'til my head ached. Grandpa Younger's will, a stack of papers about the sale of my land to Aunt Libby and Uncle Frederick ten years back so my inheritance could be put in cash bonds — which I guess old Powell figured was the smart thing to do — all water under the bridge. But what I read next made my eyes go almost blind with rage. Ma and Papa Morse borrowed funds from my trust account to pay off the second mortgage long before he took off for parts unknown and right in front of me was the second mortgage note to prove it!

And to think the horror of such deception would still be a scandalous secret if I had not knocked on the shyster's door to demand my due. I cannot believe such betrayal and I do not buy Ma's excuse that I was a babe-in-arms and she had every intention of repaying the loan in total as soon as I reached my majority and she says if I'm mad at anybody it should be Uncle Frederick because his wily ways tricked poor Mr. Powell into selling my land for pennies on the dollar when I was only eight years old and what could she do about it. I may be young but I am not stupid!

I gave Ma notice that she is overdue in paying back the loan she and Papa Morse took out without me knowing. Unless she pays it off pretty damn quick, I will take her name off my will (penniless heiress that I am!) and leave all my earthly goods to Hap. I cannot trust <u>any of them</u> — Powell, my uncle, even my own mother …

Peony Juice

Full feathered cups of
Red & white & tender pink
Swell-smelling juice to drink,
Though I prefer Blood.

How lovely it would be
To cut all your lying tongues in half
And feed to undiscerning worms.

Why linger then?
Peonies bloom,
Train whistles blow,
Justice, dear Justice, done at last.

I know God forgives my sin
As I forgive His in creating you.

VI

DÉJÀ VU

16

Threshermen's Parade

"So kind of you to give me a lift, Joanna."

"Not a problem, Tazewell," she smiled stiffly.

Yesterday at the Pontiac Library, today in County Records. This benign little man who only wanted to help was beginning to feel like a barnacle she couldn't shake off.

"Well, you mustn't worry about those trial transcripts. No doubt just misfiled. I'm sure the *Pontiac Leader* covered the Bentley trial. The Chicago papers as well. Probably quite the sensation at the time. Pretty girl, married man, all those lurid details. Perhaps I can stop by the courthouse tomorrow morning on my way to work."

"I don't want to trouble you."

"No trouble at all."

Joanna's hands were riveted to the steering wheel, her neck muscles tensing more with every mile. So tense they seemed to be cutting off oxygen to her brain. The damned Ambien from the night before had been clouding her concentration all day long.

"A lot of people don't appreciate the fact that archivists have to exercise the same intellectual skill as the most superior sleuths. Chasing down clues until we find our man — or woman — so to speak." He looked sideways at Joanna.

"Demanding work, I have no doubt."

"Oh, yes. Turning the screw inch by inch until we get to where we need to go. But very rewarding in the end," his tight smile widened. "I must say it's heartening to know how devoted Uncle Owen is to Aldine's memory. Touching."

"Your father wasn't? Devoted to family?"

Tazewell parsed his words with care. "Horatio — he always preferred that I call him by his Christian name — was a solitary man."

"I understand he could be … difficult."

The air went dead between them for a moment.

"Sins of the fathers."

"Excuse me?"

"Those brotherly grudges of the older generation. How fortunate that you and I can prevail over that silliness. We have a quest now, don't we?"

Joanna's mouth twitched, unsure how "I" became "We."

"Take the next right, dear."

Joanna did as she was told and ended up in a maze of machinery clogging the streets with yesterday. Old-time steam engines were lined in neat caterpillar rows next to restored antique tractors, each brightly painted bumper hugging another.

"The Threshermen's Parade," Tazewell sniffed in exasperation. "Every Labor Day weekend, I'm afraid. Puzzling how these sentimental rituals manage to survive."

Maneuvering around a vintage tractor, Joanna noted its black smokestack, giant yellow wheels, and shiny crimson belly.

"Allis–Chalmers, 1928," she announced.

Tazewell turned in surprise. "The city girl knows her farm machinery."

"No, I really don't. I …" she shook her head, unsettled. "Some picture … something I must have picked up from my dad when I was a kid. Odd what we remember."

"I suppose Uncle Owen would get a kick out of these junk-mobiles then. A shame he's confined."

An ugly word, "confined." Thinking of the conservatorship papers that her grandmother had filled out on Aldine, Joanna rushed to set Tazewell straight.

"He's getting better."

"Is he?"

"Every day."

"Well, that is happy news. Let's all have dinner after he's on the mend."

She slammed to a stop as he pointed to his trusty Ford camouflaged behind a row of thick maples.

"Thank you for your help this afternoon, Tazewell."

"My pleasure," he put his smooth pudgy hand on the door handle but waited to push it open until he exacted her promise. "See you tomorrow night?"

Joanna hesitated then nodded.

"Lovely. We'll have the library all to ourselves."

As she drove off, second thoughts peppered her judgment. The tension of excavating her aunt's history grew more unbearable with each passing hour. Would it really make any difference in her Dad's recovery?

"No," she said aloud. Startled by the brittle echo of her own voice, usually melodious and accommodating, she swerved to the right and bounced off the curb before skidding to a halt.

"I'm fine." Joanna sat quietly, hyperventilating. Why was she talking aloud to herself again? "I haven't eaten all day, that's the problem."

Kellogg's cornflakes and bad blueberry muffins, what the Comfort Inn called a continental breakfast, had left her digestive tract in distress for hours. No wonder she was a little shaky. Instead of turning back toward the courthouse square to find a café for dinner, she headed in the opposite direction. Out of town away from the traffic jam of tractors and combines and antique cars, toward the interstate that she and her father traveled only five days before. Toward the river.

Joanna parked near the Mill Street Bridge, one of a half-dozen swinging bridges for city residents to cross from one side to the other. Hickory trees dotted the riverbanks. Prairie wildflowers clustered here and there, splashes of burnt gold against the dark, brooding woods. Walking across the bridge, she stopped mid-point. A subtle sway unsteadied her. The wooden slats beneath her feet seemed strong enough but still she hesitated. Of course, it was safe. The sun unleashed its last glittering rays upon the water's surface and invited her to move on. One more step, then another. Just as she reached the other side, a girlish laugh greeted her. Joanna looked up to see an elderly woman seated on a park bench. Wisps of grey hair peeked from under her wig of tightly wound curls while she sucked on a grape popsicle.

"Come sit with me," she ordered, sliding over to make room. "I won't bite. My name's Lottie."

What a sweet old-fashioned name. Lottie.

"I don't want to intrude —"

"Shhh." Tossing away her popsicle stick, Lottie put a purple stained fingertip against her lips. "The river goddesses are going to sleep now."

Joanna sat down beside her. The old woman's breath was steady and even. Cares of the past days slipped away, peace and the river flowing in equal proportion. She closed her eyes. When they opened, Lottie had disappeared and so had the sun, a tangerine cream-streaked sky left in their wake.

"Why did you leave me?"

Joanna spun around. For a moment she thought she heard that same girlish laugh, now disembodied, echoing through the deepening dusk. Was she dreaming? Rising quickly, she crossed the bridge back to her car.

"About time you woke up." Lottie sat on the hood, her Mary Jane clad feet dangling. Red patent leather Mary Janes, circa 1935. "I need to bum a ride."

Startled by the old woman's assumptiveness, Joanna had to turn the key a second time before it engaged sufficiently to unlock the car door.

"All right. Sure. Where to?"

"Home."

17

The Log Cabin

Joanna drove east as Lottie directed. Curious, how she found the bossy old woman's presence comforting. The headlights of oncoming cars seemed less harsh. Even the humid heaviness of the Midwest twilight felt lighter, not ominous and foreboding as on previous nights. They rode in mutual contentment until Lottie's high-pitched voice broke the silence.

"Yep, Vern and me made it to our golden anniversary together. I told him if I ever got addle brained like some old folks he should shoot me dead but he went first. Last April."

"I'm sorry."

"Now I'll have to shoot myself when the time comes. It's hell being alone. You married?"

"Almost twenty years."

"Good for you. How's the romance department these days?"

Joanna shifted uncomfortably. "Fine."

"Take it from me, when that flies the coop it's all she wrote." Lottie looked out the window. "You went too far."

"Excuse me?"

"Old Route 66. Don't you remember how to get to the old frontage road?" She sighed in exasperation. "Never mind. Go back three blocks and turn left. Then follow the curve 'til you get to the gravel lane."

"Look, I don't live here." Joanna's cheeks flushed.

"No?"

"No, I'm just visiting."

"You like our little piece of paradise?"

"Not much." Then she added, "no offense."

"None taken. Where're you from?"

"California."

"Is that right?" Lottie took in Joanna's profile. "How old are your two daughters now?"

Joanna's grip tightened on the steering wheel.

"Cat got your tongue?"

"I'm sorry. I don't recall mentioning I had children —"

"Don't you?"

"Well, coincidentally —"

"Teenagers already, I imagine? Twins too," Lottie hooted. "Twice the trouble. Sometimes girls think they're women before their time."

Joanna waited a moment before she responded. "How did you know I have twin daughters?"

"I get a feeling sometimes … don't you?"

"What do you mean?"

"Get a feeling about things? Folks you meet?"

"No."

Joanna's tires crunched gravel as she drove past a deserted gas station. The full moon rode high in the sky, exposing slabs of old highway choked with mustard grass and abandoned railroad tracks built in another century.

"Not much to look at anymore, is it?"

"You live here?" Joanna asked.

"Behind the café. Keep going."

Just around the bend of the frontage road a roadhouse jutted out from the forlorn landscape. The foursquare cabin built with split telephone poles still stood strong, red cedar walls a last testament to the prairie forest stripped by local farmers. Next to the front door a neon Budweiser bottle welcomed all comers. Open for business. The flickering bug lights illuminated a peeling sign:

THE LOG CABIN, 1926
HISTORIC ROUTE 66 LANDMARK

Joanna's neck stiffened. This was the place where the police found her father.

"Don't you hear the music?" Lottie climbed out of the car.

What was the old woman prattling on about? Lottie tapped on the windshield. Beckoning. Refusing to leave her alone.

"Damn it," she muttered. Tentative and unsteady, her legs searched for sure footing on the graveled ground. The moment the car door clicked shut, she heard it. A jukebox playing the strains of a familiar melody.

"Ah," Lottie cooed, "one of our favorites."

Trapped in the threads of some dream just beyond memory, Joanna inched toward the entrance of the roadhouse. Pillows of freshly fallen snow softened the weight of her footsteps. Blinking lights in bright red and deep blue were strung around the perimeter of the cabin. Strange sensations bombarded her consciousness like exploding popcorn kernels.

Lottie's voice broke the spell. "They always leave the back open for me."

Through the rusty netting of the dilapidated screen door Joanna heard the old tune more distinctly. Calling her inside.

"That song …?" She was feeling lightheaded again.

"Lookin' good but feelin' bad from grievin' over you," the old woman trilled, traipsing in like she owned the place.

Joanna melted into a shadowed half-lit interior. Cobwebs hung low and inviting, ready to capture a careless insect. Route 66 relics cluttered the smoke-stained walls from top to bottom. Rusted road signs. Burma Shave billboards. Orange Ne-Hi soda tins. Framed black-and-white photos of smiling motorists snapped in the Mother Road's heyday. In the center of the room, its broad oval face glowing purple, pink and sunburst yellow, the jukebox hummed a jazzy serenade. Other than the neon jukebox, the only other light came from twin Depression era floor lamps stuck in opposite corners.

Lottie sashayed over to the glass-doored refrigerator behind the luncheon counter.

"Fried chicken and raspberry cobbler. Folks come from miles around for good home cooking like this. Hungry?"

For the first time in four days Joanna's appetite was ravenous. The two women sat down at a scratched Formica table and began to eat. The strains of one vintage song after another kept them company. Lottie fastidiously wiped a fried chicken crumb from her lower lip.

"Mama A always insisted I learn proper table manners."

Joanna lifted another forkful, the taste of ripe berries and sugared pastry still tingling on her tongue.

"Mama A?"

"That's what Aldine said I should call her, the age difference being what it was when we acquainted. She was eighteen, I'd just turned eight."

Joanna stopped chewing. The cobbler lost its flavor.

"We were both half-orphans Mama A said, my mother long gone like her father. She told me when I got older maybe we'd get a Ouija Board to reach out to my sweet mama and her dear daddy in the great beyond. You ever speak with spirits like that?"

"No."

"Oh. Well, maybe someday. You like your chicken?"

"It's delicious."

"My daddy's recipe. He worked twelve-hour days — best fry cook the Log Cabin ever had — so I was real lonesome 'til Mama A took me under her wing. Oh my, we had ourselves more fun than a barrel of monkeys, playing hide and seek, picnicking down by the river, turning cartwheels. Mama A said the river sang, the way it flowed all sweet kept her nerves at bay. She only took her very best friends there. Me and another special friend but that was for us to know and other folks to mind their own business so I can't say who," Lottie licked her finger then pointed to the small sapphire heart in the hollow of Joanna's throat.

"Your husband give you that?"

"What?" Joanna asked.

"Your necklace, silly."

"Oh, yes," she nodded, still distracted by Lottie's revelation.

"Pretty. But mine's prettier." Lottie tilted her chin and pulled an amethyst pendant from the inside of her high-necked housedress. "You ever seen such a darling thing?"

The lavender stone rippled with light, its facets framed by delicate filigree in the center of a gold linked chain.

Joanna stared at the pendant, mesmerized by the amethyst's glow.

"Mama A always had a rich girl's taste. Gave it to me for my 10th birthday in a velvet box. 'A young lady deserves the finer gifts in life,' she said. Wrote me a poem too. Her words, not some silly rhyme copied from a storybook. Mama A promised to show me how to write verse too when I got big but then the bad angels took her away," the old woman's bright eyes scanned Joanna's. "You want to go see where it happened? Rooks Creek Bridge is just down the road."

Rooks Creek Bridge. Joanna recoiled at the name.

"Another time then. It's spooky at night anyway. Poor thing out there all alone with that drunken fool. Midnight. Dead of winter." Lottie shivered. "Afterwards folks used to come from miles around to study the spot. Fascinated something awful just like they were with Bonnie and Clyde's death car when it went on tour up in Kankakee and Chicago. That's how some people are. Acted like they were on their way to see a high-flying girl in a circus. But the girl was gone and the circus had already left town. Mama A would've laughed at the whole bunch of 'em."

"Would she?"

"Soft as silk, tough as nails, my daddy said she was." Lottie's head bobbed in a hypnotic jig, keeping time with Fats Waller and his piano. "Oh, listen to this swell tune."

Underneath the music a whisper rose and fell.

Joanna looked over her shoulder. "Is someone else here?"

"Just you, me, and the music." Lottie laughed. "Let's dance!"

She reached for Joanna and pulled her to the floor.

"Don't you just love to trip the light fantastic? Mama A cut a rug like nobody's business." Lottie twirled her partner round and round, their fingers entwined.

The colored lights of the jukebox swirled. The room swayed. The music faded and the voices — a man's and a woman's — grew louder. His words were slurred, her tone defiant. Drowning out Fats's happy refrain …

"… get off my case for Christ's sake …"
"… only a few miles up the road …"
"… I said drop it …"
"… maybe your sweet wife will drive me …"
"… keep your goddamned voice down …"
"… Give me the keys …"

Her head spinning, Joanna slipped out of Lottie's grasp.

"Too much, dear? Maybe we should sit down."

The older woman escorted the younger back to their table. Joanna sank into the chair and closed her eyes.

"You need to get out on the dance floor more." Lottie leaned closer. "How's Junior?"

Joanna opened her eyes. Again, the old woman had struck her speechless.

"I'm not surprised about that bad spell of his. Chickens always come home to roost."

"How did you know about my father?"

"You told me when we drove up."

"Did I?"

"You been working too hard, honey. This past Monday night, wasn't it? When your dad made his way here?"

"The police said he didn't know where he was —"

"The police don't know shit from Shinola." Lottie's chair scraped against the worn floor as she rose. "I'd best lock up now. Off you go."

Startled by the old woman's sudden shift, Joanna stood up.

"Don't worry," Lottie scooted Joanna toward the exit. "You and me, we'll meet up again."

Joanna followed her. "I'm not sure how long we'll be in town —"

"Long enough, you'll see." Lottie opened the screen door. "Maybe I'll stop by the hospital to see your dad. Chew the fat over old times. Cheer him up. Do us both good."

Joanna made no move to leave.

"Something wrong?"

"I can't believe you knew my aunt."

"Call your husband, honey," Lottie nudged her guest out then peered through the screen. "Before he gets tired of waiting for you to eat humble pie."

The door with the peeling paint closed tight and the porch light clicked off. Joanna stood alone in the dark. She tried to recall when she told Lottie that her father was in the hospital, but the moment eluded her. News travels fast in a small town.

18

Queen of Spades

All things considered, Joanna told Peter, the situation was looking brighter. Even though her father's mood swings continued. No doubt his mind would clear as soon as Lottie came to visit.

"Who's Lottie?"

"This old woman who knew my dad's family. The most amazing thing, Peter, she was best friends with Aldine!"

"Who's Aldine?"

"Jesus Christ, Peter, you sound like a broken record. Aldine was my dad's older sister. The one who was killed? I told you about the newspaper clippings, I know I did many times. The ones I found when I was a kid and my dad wouldn't talk about? You never listen."

"Joanna, please. You're talking a mile a minute."

"Because you're not hearing me. I'm trying to bring you up to speed is all. Isn't that what you asked me to do last time? Said I should call you, right? Keep you informed? Even though this is really none of your concern."

Now Peter's voice rose. "You're my wife."

"That doesn't mean I have to eat humble pie."

"Humble pie? I don't understand what you're talking about —"

"Never mind, it's not important." She took a deep breath. "How are the girls?"

"Missing you. Sarah said they left a message yesterday, but you never called back."

"Is something wrong? Are they all right?"

"They're having the time of their lives. I think Lizzie's got a crush on some tour guide she met in Venice."

"Tour guide? Their host family's supposed to be chaperoning them."

"I'm sure they were there."

"Did Lizzie confirm that?"

"Well, no."

"Exactly. This guy is probably a creepy Italian gigolo twice her age."

"She said he was a graduate student from Copenhagen."

"That may be what he told her but he could be anything — con artist, criminal, a serial killer for all we know."

"Honey, your imagination is running wild."

"No, I am being a responsible parent. You need to ask questions."

"I'm not going to give Lizzie the third degree, for heaven's sake. I trust our daughter."

"Then you're a fool. These are vulnerable young girls. You think Lizzie would recognize a sheep in wolf's clothing? Do I have to handle everything? Don't I have enough on my mind now? I'm trying to save my life here!"

A long pause. "What do you mean, save your life?"

"My father's life, I said."

"No, that's not what you said."

"Okay, we're having problems communicating again. Let's call it a night."

"Joanna —"

She hung up, the warm glow that had preceded the call now gone. He never paid attention to what she was trying to tell him. Never listened to what she wanted. Why on earth did she imagine he could ever change?

She grabbed the phone when it rang again. "What makes you think I need you anyway?"

Silence. Except for his breathing.

"I don't. You hear me?"

His silence mocked her, kindling something deep and desperate. Words spewed out, words that made no sense —

"You want to walk out on me? Go ahead. I don't give a damn."

But still no sound on the other end.

"Answer me, you son-of-a-bitch!"

The voice was impassive. And soft. Very soft.

"It's your cousin."

"I …" she swallowed, her head swimming with confusion. "Tazewell?"

"Yes."

"I thought … I was expecting someone else."

"Is this a bad time?"

"Well, I … actually I was just about to turn in early."

"I can call back."

Joanna mustered a semblance of control. "What is it, Tazewell?"

"I found the full archive."

"The archive," Joanna repeated.

"Of the Bentley trial? The *Pontiac Daily Leader* covered the daily proceedings, so you don't need the court transcripts after all. Isn't that good news?"

He waited.

"Well, thank you."

"Oh, it's my pleasure to be of service."

A dead space hung in the air between them.

"Good night then, Tazewell."

"See you tomorrow, Joanna."

"Tazewell, wait." she blurted.

"Yes?"

"How did you know where to reach me?"

"I'm a detective, remember?" He laughed. "Sleep well."

Joanna hung up. The pulsing light on the phone indicated a message. Peter no doubt, but she was still too angry to talk with him and didn't know why. Maybe Sarah or Elizabeth? She should call her daughters, she really should. But not tonight. Instead, she instructed the motel operator to direct future calls to voice mail.

For the second night in a row she was too exhausted to wash her face or brush her teeth. Yet when she closed her eyes, sleep refused to come. Despite the unpleasant hangover effect of the previous night, she swallowed two more Ambien and crawled between the sheets. Tomorrow, whether she was ready or not, would soon be here. Drifting in and out of consciousness, she heard music. The old tinny tunes from the Log Cabin jukebox. Sweeter, more melodious, almost magical. Rocking her like a baby's lullaby ...

Until the shot rang out.

Joanna's eyelids quivered. She could feel herself moving toward the sound of the gunshot, past the jukebox, into the middle of the dance floor where a black-figured card stood five and a half feet tall. The Queen of Spades, a bullet hole straight through the heart of its lovely profile, collapsed.

19

The Last Time

"Conservatorship?" Joanna repeated, mirroring the physician's monotone. That word, once foreign and un-relatable, resonated. She'd come across it before. Recently. Yes, she was sure of that.

"Quite simple really. It's not even necessary to get a lawyer involved at this stage. Rexall's down on the corner has the standard forms ..."

The voice faded, muted by a flickering parade of images Joanna needed to put in order. Her father's warm brown eyes. The way he used to laugh when she was a child, a big-jawed smile that split his face in two. The un-expected strength of his gnarled hand squeezing hers outside the Pontiac courthouse —

"... the sooner the better. So we can start processing the paperwork."

"No."

The new doctor raised her eyebrows. Not the same doctor as yesterday, the one who agreed with Joanna that the patient's progress was guarded yet hopeful. A new doctor because this was a holiday weekend and hard-work-ing medical gods needed time off to play golf.

"I don't think you understand the level of deterioration, Mrs. Giorda-no."

"Too fast," she mumbled.

"Yet, I'm afraid things can move pretty quickly at this stage. Unfortu-nately, Mr. Morse is no longer capable of making decisions for himself."

The second doctor, the one she had spoken to only yesterday — or was it the day before — what was his name? The second doctor said —

But the new doctor was already listing Owen Morse's offenses over the past thirty-six hours; "escalating mental disorientation, inability to control bodily functions, violent behavior toward staff, refusal to eat —"

"There must be other medications you can try?"

"Medications take time. Better to move him to Peoria. It's one of the better psychiatric wards south of Chicago. Unfortunately there are no beds available right now. Maybe by tomorrow or Monday." She glanced up from her clipboard. "I leave at 3:00 today."

Joanna stared blankly.

"You'll need my signature on the conservatorship form."

Joanna wanted to kill. Stab the new doctor through the throat with the ballpoint pen perched in her white breast pocket. The one with the blue ink that would certify Owen Morse was no longer an independent, functioning human being worthy of dignity and respect.

Instead of committing homicide Joanna marched into her father's hospital room and ordered the nurse to remove all three vases of white roses. The third one had been delivered only an hour earlier. Those rosebuds were still lightly fragrant but the pungent odor of the older roses already permeated the room, a wilting sweetness that filled Joanna's lungs until she could barely breathe.

"We hooked up the IV this morning," the nurse announced. Owen's mouth was half open, his loud snore piercing the quiet buzz from the overhead fluorescents. Intravenous fluids trickled silent and steady into his left arm.

Joanna ignored her. "I'll feed him when he wakes up."

"He won't take anything orally. Medication. Food. He refuses everything."

"My father likes his eggs over easy. Pork sausage. Sourdough toast. Coffee, black."

"The breakfast trays have already been removed."

"Lunch then. Anything with gravy."

"The hospital kitchen does not serve gravy."

"Okay, chicken, Jello, pudding, whatever. Where's the damned menu?"

After the nurse relented and promised to send an orderly with the daily selections, Joanna pulled a chair up to her father's side. She watched his diaphragm rise and fall and felt herself rising and falling with each breath he took. When she reached for his hand, his fingers twitched out of her grasp. His eyes opened. No focus, no recognition, just a groggy flat stare.

"I'm here," she whispered.

Owen tilted his head back and fixed on the ceiling.

"Guess who's coming to visit, Dad?"

He did not answer.

"Lottie McKeown. Do you remember her? Aldine's little friend? She remembers you. A big handsome strapping boy, that's what she said." Joanna's voice cracked.

Her father closed his eyes again. For three hours she stayed by his bedside. When the broiled chicken and rice pudding arrived, she patiently lifted spoonfuls to his dry lips. His only response was to shake his head and turn to the wall. The nurse stepped in to adjust his IV tubing and didn't look in Joanna's direction when the uneaten food was removed.

While Owen dozed, his daughter tried to recall a centering meditation from yoga class but instead found herself replaying an endless loop of what-ifs. What if her father's condition did not improve? What if he ended up in the psych ward in Peoria and could not travel back to California? What if she had to stay in Illinois? And the girls still in Italy with that lecherous tour guide? Then Peter would just have to bring them home early. He'd understand if she insisted. Yes, the girls would be fine.

It was her business that would suffer. What if she lost clients? Or her financial portfolio tanked? How would they meet the mortgage payment on the beautiful gabled house they had restored down to every detail? The lathe and plaster walls, the Batchelder fireplace, the dormers that looked toward the glorious San Gabriels? Her entire bastion of security was crashing, disintegrating, disappearing.

"You're here." Owen looked at his daughter.

"My God ... Daddy?" She buried her face in his chest half-crying, half-laughing with relief. He patted her head as she clung tightly, the IV caught in her hair like a tangled umbilical cord.

"You ..." his voice was low, strained.

Joanna lifted her head.

"You … never …" he began again.

"What?" Her heart beat faster. What had she failed to do?

"… should've …"

"Dad?"

"Come … back."

Unsure what he meant, she covered with the smile he always loved. "We're going home, Dad, as soon as you get well."

He went silent again, looking into her eyes as if he wanted to tell her something she should already understand.

"What do you need? Are you hungry yet? Maybe a piece of pie?"

A small smile seemed to hover at the corners of his mouth.

"What kind? Banana? Peach? I know, your favorite! Coconut cream like Mom used to make with meringue on top?"

Yes, he nodded, coconut cream. Joanna was sure of it.

By the time the nurse arrived to announce visiting hours were over until evening, Owen had drifted back to sleep, his hand held tight by his daughter.

"He recognized me," Joanna said. "He knows who I am."

20

Detour

Joanna informed the doctor that her father had regained his mental clarity and no conservatorship would be necessary. The doctor informed Joanna that one moment of lucidity in no way indicated full recovery. The Rexall with the standard conservatorship papers was just around the corner.

And so it was. A corner Owen's daughter passed without a glance as she drove out of town toward the interstate and the broken pavement of Old Route 66. By the time her tires traced their way back, the Log Cabin's lunch crowd had come and gone. No matter. The Budweiser bottle still burned a bright neon welcome.

Joanna strode in the front door, feeling an immediate sense of comfort as soon as she sighted the jukebox in the corner. At a nearby table two old farmers in bibbed overalls were playing chess. Otherwise the place was vacant. Except for the counterman scooping stacks of coins out of the cash register.

"We stop serving in seven minutes," he said, eyeing the clock as Joanna started to sit down. Dirty stuffing splayed out of the torn red vinyl stool cover. She decided to stand instead.

"This will be quick," Joanna assured him. "One piece of coconut cream pie with meringue to go."

"Pie's sold out." The counterman kept counting coins. Not even a "sorry, ma'am."

A vintage malted milk machine, tall and tantalizing, sat on the shelf behind him. Funny, Joanna hadn't noticed it the night before. Such a soothing shade of green, the same color as the porcelain spittoon in her childhood dentist's office where a circular drain sucked up all the bitter debris after the drill did its work.

"Chocolate malt," Joanna brightened. "Make it two, one for my friend next door." Lottie will direct her to the best pie shop in town and then they'll go back to the hospital together to visit her dad and the two of them can reminisce about old times —

"Malt machine's out of commission."

"You're kidding."

The counterman lifted a shaggy eyebrow. "Do I look like a kidder?"

"Okay then," Joanna sighed, rejecting defeat. "Two root beer floats. To go."

"Take out is twenty-five cents extra. Each."

"I'll splurge," Joanna turned around to admire the jukebox. "Does it take coins?"

"Nope," the counterman grunted, slapping away at the hardened ice cream with an old scooper.

"How do you turn it on?" She walked over to the jukebox, patting its opaque yellow horseshoe frame as if it were a long-lost pet, and peered inside the window at the stack of 78s on the record changer.

One of the chess-playing farmers cackled as she looked for the magic switch.

"Is it unplugged?"

He lifted his opponent's pawn then turned his loose jowls toward the counter man. "Ed, we got a tourist needs some help here."

The counterman gave his Juicy Fruit a couple good cracks before responding. "Been broken for twenty years."

"Forty," the farmer corrected, setting the know-nothings in the room straight.

"It never stopped playing yesterday," Joanna protested.

The men exchanged glances.

"Not that piece of junk." The counterman plopped a couple hard-won vanilla spoonfuls in a paper cup.

"I was here. I heard it last night."

"We were closed last night like we are every day after four sharp." Another shaggy eyebrow lifted. "Almost that time right now. Four sharp, we close."

Joanna ignored the man's rudeness. "My friend next door let me in. Apparently she has an understanding with the owner."

"Never heard of the skinflint owns this establishment having any 'understanding' with folks," the old farmer drawled. "You, Ed?"

"Nope."

"This lady lives in the little cottage behind the gas station."

"That old supply shed? Nobody lives there 'cept the rats." He served up two sad-looking floats and moved to the cash register. "Four fifty with tax."

Joanna gritted her teeth and dug in her purse. Lumps. That's what they were. Fellows who couldn't see anything not right in front of them.

"She must live just down the street then. Keep the change."

Ed regarded his tip with disdain.

"Lottie McKeown's her name. Maybe one of you can tell me where I might find her?"

The second farmer, the silent one, fixed his watery eyes on Joanna. "I expect so."

"Yes?" Was the old coot going to make her beg for directions?

"The Holy Family Cemetery down in Flanagan."

"Excuse me?"

"Her and her better half." He peered over his spectacles at his chess partner. "Remember what happened with those two, Wayne?"

Wayne was now too busy studying his trapped queen to give a damn.

"Her husband had a bad case of liver cancer so Lottie took him out of his misery then turned the gun on herself. Back in '89, I think it was."

"Oh no, that can't be right," Joanna shook her head.

"Yep, papers said so. Neighbor lady found 'em."

"I think you must have her confused with some other lady."

"Husband named Vern?"

Joanna stared at the walls papered with Old Route 66 memorabilia, the same rusted relics she had seen the night before. The same glass-doored fridge behind the counter. The same ancient jukebox —

"Straws?" Ed glared at the twin puddles dirtying his counter. Two root beer floats sinking by the minute. "I'd take some straws if I was you."

"Fried chicken and raspberry cobbler —"

"Lady, the kitchen is closed."

"— isn't that why folks come from miles around? Your fried chicken and raspberry cobbler, the best in the county, right?"

"Not in my lifetime," he hooted, his grin displaying gobs of Juicy Fruit stuck next to a gold molar.

Joanna did not join in the laughter.

"You want the straws or not?"

"Forget the goddamned straws and keep your lousy floats."

Joanna did not care that the gold-toothed counterman was staring out the window when she banged on the door of the small house that Lottie said was hers. Nobody answered. And it did look uninhabitable, more decrepit than had been visible in the gauzy glow of the moonlight. How could anyone live here? And yet last night they talked, they ate, they promised to see one another again. Ignoring the mocking males in their log cabin citadel, Joanna lifted her head high and walked back to her car.

21

The Vermilion

For two hours Joanna waited on the banks of the Vermilion at Mill Street Bridge. Enough time to reconsider her recollection of the previous night's events. The big gold ball rolled lower on the horizon just like the day before when the river goddesses went to sleep. Sundown. Still, the old woman did not appear. And why would she, Joanna chastised herself, rising at last from the wrought iron bench they had shared. If the farmer's tale were true, Lottie was just some eccentric refugee on the lam from an old folks' home pretending to be someone else. Maybe this loony imposter had been a friend of the real Lottie before … Joanna's scalp tensed trying to sort through the strange coincidence that "Lottie" — or whatever her name was — knew Aldine. Or so she'd said. Then again, her father had made no response, none at all, when she mentioned Lottie's name at his bedside.

She pushed the old woman out of her mind, focusing instead on the day's good news. Her father was returning to himself now — that's all that mattered. Soon this terrible stress would be over and life would go back to normal in California. Better than normal. They should clear at least a couple hundred thousand from the sale of Horatio's property, plenty to pay off the mortgage on her dad's old house and get him set up in a nice condo in Pasadena near his grandchildren.

How happy her mother would be to know that her daughter had mended the torn fabric of family hurts. Joanna breathed deeply, savoring the beauty all around her. In the last wisps of cirrus clouds, streaking like music notes across the amber sky, she could see her parents arm-in-arm together. Their first dance, the dance that sealed them together for all that came after. Embracing. Laughing. The light of love in their eyes so strong there was no room for anything less. The image stayed with Joanna as she drove away from the river, even as the spectacular dusk slipped into night.

On her way back to the hospital she pulled into the first truck stop she saw and there it was in a glass box behind the counter. A plate of coconut cream pie, whipped meringue topping toasted to perfection, with her dad's name on it. The last piece. Nibbling on a club sandwich while the waitress packed the pie in a perky red and white checkered box, Joanna reveled in her good fortune. Yes, everything was going to be all right. Then she noticed the black hands creeping closer and closer on the wall clock above the café grill. Almost 6:30 …

And she remembered. The library. Tazewell. What time did he say? She wished to God she never said she would meet him. All the tragic business about her poor aunt seemed irrelevant now that her father was recovering. She wanted it to be irrelevant, she knew that much. And there was something about her cousin … his presumptuousness, perhaps? Joanna swallowed the last bite whole, almost choking on the charred bacon that caught in her throat.

～～～

"You're late," Tazewell unlocked the library door, ushering her in with a frosty glare. "I've been waiting an hour."

"I'm sorry. It's been a busy day. I was visiting my father at the hospital. He's much better."

"So glad to hear it," he smiled. But he did not look glad.

The library was dark except for the glow of a pair of table lamps. Dark and hot and stifling. No ceiling lights, no air conditioning. The place reminded Joanna of a pharaoh's tomb that she and Peter had visited during their fifteenth anniversary trip to Cairo. And for some reason she wondered what her husband was doing at this moment. Was he missing her as she was suddenly missing him?

"My apologies."

"Excuse me?"

"The stuffiness. Our city fathers are such cheapskates with the electricity. Six o'clock and we turn into a pumpkin. If you'd been on time —"

Joanna ignored the rebuke. "Well, I can't stay long."

"No?" His face clouded over like a pouting child. "After I worked so hard to find this treasure for you. Family history is a treasure, don't you think, Joanna?"

"I appreciate the time you've put into this for me."

"For us." Tazewell corrected her. "You've piqued my interest about our dear departed aunt."

As he led the way to the microfilm reader, Joanna noticed for the first time that her cousin was losing his hair. The shiny pink disk in the back of his head was surrounded by a halo of blond wispiness, the look of a medieval monk devoted to self-flagellation.

"Sit down," he ordered, pulling a chair next to her. "This is the issue of the *Pontiac Daily Leader* from the first day Asher Bentley was called to testify. He denied killing her, of course. Even though they found her blood splattered under the left fender of his car."

Tazewell rotated the microfilm wheel. Very slowly, so Joanna could read every detail herself. "You have to admire his cleverness, the way he manipulated the situation. They were driving back to Pontiac but he had 'one too many' so she took the wheel according to Bentley. Somewhere along the line the headlights went out. A neighbor driving by in the opposite direction saw a young woman in the driver's seat of a slow-moving vehicle without any lights. He stopped to see if he could help."

Joanna squinted through the witness's testimony as she read aloud:

"I asked the young lady where she was headed … and she said, 'to Pontiac or Dana, I don't give a damn.' I offered to give her a ride but she informed me she could handle it herself so I left."

"The boy never saw Bentley," Tazewell's tongue flicked over his upper lip. "Old rascal was hiding in the back seat supposedly 'sleeping it off' according to his defense attorney."

Joanna's eyes ached. The tiny type was making her nauseous again. "My father said he killed her because …" she hesitated, uncomfortable with her cousin's hand only inches from hers. Why did he make her feel like she wanted to run away?

"… she wouldn't give him what he wanted."

"Yes, I heard that one from my father too. Brothers want to protect their sister's reputation despite evidence to the contrary."

"What do you mean?" Joanna's neck stiffened.

"Right here. Bentley says they met at the Wilmington Gun Club —"

A gun shot rang out! A warning déjà vu echo, and then the Queen of Spades collapsed …

"Wait, what did you say?" Joanna, jolted by the memory of last night's dream, abruptly cut off Tazewell. "Why would a teenage girl go to a gun club?"

"A speakeasy!" he set her straight. "One of those fancy roadhouse speakeasies they used to have up north during Prohibition. They had all sorts of covers. Men's gun clubs, dance clubs, whatever threw the law off. Says here Bentley called her 'a good fellow to drink with' and admitted knowing her over four years."

"So he acknowledged they were … intimate?"

"Intimate? What a quaint word. No, of course not. Said they'd never been alone together. Liar!" His high-pitched giggle startled her. "Not until that night when they left the Log Cabin."

"They were at the Log Cabin? The old restaurant west of town?"

"You know the place?" He looked amused.

"I … I've seen it."

"Ugly dump. Should've been put out of its misery years ago."

Joanna went quiet, remembering what Lottie — or the woman pretending to be Lottie — said about Aldine coming by to play music and dance to those mesmerizing old tunes. Aldine was a wonderful dancer, her father had said. Wonderful.

"Shit-faced, apparently."

"What?"

"Bentley admitted under cross examination that he was making such a drunken fool of himself, the owner asked him to leave."

"And she went with him?"

"Not only that, witnesses corroborated that our aunt asked Bentley to drive her to a dance over in Dana so she could check up on some ex-boy-friend who was two-timing her," Tazewell guffawed. "Doesn't that take the cake?"

"Maybe …" Joanna speculated, "… she was trying to make him jealous."

"Well, she did that all right. The hired man at the farm across the road from where they found her body heard them quarreling."

Joanna peered closer, the type in front of her doubling as Tazewell capsulized the next page of newspaper coverage:

"The prosecutor presented a block of wood found in Bentley's car as evidence during the Sheriff's testimony. They figured he knocked her unconscious and then drove over her body to make it look like another car hit and run. Bentley denied it, of course, said she decided to walk back to town when the car broke down and left him to sleep if off. You believe that, cousin?"

"Why would she head back in the middle of the night by herself?"

"That's what the Sheriff didn't buy." Tazewell spun the microfilm reel. "Here's testimony from the morning they went to Bentley's house to arrest him. 'We want to help you all we can, Asher. It would be a good break for you if you could remember where you lost this girl out of the car.' And what does Bentley say? He swears she got out, maybe jumped. 'She was crazy like that.'"

Tazewell twisted the wheel a few good turns. "Take a gander at this. Another witness swears the woman he saw on the road later that night wasn't walking anywhere."

Joanna struggled to decipher the column text that came up next.

"MYSTERY CAR IN DEATH PROBE"
Lyle Raber, a young farmer returning from a party short-ly before the girl's body was found, testified that a woman appeared in the middle of the pavement and screamed as though she wanted him to stop or was badly scared. He was unable to hear what she said and did not stop …

Joanna turned away from the viewfinder. "If he'd stopped, if he'd offered to help —"

"No doubt that's what the jury thought," Tazewell sniffed. "So Bentley's defense brought up another witness to stir the pot: 'John Smith, a Gramont famer, told of meeting a speeding car with blinding head lights just before he came upon the mangled body of Miss Younger.'"

Joanna recoiled, sinking back in the chair and rubbing her brow.

"Sad," Tazewell murmured, "so sad, isn't it?"

Hearing no response, he stared a long moment at his cousin before speaking again.

"Beauty can be so seductive."

Joanna sat up straighter. "It's getting late. Let's leave the rest for another day."

Tazewell gave no indication of hearing. His fleshy elbow brushed against her shoulder as he turned to the testimony of Will Haskell. "Here's what the hired man at the Hutson farm swore under oath," Tazewell began, clearing his throat.

> I heard a man's voice say, 'by God, do you think you can go out with me then flag a ride back to town with somebody else?' And then a woman's voice 'when a girl goes out with you, you never treat her right.' And then the man's voice said, 'Yes, and you told Clara not to go out with me. I will be goddamned if you can do that and get by with it ...' I heard a scream, went to the upstairs bedroom window and saw a grey object in the road. A man stood over it and then I saw the man run west into the shadow of the big cottonwood tree on the south side of the road then I heard a car door shut and a motor start and after the driver got out on the pavement he drove up to about fifteen feet of this grey object and drove over it.

Joanna shook her head, feeling dizzy. The stale air, the harsh glare from the light on the machine, the acrid odor from her cousin's sweat-soaked armpits.

"I've got to go."

"So soon?"

"My dad's expecting me."

"Oh? I thought you said you spent the day with him."

"I have to get to the hospital before he goes to sleep." Joanna stood up so fast she knocked her chair backwards. It hit the floor with a loud crack. "Oh dear. Sorry."

"Not to worry," Tazewell picked up the chair and smiled. "Nothing that can't be set right."

"You've been very kind. I just have to go now."

"We're family. I understand. Uncle Owen needs you."

"Yes."

"Oh, almost forgot. I have a surprise for you."

"Tazewell, really —"

"It'll only take a minute." He headed into the darkness of the back library before she could stop him.

Joanna waited. Listening to the quickened thump of her heartbeat in the silence. One minute passed. Two. Three, going on four. Her head throbbed at the base of her skull. A merciless vise squeezing —

"Ta-Da!"

Tazewell was at her side again, presenting the thick manila envelope with a child's delight.

His cousin looked at him without comprehension.

"The witness depositions from the Bentley trial."

"How did you —"

"Oh, I have my ways. Only caveat is I need to return them to the courthouse archives first thing Tuesday after the holiday. Perhaps you can read them tonight."

"Tonight?"

"Yes. You can give them to me tomorrow."

"Tomorrow?" Her voice had become an echo chamber separated from reason.

"I'll want to go to the hospital to pay my respects to Uncle Owen during afternoon visiting hours."

He escorted her to the exit. "Will I see you then?"

Joanna hesitated.

"I'll give you a jingle. You don't mind that I call you at the motel?"

"I may be conferring with the doctors."

"I'll try anyway."

Unlocking the door so she could leave, he lowered his voice. "She didn't suffer."

Joanna looked at him.

"Our aunt," he cleared his throat. "You haven't read the medical experts' testimony yet. They said she died instantly. That's what happens when the brain is torn from the spinal cord."

Joanna lowered her eyelids, turning away.

"Good night, Tazewell."

"Good night, Joanna."

~~~~~

By the time she arrived at the hospital with her father's dessert, both dinner service and evening visiting hours were long over.

"You can bring it back tomorrow morning for breakfast," the receptionist chirped.

"Can't I at least go in to say goodnight?" Joanna asked a passing nurse.

"We just turned the lights down for Mr. Morse. He's resting peacefully."

"Well, thank you."

But as soon as the nurse rounded the corner, Joanna slipped inside her father's room and kissed him on the cheek.

He stirred ever so slightly.

"Sweet dreams, Dad."

22

Witness

The soft, cooling twilight breeze Joanna had felt on the banks of the Vermilion was gone. Inside the sweltering motel room, a cranky air conditioner threatened to give up the ghost. At least a mini fridge under the desk and the ice machine down the hall were still working. She scooped cubes from a chilled bucket into a washcloth and pressed the cool relief to her forehead. Two tablets of Advil had not yet done their job.

The silent phone was still silent. Sweeping away the greasy wrappers from a barely touched Big Mac, she wondered if it was too late. Midnight in the Midwest was ten o' clock on the coast and Peter was always early to bed and early to rise — even on weekends. Finally, she reached for the phone and dialed Peter again and once again got his answering machine. She hadn't left a message on her previous attempts. This time she had a change of heart.

"Peter, I … I'm sorry about the other night. You were right. It's been a stressful time and I just … just wanted to reassure you I'm fine. I really am … My dad woke up and recognized me today." Her voice started to crack. She took a deep breath and tried for a stab at humor.

"You know what they say. True love never does run smooth. Please stay safe." As she hung up, she made puckered kissing sounds the way they used to do when she and Peter were newlyweds. Before the babies and the mortgage and all her dad's troubles.

Then she pondered, considering what she could have said better.

Please stay safe? Stupid. Stupid. Why would she say something so stupid? Because that is what Marcus Washington had said to her when she left his house the day before. That didn't make any sense either. She shook off her second thoughts, gave her temples another ice bath, and decided she had better get to bed.

On the night stand a manila envelope waited.

Joanna, now unsure how reading any witness statements from the Bentley trial could contribute to her father's return to health, stared at the envelope for a good five minutes. But it was a gift from Tazewell, the teenage godfather who had held Joanna as a baby, and needed to be acknowledged.

Paulina Morse wanted to bring her blended brood together through the sacred rite of Baptism, her father had said. The bad blood between a mother's sons could be healed by the next generation with enough faith, trust and loving intent.

In an act of homage to her Grandmother Morse, Joanna lifted the brass-colored clasp ... There were more than she expected. One old typewritten deposition on top of another with names she did not recognize. Until she came to F. B. Stickerling, the lawyer who had handled her grandmother's many legal entanglements. Why had he been subpoenaed? My God — he had been called as a character witness by the Bentley family. She began reading.

~~~

WITNESS STATEMENT of F.B. Stickerling, Esq.

To begin, I'd like to clarify for the record that my former client, Miss Aldine Younger, came from fine stock. The finest in these parts in my professional opinion.

There were two William P's in the olden days. William P. Younger, a local man of English extraction, exceedingly good mind for business investments and such. William P. Heinemann, German-born, a fellow active in township politics and head of the Village Board, came to America selling goods from his father's damask factory then put his profits into land just like Younger. In common parlance one could say that these two captains of the prairie carved up the prime real estate of Livingston County like a butchered hog. Being smart men they knew blood was thicker than water so they merged their interests so to speak. Younger's girl, Libby, married Heinemann's boy, Frederick. No question that proved a sound investment. Frederick supervised his father-in-law's property with a sharp eye. A few years down the pike, Heinemann's daughter Paulina married Younger's son, Billy.

Now, for the record, this was not Paulina's first marriage. Quite the story there. Her first husband, John Billingham, got mowed down by an Illinois Central freight train when he was hauling a load of corn to the grain elevator. The man and his horses never knew what hit them. But I digress.

As I was saying, the Widow Billingham wed Billy. Less than two years after their wedding, which I had the honor to attend, Mrs. Younger became the Widow Younger when her husband died. At that time she engaged my services in consideration of the years I had advised her late father-in-law, William P. Younger. It fell to me to support the legal interests of Billy Younger's only heir, his one-year-old daughter, Aldine, for whom the Widow Younger served as guardian. Because of Billy's untimely passing, tuberculosis I believe, the child inherited one half of her grandfather's property.

Unfortunately, when Miss Younger reached the age of eighteen, there was trouble afoot. And this is where we get to the matter at hand concerning this girl's character.

Paulina, Mrs. Morse after her third marriage, met privately with me concerning several issues of familial concern, which I will not specify according to attorney/client privilege. What I can say is, in my professional opinion, Miss Younger did not always exhibit common sense or sound judgment.

In one specific instance she demanded, rather hysterically as I recall, that I serve papers on Herbert Powell, the executor of her bequest from Mr. Younger, Senior, because there had been an unexpected delay in accessing her full inheritance. This course of action struck me as rash and ill-conceived for two reasons.

Firstly, I was well aware of Mr. Powell's stellar reputation. He and I had become acquainted when he acted as executor of Mr. Younger's will.

Secondly, he is — or was, until recently — the president of the bank's board of directors on which Miss Younger's own maternal uncle, Mr. Frederick Heinemann, sits with distinction.

My argument for patience and restraint regarding Mr. Powell, made no impression on Miss Younger. She engaged a new attorney — a colored man in need of work — to stir up a hornet's nest against Mr. Powell. Nobody was more surprised than I when the D.A. filed charges against him for embezzlement. With the mental strain of the times, even our most decent men made unintentional errors. But I digress.

In summary on the issue of Miss Younger's character and behavior, I would say she was a person unpersuaded by reason.

However, for the record, whatever happened during the tragic accident involving Miss Younger and Mr. Asher Bentley, I am not qualified to comment.

WITNESS STATEMENT of Sheriff Pemberton

A bad accident, I called out when I knocked on the door of Mrs. Morse's house that night. She and the boys ran down, all bundled against the cold, and I escorted them to the morgue where that poor mother had to identify her daughter's body after what happened!

The lady has already seen too much loss in her life but I do believe the worst was having her daughter taken the way she was. The morning of the funeral my wife, Mrs. Pemberton, played the organ. I will say I think that gave Mrs. Morse some peace.

To this day, I can't figure why Aldine Younger took up with that hoodlum Bentley. "Skinny," his pals call him. Pretty as she was, she could've had her pick of the marriageable men in this town, and she settles for a drunken cheat twice her age. But what does an underage girl know about a reprobate preying on her innocent affections? This college boy — big law degree he got himself and let everybody know it — looked me in the eye and swore that the only time he'd ever been alone with Aldine was the night she died. And if you believe that, I got a bridge in New York City I'll sell you for a quarter.

First time he fixed on her was five- and one-half years before at the Wilmington Gun Club, the roadhouse north of town frequented by bootleg lowlifes from Decatur. Oh yes, we found witnesses to that effect. And her being only fifteen! Of course, Aldine had no business going someplace where illegal liquor was served though that little girl did love to dance, and like her mother said, she always had a mind of her own. A decent man wouldn't touch a child, but Asher Bentley was no man and decency never knew his name.

If we can't protect our precious children from the wicked, at least we can endeavor to rid the world of their devious kind. But I owe my allegiance to the law. So I follow due process every step of the way. And I trust the solid citizens of Pontiac to deliver the right verdict. Justice speaks louder than money on my watch.

WITNESS STATEMENT of Paulina Morse

I warned my dear daughter. Time and time again, I warned her against the temptations of earthly life. The nail that sticks up gets pounded down. I feared that she might carry the same weakness for liquor her poor dead father had. To be fair, my second husband only took up whiskey to ease the pain of sickness in his final days. With Aldine it was the bad company at roadhouses that sent her down the devil's path.

Lord knows I did my level best to put a stop to the shameful business with Asher Bentley. That's why I sent her out of the house to live with my older daughter and her husband soon as they got married. Bertha always kept her feet on the ground, but her sister was different. Trouble seemed to follow Aldine like bad cigar smoke.

Terrible times for our family what with Herbert Powell's nefarious thieving of her inheritance! Aldine started running up debts like there was no tomorrow, and me having to make restitution to the shopkeepers. The bills keep coming, even now after she's gone. Come to find she spent $50 on a gold amethyst pendant and never wore it, not even once. Another $12.50 on some sort of leather writing book I've never seen hide nor hair of. Who knows what she did with these frivolous things? Lost, just like the money she sent to that Holloway fellow who misled her affections. I warned her against him too.

I've thought long and hard about that awful night and know it must have been the drink that clouded her mind when Bentley's auto broke down. Why else would she turn away the boy in the car that stopped to help? Her one chance to get away before that drunken good-for-nothing ran her down and she says no to a Good Samaritan who could've saved the day? Makes no sense. A lot of what Aldine did still makes no sense to me, but the Lord knows no mother tried harder.

Piano lessons and singing classes, because Mrs. Lawson said I should afford my gifted daughter the higher cultural advantages. Deportment classes at Miss Evangeline's every Thursday after school too.

Fancy hats from Walton's on Main Street and georgette fabric sent special from Chicago, new outfits spring and fall without fail. Bertha, the boys and I had to make do, but Aldine never had to forego her heart's desire. Her late grandfather and I saw to that. I did my duty in protecting her income day in and day out. Every dollar, every cent accounted for on my monthly ledgers. It was only proper that I charge Aldine for my dressmaking services. Room and board too. Seven dollars a week, mind you, a bargain during these hard times. Services rendered, services paid. My daughter was getting $1100 a year annual income, tax free. She owed her family a little help, considering all the blessings in life she inherited, and she obliged with no argument whatsoever.

My children have been much aggrieved since the loss of their sister, especially her younger brother, Junior, who stopped school due to not being able to keep proper attention on his studies. Idle hands are Satan's playground, so I hired him out to the neighbors. Our family can use the money. As it is, we must cut every corner to make ends meet.

Waste not, want not. I even stitched up Aldine's fur coat from the night she went to her Maker. It would have been a sin to throw out a good winter wrap. Her being so tall, it fit me fine after I cut off the bloody part that got soiled on the road. Only another mother can appreciate how that coat gives me comfort. I can smell her perfume in the silk lining like she never left ...

Let the record show Mrs. Morse requested a short recess to regain her composure.

The only thing left to say is that my father, William P. Heinemann, provided the funds to build the Methodist Church in our township. He was a Christian man of means who believed in the Word of the Lord. My brother, Frederick, follows a different path. I pray that my daughter's killer and any unknown cronies who conspired with him, will be punished for their evil deeds.

~~~~~

Joanna leaned back against flattened pillows and closed her weary eyes. Now she understood what her father had tried to explain about Grandma Morse's suspicions that her brother Frederick's avarice knew no bounds. If he were a thief — in league with the embezzler Herbert Powell as Marcus Washington had suspected when he revealed that Powell's conviction had been overturned — her grandmother thought that he could be a killer too.

But in researching her aunt's death Joanna had found nothing to indicate that Frederick Heinemann had any relationship with Asher Bentley or that Bentley could have been "hired" to kill Aldine. Bentley had all the money he needed. No, according to all the evidence Joanna had read about the last night of her aunt's life, the finger pointed to Bentley alone as the man capable of murder. As to her great uncle's own culpability in stealing from his niece, perhaps that justice would come in the next world, as Marcus hoped. There were more witness statements but none that she would read tonight ... or maybe ever.

The good people of Pontiac convicted Asher Bentley and Herbert Powell for their crimes against her aunt but ultimately there would be no reparation for a life and fortune lost, or a family broken. Not in this lifetime.

VII

HARVEST

Private Musings & Verse by Miss A. Younger

SEPTEMBER 30, 1931

My sleep suffers terrible these days. Sweet dreams stay away no matter how bad I long for escape, last night the worst of all. When the clock struck midnight I sneaked out quiet as a mouse so Sister would not hear me getting my Chesterfields from under the porch steps. On and on I walked blowing smoke rings until I reached the south bridge above the Vermilion River. Looking into the black water, I sensed God's Hand on my back pulling me close. The red maples on the bank stirred. Whispering my name …

All of a sudden the new moon waxed and waned in the blink of an eye! I felt myself a windmill spinning in a tornado let loose on the land! So beautiful, all of nature so beautiful! I stood crying and laughing with joy for who knows how long? Hours? Days? Years? Sunrise reigned forth in all its golden brilliance until I near burst from the sight. I yearned to stay forever but it was morning and the harsh call of home broke the magic spell.

I trudged seven miles, maybe ten, not feeling a bit of cold until I was climbing up the back stairs to Sister's kitchen. That's when the shivering came upon me. Bertha stood at the stove frying runny sunny sides, her belly big and round now that she's in the family way. Conley as usual was buried in his morning newspaper at the breakfast table. A year since wed and already they look like an old couple. Faces long and sober and full of grievous regret.

"Where have you been, Aldine?"

"Walking. You and Conley ought to take a stroll down to the river. Hear tell it's a nice Lover's Lane if you're in a necking mood."

My brother-in-law blushed over his sunnysides. "We got jobs to go to."

"Well, have fun then." I turned to go upstairs but Bertha's greasy hand slicked my elbow.

"Conley told me you didn't show up for work yesterday. You know he needs help with the inventory."

"I had to take my little friend Lottie shopping for school supplies. A darned shame when a girl has no mama to do right by her."

Sister did not miss my point. "Our Ma's done right enough by us raising five kids on her own and don't forget it."

I took my shaming without a word.

"You better be at the store today."

"Yes, Bertha. I will."

Then before they could stop me, I ran upstairs to make my trousseau list for the train ride West. Will Hap accompany me to my poetic studies this fall or abandon the brutal cold of Illinois in December for a holiday reunion amongst the orange groves? If we could talk directly about this vital matter my mind would be more at ease. But every time I call, Hap's old battle-axe mother says he is too busy to come to the phone and I cannot vex him at the market with personal affairs as he would get in trouble with his boss for sure. So I must carry my own counsel for the many things to prepare and pack.

Maybe my robin's egg blue chemise with that smart new pair of spectator pumps I saw in the window of the Antoinette Shoppe when I put the pretty fox on layaway. Ma made a solemn promise to repay every penny of the mortgage loan to my account in plenty of time for my birthday, so I can settle my account with Mr. Cabaleri. My fox and I will soon be constant companions! Whatever harsh winds may blow, her soft furry arms will keep me warm and that gives me solace.

Ay

DECEMBER 25, 1931

Psalm 147:19-20 — *The Lord declares his word to Jacob, his statutes and his judgments to Israel. He has not done this with any other nation.*

Ma has gifted me with these words so that I may understand the Good Lord has made a Covenant with me and my tribe too. If we follow his Word and love one another, we will prosper in Wondrous Ways. But such a miracle cannot take place until I renounce my imperfect foolishness first!

Yes, I have stumbled bad but not on purpose so much as on account of faulty vision. Last Sunday I drove Ma and the boys to the church supper and Absher was on her lap and I hit the brakes hard and my little brother hit the window and bled awful and needed stitches and scarred bad but the windshield was terrible dirty and it was a dark night hailing cats and dogs. I could not see what was two inches in front of my own face. Faulty vision, Ma, that's all it was.

As befits a Christian lady my dear mother talks a blue streak about how Jesus surrendered his body and blood to save mankind and I understand now we all must make offerings to lay on the Holy Altar. The choice to walk this earth is the first supreme sacrifice. Coming from a sweet safe space of nothing is an act of faith not to be taken in light regard. As I think on it, I accept the fact that all of God's creatures must toss aside what they most dearly cherish to serve something Greater. The corn casts off its seed, the apple tree drops its precious fruit, even cattle go to slaughter, if not gladly, at least in keeping with their purpose. Every web weeps from its center. First the spiders feed on the flies then the ducks scoop up the spiders and soon enough those high-flying birds get blown to smithereens by hungry hunters just so our kind can quiet the screaming pangs of the human belly!

It is the Way of Nature I cannot deny.

On this Holy Day of Jesus's birth I pledge to sacrifice my selfishness and be a comfort to my family.

Little Maggie is six weeks old now and needs her auntie to cradle her when Bertha is busy with kitchen chores and I don't mind. She is a dear sweet babe, so sweet sometimes I can hardly bear to look at her without sad, wishful thoughts troubling forth. But Ma instructs me to do my duty first and I will not disappoint. In Jesus's name. Amen.

Ab

VALENTINE'S DAY 1932

A measly box of drugstore chocolates?! What about my diamond ring you promised?

Hap could not even look me straight in the face. Just moaned and groaned about times being tight and maybe we're too young to get engaged so soon.

"Is that you or your mother talking?"

"That's not fair."

"Fair? Don't talk to me about fair with what I've been going through. Have you no pity for me after all my legal tribulations?"

"You're a strong girl. You'll see to it Mr. Powell does right by you —"

"What about you, Hap? Will you do right by me?"

He looked so unbearable perplexed I told him he could go to hell and take his damned chocolate creams along for the ride.

A sage once said there can be no romance without finance. Truer words were never spoken. I am wiser and no longer in need of any sweetheart by my side. A modern girl has to be practical. Focus strictly on business and such if she is to make her way in the world. My one and only comfort now is that Ma finally saw the light and fired old Stick-in-the-Mud Stickerling.

Thank goodness for Marcus Washington, the new lawyer we found to engage our case for a fee that won't break our pitiful bank. He is a nice-looking, upstanding young colored man with kind eyes who will take our side against the villains in town.

His father, Mr. Washington senior, acted a bit of a cool cucumber when Ma and I first made his acquaintance, but he warmed up soon enough after she told him we'd give him a cash deposit straightaway from the last of my account interest.

I intend to celebrate my lost fortune's return any day — with or without the butcher boy!

APRIL 3, 1932

Summer died early
Fell down a rabbit hole
Tell me, Beautiful Boy, so blessed
Your thick golden hair,
Your warm golden touch,
Your fine golden words,
Why am I less —
Or am I more —
Than what you want?
All those promises
Gone without a backward glance.
My beautiful, beautiful boy
You used to be a Man.

Medea the Battle-axe sent her son away to spite me!

"Off to Muncie, Indiana, you must go to work for your brother," she orders and in the snap of her fingers, Hap does her bidding.

"No," I said. "No! Meet me in Chicago at Union Station and we can buy tickets to Pasadena and my architect friend will surely welcome us with open arms!"

Though he swore he would come when he could and pledged to deposit every penny of the $300 I gave him for our future elopement, my heart quakes. Maybe I am a spendthrift like Ma accused, frittering away my own self with no true value received in return ...

JUNE 28, 1932

My mother lost her wits, no doubt about it.

I arrived at the farm in good cheer to visit Junior and Absher and bring them the rock candy they love and what horror did I see? Ma bent over her homemade still, churning out fresh cups of bootleg beer! Worse, my poor little brothers, her slaves and partners in crime were putting on the bottle caps!

"Ma, what if the Sheriff finds out? Or our new lawyers, Mr. Washington and his proper fearsome father? Not to mention that hell's bells snobby gossip Mrs. Holloway? All the so-called decent folk in Pontiac will run our family out of town on a rail!"

"Daughter, you think we're the only ones in the county bringing in extra nickels where we can?"

"But Mr. Washington said we should take care to court our neighbors' sympathy with the trial against Powell down the road and here you go creating more scandal than me and turning your own sons into lawbreakers."

Was that sweat or tears glistening on my mother's cheek? I will never know for she turned back to the work at hand and muttered so low I could barely make out the words.

"It's best you go home, Aldine."

"Home? I have no home."

Bertha so busy with her precious baby girl and all a-flutter because I hold on too tight when I cradle Maggie to calm her cries in the night. And now my own California cottage stands empty, the hearth cold, the garden untended, the door closed!

"You're not listening to me, Ma —"

"At least I'm not swilling the nasty stuff like you do, am I?"

Such hypocrisy let loose a fury I could not stop and I don't care that our hired hand got an earful or anybody else for miles around either. The only thing to do to rescue Junior and Absher was destroy that goddamned still then and there, so I brought out the ax from the woodshed raring to go, but Ma wrestled it away.

Even Bertha took my side when I told her about Ma's shenanigans.

It wasn't long before Sheriff Pemberton got word and showed up to talk sense into Ma and she listened to the law all right. Though she never listens to me.

My only regret is that the boys got upset and troubled at the big fuss. Someday they will be grateful that their sister had their good names in mind.

Why should I feel any shame for what I tried to do?

I don't.

I won't.

JULY 22, 1932

"Poor little rich girl," the hypocrites hiss, "she's reaping what she sowed."

In my mind's eye I see fallow fields spread far and wide, black earth aching for the feel of sure hands to plant strong roots and high above, blue sky bigger than the universe. That was my land before my uncle and his crony Herbert Powell did me wrong — my land! But in the wet heat of my 19th summer, the days so sticky cotton voile sucks my skin like a mosquito hankering for blood, I have no fight left.

And no guardian to keep the enemy at the gate.

Skinny is a rich man's child — what I was born to be before my family trespassed against me — and he will not stop 'til he owns me again. If I deny him he says he will collapse of broken heartedness, and I'll be doomed to live with a guilty conscience for the rest of my days. Thou shalt not steal, the Bible says, but my rightful legacy has been stolen by jackals in the night! And S is courting me all the while his bird-necked wife looks the other way so what am I to do? I am penniless now except for the $300 Hap is holding in the Muncie bank but he writes seldom and takes no bother about his rival's advances.

I am sick to heart of being cast aside — don't I deserve to get something while I can? Eve took what caught her eye and made the best of unexpected calamity and why shouldn't she with old Adam snoring away not paying any attention. Our Mother Eve — though maligned by so-called Christians — was smart enough to find a path out of the Garden. Even a serpent can be good company during mean lonely times.

For the Ones I used to Love

I wonder where midgets live.

Do they cluster with their own kind,
Shoulder to shoulder in
Deep dark drowning tubs

HARVEST

Spiked with steaming bubbles and lavender gin?

Open wounds and lies
Fester
With a touch of alcohol, you know.

The faucet too far
Away to touch,
The temperature rises,
The blistering begins.

Until a human being no longer feels human.

Overcooked lobster in oval porcelain.
Red, silent, screaming
Is about to be served.

A troll is waiting for his supper.

The telephone rings,
Prairie Central party line connection,
The operator says

"Jesus calling"

All the misbegotten who are so very weary
Of filling another's belly and pretending to be

Small.

AUGUST 19, 1932

"You'll be happy when you get back the money the bad man stole," my brother promises when Ma let him visit, "then you can go to Paris like you always say."

"Can you keep a secret, Junior?"

"Cross my heart and hope to die."

"I'm taking you with me."

"To Paris?"

"California! Just you and me, would you like that?"

He hugged me tight and I squeezed him close. But above his head in the distance behind the clouds I could see an unnatural glow, the sun's gold besmirched by smoky ash.

"Do you smell the fire, Junior?"

"My brother shook his head."

All across God's face blackened cinder and burnt dreams as far as I could see.

SEPTEMBER 6, 1932

The church walls weep with honey from morn 'til night since the buzzing hive started clinging for dear life to the old Methodist eaves.

"Look out for the bees!" screamed darling Lottie, my only playmate since Ma moved Junior and Absher back to the farm.

Hap paid me one last visit and now is gone for good, leaving me with hard news to remember him by. He said the bank in Muncie failed so our marriage money is gone through no fault of his own. Gone. Frittered across a sea of prairie grass. Such a shame but we live with tough times 'round every corner. Not a time to settle down and start a family.

"Do you love another girl, Hap?"

"We had some good laughs, pea-pot, don't spoil 'em, okay?"

He wanted to shake hands goodbye because it seemed the right and proper thing to do. I slapped his face instead. It seemed the right and proper thing to do.

But I hope my sweet little friend Lottie will never ever feel a slap in all her days to come! I pulled her close to keep her safe in my arms.

"The bees won't sting."

"No?"

"No, they only want to scare away invaders to protect their queen the same way I protect you."

Such a precious girl, so fresh and innocent, her long curls the same shade of bronze aster that used to grow in my mother's garden. Some nights we dance to the jukebox at the Log Cabin when her papa is working late and I tell her stories. Tales of great heroines like Esmerelda, the beautiful gypsy girl — a good gypsy — who befriended Quasimodo and made him fall in love with her so she could take sanctuary in the church away from the king's soldiers.

"Like the bees?"

"Yes, exactly like the bees."

Indian summer has come, Demeter's last warm tender breath before the frostbite of autumn. On Saturday afternoons Lottie and I go down to the river where it's peaceful to high heaven and we can ease our sad spells and pick wildflowers to decorate our tresses like fairy princesses of old.

"I only allow my very best friends to come here with me."

"Am I your very best friend, Aldine?"

"You and Marcus."

"The dark man that came to our picnic yesterday?"

"He's going to find my lost treasure and when he does I'll buy us long feather boas and we'll strut around just like the glamour pusses in the picture shows."

"Oh, Aldine, I love your stories! Tell me about the Lady of the River."

"I always tell you that story."

"Tell me again."

"Once upon a time a Great Lady dripping in diamonds and rubies and purple amethyst robes arose from the river bottom, the most gorgeous thing I'd ever seen. She took a keen liking to me and do you know what she said?"

"What?"

"All the wondrous things we're seeking are seeking us at the same time. We just don't know when we'll meet up. And then the Great Lady shared the secret spells hidden inside her laurel crown."

"What kind of spells?" Lottie wants to know.

"*Magic* spells, the biggest and most powerful kind that make folks do your bidding whether they want to or not."

"Can you teach me?"

"Maybe someday when you're older. Magic is like playing with matches. You must be full grown so you don't burn yourself."

"Oh," she said, her face all melancholy. I could not bear to see my sweet Lottie in misery. How her eyes lit up the next day when I presented her with my amethyst pendant, the one I bought to wear with the grey fox for my travels west. Better to make Lottie smile than chase a silly dream that will never come true.

"I've never had anything so pretty to call my own!"

"Hold tight to the magic stone and spin around three times

whenever you feel lonesome and want to talk to your mama in heaven," I told her.

"Will she talk back?" Lottie's freckles popped round and orange and big as could be.

"Of course, but her voice won't sound like yours or mine. Spirits speak really low and deep because their words are only for those they love and nobody else."

"Then how will I know she's talking?"

"You must be very quiet and let the feeling rise up to cover you like when you slide into a warm bath."

"How do you know these things, Aldine?"

"I listen to spirits myself."

Last night when I dropped by the Log Cabin for one of our jukebox parties Lottie pulled out her pendant for me to kiss then put her little finger to her lips.

"Shhh," she said, "Mama's talking."

DECEMBER 12, 1932

'Tis been a bitter winter
The Falls of Niagara froze
Icicles twist into daggers
Faces change

Loose flesh in my mother's cheek
Drops low and heavy
Grief is cruel

Each stinging tear
Maroons
Consumes
Entombs

I am frozen in salt

Deep inside the looking glass
A purple phantom laughs
The Younger Girl
Is
No
More

1933, THE YEAR OF OUR LORD & MY WILD 'N MIGHTY JESUS

I hate it when Ma moves the maidenhair fern to the south window and without asking cooks up a cauldron of chicken broth to mist its lovely leaves because she thinks they have the sniffles and need to be tucked in for a mid-winter's nap!

But how on earth can a fern sleep?

It's lived forever, crawling out of wet-nosed jungles even before the Sun of God walked this earth. Ferns do not sleep! They abide and surmise and survive. Can the fern ever forgive the chicken broth baths? Will she forgive her own watery depth buried in a long dead past? A fern by any other name is Daughter Dinosaur Divine, the baby egg that jumped into a baby green fist so she can slide into birth on a California porch —

But there will be no California.

No matter what the courts ruled, Powell will never repay what he stole now that his crooked lawyers have filed an appeal! Marcus, my one true friend, tried to comfort me but how could any comfort be had? I have no cash left for Marcus and his father to fight the crooked son-of-a-bitch.

The last of my savings were buried in a Muncie graveyard Peapot sweetheart Hap are you dancing with your new love while Skinny turns a deaf ear to my desperate plea for money to fight the goddamned appeal?

VIII

REVELATION

23

All Your Family Needs

Vacant. The bed was empty. Puzzled, Joanna double checked the number next to the door. All these godforsaken sterile rooms looked alike. No, she was in the right room, but her father wasn't. *Just when he's improving they move the poor man.* Or what if he had a relapse? Did the damned doctors have the audacity to ship him off to the psychiatric ward in Peoria without consulting her? Still clutching the box of coconut cream pie she'd kept chilled in her mini-fridge since last night's visit, she steamrollered to the nurses' station ready for battle. This morning, however, there were no opponents to challenge or defeat. Only one young RN's quiet voice.

"Mr. Morse?" She looked down at her charge sheet. A holiday weekend staff replacement, she wanted to be sure.

"Yes, Owen Morse. Room 232. Moving him at this point in his recovery is unconscionable."

"I'm sorry, ma'am —"

"You should be. Where is he?"

"Mr. Morse died earlier today." The young nurse informed her that the doctor on call left a message at the designated number, the Comfort Inn according to their records, and that Mr. Morse's body was now in the hospital morgue awaiting transport to the local mortuary for arrangements. If there was anything they could do to be of further assistance —

"I was with him last night!"

Joanna stood her ground. If she did not move, the nurse's words would hold no power.

"Yes, ma'am."

"He was recovering, he was fine." She had seen this with her own eyes.

"The cause of death is listed as cardiac arrest at ..." she checked her notes, "yes, 3:47 am."

"He had a heart attack?"

Like her mother.

"The staff attempted resuscitation without success."

Like her mother.

And then Joanna noticed the September calendar on the wall. Today was September 2nd. The same day that her mother died twenty years before.

Owen Morse may not have been a regular churchgoer but he and his kin carried sacred dates in their DNA as prescient as Ezekiel's prophecy. Her father, partial to recrimination more than reflection, had surprised her once by bringing up the question of a Holy Ghost master calendar that coordinated family comings and goings. Owen's mother died on Aldine's birthday, his grandmother the same day as her husband two years earlier, Aunt Kate on the first anniversary of her little brother Jonah's passing ... The list of morbid anniversaries went on and on.

"Why do you think that is?" Owen had asked his daughter.

Coincidence, Joanna started to say, but decided such a reply would be flippant and perhaps not altogether truthful. "I'm not sure, Dad."

"Do you think I'll die the same day Mom died?"

Trying to make a joke of a question neither one of them wanted to consider, she replied, "Only if you want to."

The nurse was standing now, repeating herself for some reason. "Mrs. Giordano ... Mrs. Giordano?"

"Yes?"

"Your father's personal belongings."

She thrust forward a white plastic bag, its square handles open to reveal the former patient's clothes. Checkered shirt, denims, boxer shorts, leather belt, a half-filled White Owl Cigarillo box and the gold Bulova she bought him for Christmas so that he would always know when to take his medication. All no longer needed.

"Oh, I almost forgot." She slipped back into her cubicle and presented Joanna one last memento of the evening. "Mr. Hartwig's card."

Joanna looked at the laminated four-color card with the proprietor's smiling face: "For All Your Family Needs."

~~~~~

Awaiting her arrival that afternoon at two o'clock sharp, Charlie greeted her with a respectful nod carefully balanced between welcoming and mournful. After the well-rehearsed condolences, he began listing their litany of services.

"Cremation," Joanna interrupted, saving them both further effort.

"Of course. A return to your lovely Pasadena for dispersal, no doubt?"

"I'd like to see my father now."

"Certainly."

"I'll need a bowl of water and clean cloth."

He looked surprised but, being in the service business, did his best to accommodate the client. "Whatever you like."

"Warm water."

"Warm water," he nodded. "Won't you have a seat while we prepare?"

Joanna sat down in the Victorian parlor next to the chiseled lead glass bay window. What would her father say about such an indignity? His lifeless body parked in the back room of the "mansion" where his sister's killer lived, laughed, and eluded justice.

"Son of a bitch," she whispered, saying it for him. Her throat was raw, her eyes red from crying jags that started, stopped, then started again throughout the day ...

Calling Sarah and Elizabeth had been the hardest. First she inquired about their host family, the trip to Venice, whether they felt welcome in this new land. And how was Grandpa Owen, they asked. Only then did she break the news with a steady voice. They needed her strong maternal front, she reasoned, because their grief would be more profound. If they had lost a devoted grandfather, at least there would be a thousand strands of happy memory left. Instead a familiar stranger they would now never know better had galloped off to the happy hunting grounds without so much as a wave goodbye.

First there was an awkward silence then a tearful choking sound from the more sensitive of her two daughters. The one that locked herself in her room when she learned their grandfather was feeling too "under the weather" to attend their high school graduation. This was the girls' first experience of death in the family and the word seemed as unreal as the event. Unsure how to comfort their mother (as unsure as she how to comfort them), they tripped over one another trying to fill the long-distance space with recollections from the rare occasions in their grandfather's presence.

They especially remembered his love of animals ... all those cats and dogs and rabbits from the foothills behind his house!

"Yes," Joanna agreed. No wild thing went without food and shelter in Owen Morse's universe. She revisited her childhood horror when she witnessed the family calico pummeling a mouse corpse, belly torn, jaws frozen in rigor mortis, to and fro like a hockey puck.

"Good mouser," her father laughed. Then he welcomed the calico back inside the house, chucked him under the chin, and poured a saucer of milk.

"That's how you win an animal's loyalty, Joanna. Reward 'em for being true to their nature."

And then both girls brought up the ritual bear hugs that always opened and ended each visit with Grandpa Owen, his warm arms wrapping their slender frames in a vise until they squealed for release. Still he held on.

"Like he never wanted to let go, Mom."

It was Peter who recognized that it was Joanna, as well as her dad, who had never wanted to let go.

"You did everything you could for him," her husband comforted.

"Did I?"

"Not just these past days, your whole life."

"But, I was too late!" Five minutes of sobbing and hyperventilating passed while the orphaned daughter battled to regain her equilibrium.

Peter waited. When she sensed he would wait forever if need be, she calmed.

"I should have been with him at the end."

"What more could you have given him, sweetheart?"

Joanna had no answer.

His strong voice softened. "God, I love you. Come home so I can hold you ..."

"I want that, Peter. More than I can say. I —" She choked.

"Yes?"

"I've been missing you."

"I've been missing you too. That's why I kept calling."

"Yes, yes, I know, but I meant ... I've been missing you for a long time."

Despite the death of her last parent she no longer felt alone and promised her husband she would call again soon. Then her wrist brushed the red-and-white pie box still sitting on the bureau. The coconut custard was room temperature, the meringue damp and weeping, its toasted crispness gone. She scooped the wedge into her hands and inhaled every crumb. A few minutes later she lost it all, lumps of yellow and beige circling down the toilet drain. Only the bittersweet remained.

"Mrs. Giordano?"

Her head turned. The pocket mahogany doors shielding the Victorian parlor from uninvited guests creaked open.

"Your father is ready now," Charlie Hartwig announced.

Joanna rose to say goodbye.

24

Visitation

The porcelain bowl filled with water sat next to a powder blue washcloth on the side table. A modest sheet had been tucked with care under the chin, draping the body like a light snowfall. The only exposed flesh in the room was his face, and Owen Morse's face was not his own. To a casual observer, one who had not truly known him, his features might seem to be the same. The jaw still strong, nose still high and broad, eyelashes still coal black even as the once wild head of hair had thinned and greyed. But meaning and power and purpose had been carried away on death's shoulders.

Joanna caressed her father's cheekbone. Cold. No feeling, not even a mirror of feelings come and gone. The essence of the man whose seed had given her life had evaporated, leaving a visage that looked like nothing more than an empty stone tomb. The person she'd loved beyond reason had escaped into a distant ether beyond human touch. All those years of trying to "save" him from an earthly end he came to in his own way and time that had nothing to do with her …

Joanna folded back the bottom edge of the sheet so that she could soak his feet — always cold even in life — with warmth. The water was clean and clear, a prayer for mercy in every drop. First she bathed the left foot, then the right. The skin, protected daily as it had been by his athletic socks and heavy boots, was as delicate as a baby's cheek. She blotted the wetness with reverence, just as she had watched the Episcopal priest perform the ritual when her infant daughters were baptized in preparation for their lives to come. She covered her father's feet and turned away.

Walking to the door she told herself she would not look back. She would not. But she did. And in that instant she saw a different body. A young girl in a grey fox coat, her skull bloodied and split, her limbs splayed like a rag doll. A mother's scream punctured the air. A terrible scream. Joanna blinked. The bodies of the girl and the old man now lay side by side, discarded shells of what they once were. Slamming the door behind her, the woman who still lived stepped into the hallway, but could not catch her breath.

"Mrs. Giordano, are you all right?" Charlie Hartwig was advancing in her direction.

"Of course," she answered, her heart racing.

"I thought I heard —"

"What?"

"Ah, well, nothing." He spread his hands, ushering her back to the parlor. "Is there anything else —"

"No. Thank you, Mr. Hartwig."

"Please, Charlie, remember?" he reminded her, beaming with beatitude, "I took the liberty of notifying family on your behalf."

Before Joanna could ask what family that might be, she heard Tazewell's voice.

"Cousin Joanna, I'm here to help." His hands reached for hers.

~~~~~

All she wanted was to leave. Proprieties dictated otherwise. At Tazewell's insistence Joanna accepted a half-cup of tepid coffee in the waiting room of the funeral parlor.

"Please accept my deepest condolences."

After several intolerable minutes commenting on the mutual loss of their fathers, she stood to go and he walked her to her car. But when Joanna turned the ignition, the engine failed to turn over.

"Something wrong?" Tazewell tapped on the passenger side window.

She rolled down the window. "I don't know what the problem is."

"Perhaps I can help," he smiled, motioning for her to lift the hood. "I'm handy with mechanics."

It had only taken a moment to remove the distributor cap when he arrived earlier. His cousin's extended grieving over her father's body had given him time to spare.

"A bad alternator," Tazewell announced, slamming shut the hood with authority. "I'll go ask Charlie to call AAA."

Joanna collapsed against the headrest. Her father's passing had squeezed her dry. Bone dry. She heard the occasional car drive by ... the birds chattering ... leaves rustling in a late summer breeze ... the lullaby of sound rocked her into a deep, drug-like repose. So peaceful, so very peaceful.

"Joanna?" his soft voice intruded.

She lifted her lids and looked into her cousin's eager eyes. Grey? Brown? Hazel? Some indeterminate color she could not name.

"It'll be several hours, I'm sorry to say. The Labor Day weekend."

Joanna rubbed her eyes. Yesterday was Saturday and her father was alive. Today is Sunday and her father is dead.

"You don't look well," he leaned in. "A little lunch might do you good."

"I'm not hungry."

"Something light. Uncle Owen would want you to take care of yourself, don't you think?"

Her throat tightened, so fierce and taut she could barely speak.

"I ..." She began. Stopped. Began again. "I might miss the repair truck."

"Oh, don't worry about that. Charlie's putting the service on his card."

"That's kind of him."

"Yes, it is.

"I guess I could use another cup of coffee."

"Of course," Tazewell opened the car door which Joanna, in her distraction and fatigue, had failed to lock.

"May I have the keys?"

She hesitated, her mind still clearing.

"To give to Charlie in case they get here early?"

Embarrassed at her slowness, she pulled the keys from the ignition and placed them in Tazewell's palm. Always a gentleman, he escorted her to his ten-year-old Ford, a vehicle sturdy and dependable like himself.

"I'll be right back after I give this to Charlie." He smiled, "You take a load off."

They rode in silence the first few minutes, which Joanna appreciated. An eccentric personality, no question, annoying at times but not without compassion.

"It's a hard season for us, isn't it Joanna? Losing our fathers."

"Yes," was all she could manage.

"I'm glad you have a husband and children waiting for you back in California. You're very fortunate in that respect."

The Ford began to slow as they approached the Baby Bull, the café where Joanna and her father lunched after the visit to his sister's grave. She stiffened. Not there, not while the memories were so fresh —

"Tazewell —"

"Yes?"

"Never mind." As he passed the Baby Bull and turned left at the next corner, her body shuddered in relief.

"Something wrong?"

"No, I …" she struggled to collect her thoughts. Make polite conversation. "I was just wondering. How long has it been since your dad —"

"Four months on Friday."

"I'm sorry," she sighed, not remembering if she had expressed her sympathy when they met at the courthouse.

"At least he's not in pain anymore. Doctors can be such cruel hypocrites with their miracle medicines and false promises. At the end I insisted he be in his own home where I could give him proper care."

Tazewell turned north, driving across the Vermilion River toward the outskirts of town.

"You reconciled then?"

"What do you mean?"

"I heard … there was some difficulty between the two of you."

"Who told you that?"

Joanna hesitated.

"It was Hornbeck, wasn't it?" Tazewell pressed. "I have a close confidante in his office. She'll tell me. I have a right to know who's besmirching my reputation."

"I don't think he intended —"

"You are not taking his word over mine, are you? I would be so hurt."

Joanna massaged her forehead, tension pulsing under the skin. "Obviously Mr. Hornbeck was mistaken."

An uneasy silence filled the space between them.

She looked up the road. "I could use that coffee now. McDonald's is fine."

"Oh, we deserve something nicer than that." He sailed past a pair of golden arches. "There's a place not far ahead."

Joanna nodded, hiding her irritation.

"Interesting how family tragedy binds us together. Just before Charlie called with the sad news about your father, I was considering Aunt Aldine."

Joanna looked out the window as the City of Pontiac rolled by. Bailey & Sons Crop Hail Insurance … Richard Kauffman Farm Drainage and Conservation … Evenglow Retirement Home …

"She was a weak woman, Joanna. We must accept this. Drinking and carrying on with a married man? Bentley would never have left his wife and property for her. I think she knew this and decided to punish him. Make him look like the villain …"

Joanna kept her face turned. If she ignored him maybe he would stop talking.

"… and that's why she stepped in front of the oncoming car while Bentley was sleeping it off in the back seat." Tazewell's brow wrinkled in consternation. "The poor thing was already dead when he woke up. The fact that he ran over her corpse was just … well … an unfortunate detail —"

"Tazewell, please!"

"What is it, Joanna?"

"No more talk about our aunt."

"Oh, I'm sorry. I didn't mean to give offense."

"Let's just … let her rest in peace, okay?"

"Yes, you're right. None of that old family business matters now anyway."

She closed her eyes. "I wish you would've told me how far the café was."

"Almost there. Only a couple more miles."

At the last four-way stop before the interstate, Tazewell turned right, proceeding down a ribbon of hard road that sliced across acres of corn and soybeans then descended into pockmarked WPA era blacktop.

Startled by the bumpiness, Joanna opened her eyes. "Where are we?"

A beat-up pick-up passed by in the opposite lane, a grizzled old-timer at the wheel barely doing thirty.

"A special place I know Uncle Owen would want you to visit."

Joanna's empty stomach ached for sustenance. "You promised me lunch."

Her cousin did not answer.

"Tazewell?"

Awake now, finally fully awake, she felt a slow-brewing alarm crawl up her spine.

"Soon, cousin."

Joanna sat up straighter, scanned the vast acres of land passing in a blur and thought for an instant that she spotted a lone woman on the opposite side of the road. The hitchhiker raised her right arm just as Tazewell turned off the blacktop into a rutted dirt path that ended in front of a weather-beaten farmhouse. A picket fence had collapsed atop snaking vines and heavy-headed sunflowers drooped low in the prairie heat. The home's stone foundation peeked through the overgrowth. Beneath the earth a storm cellar, once a hiding place from tornadoes, blizzards and all manner of nature's excess, nestled.

"Welcome to the family homestead." Tazewell, his moon face impassive, killed the engine.

25

Homestead

A canopy of sugar maples shadowed the cousins as they walked together toward the house. When Tazewell petted her hair, she did not pull away. When he asked if they might hold hands, she did not reveal her revulsion. When he led her to the corner of the yard where the family felines were buried, she did not flinch.

"Cats can be so cruel. Scratching, biting, eviscerating poor defenseless creatures half their size ..." His eyes measured Joanna, waiting for her response.

"Yes," she began, mouth sandpaper dry, mind spinning. "My father ..." the words caught in her throat like a sob. "My father said it's their nature."

"Exactly. They're afflicted by a superiority complex and there is only one solution for that. Arrogance must be humbled."

Joanna had no reply.

"You've been very patient, Joanna."

"Have I?"

"Oh yes. Patience is a gift. Horatio, unfortunately, was not a patient man. Especially when we both knew death was inevitable," he leaned closer, his words barely audible. "None of his medicines were working. That's why we had to throw them away, even the morphine. But did he thank me?"

Tazewell pulled Joanna toward the front porch. A once grand hydrangea bush, dead leaves the color of tarnished gold, squatted in the rich Illinois soil next to the peeling handrail. As he started to lead her up the rickety steps, Joanna fell back.

"Let's have lunch out here, Tazewell. A picnic under the trees?"

"Not today. Our business is inside."

Joanna's hand jerked, slipping ever so slightly out of his grasp.

He tightened his grip. "Is there a problem?"

"Of course not."

"You look afraid, Joanna."

"You're hurting my hand."

"Am I?" He seemed surprised but did not lessen his hold. "Well, that's your fault for not listening. It's important for a person of character to be respected, don't you think?"

"I respect you, Tazewell."

"Then you must come inside, Joanna. It's time to do the right thing."

~~~~~

The family homestead was an oven. A hundred-degree oven of abandonment and despair. Everywhere she looked, hollow-eyed decay glared back. Hardwood floors scarred, walls stained and stripped bare, the entryway's torn wallpaper the only visible decorative art. Sheets shrouded odd sticks of furniture revealing neither design nor function.

"Disregard the dust," Tazewell muttered, leading Joanna through the parlor and dining room into the dilapidated kitchen. Behind a few remaining drawn curtains, the windows, like every other window in the house, were sealed. A pine table with two mismatched chairs occupied the center of the room. On the table's scratched surface a stack of papers awaited execution.

"Sit down." He pushed her into the closest chair, his hands heavy on her shoulders. "Do you see the pen, Joanna?"

A ballpoint with red lettering on its plastic green case — "Happy Holidays from Kessler Farm and Home Realty" — had been placed at a perfect right angle on top of the papers.

"Yes."

"Good. Pick it up and sign where designated." Tazewell had attached yellow post-its for her convenience next to the signature lines.

"What am I signing, Tazewell?" Joanna rasped, her focus growing woozy in the stifling darkened room.

"Read it yourself," he snapped. "It's there in black and white."

Joanna did not move. "Can you open the curtains for me, Tazewell? So I can see better?"

"No, it's cooler this way."

"A light then." She squinted up at the old, globed ceiling light.

"Electricity costs an arm and leg, Horatio always says. You can see just fine."

"It's very hard for me, Tazewell. My glasses are at the motel. If you drive me back —"

"Oh for cripes sake!" Tazewell's index finger pummeled the document as he read over Joanna's shoulder:

"Illinois Statute 7551LCS27, Section 5 — Residential Real Property Transfer on Death Instrument. Definitions. In this Act: 'Beneficiary' means a person that receives residential real estate under a transfer on death instrument …"

Joanna's head tightened as she followed paragraph by paragraph. Tazewell's voice rose higher with each word.

"… permitted under the law of this state … if another instrument contains a contrary provision … capacity of owner and agent's authority … (1) must contain the essential elements and formalities of a properly recordable inter vivos deed —"

"Excuse me, Tazewell, I need some water."

"After you sign."

"I'm not feeling well —"

"You're not cooperating, cousin. I find that upsetting. Very upsetting."

Joanna slid off the chair, out of his grip onto the filthy cracked linoleum.

"Joanna? … Joanna!"

She kept her eyes closed. Waiting. Buying time. Praying the bluff would work. Finally she heard the faucet running, felt the plastic cup pushed to her lips, tasted the water spilling down her parched throat. All the while, her mind struggled to take back control.

"Get up," he pulled her limbs in a wild frenzy.

"Thank ... you," she stammered, slowly sitting. "I'm so embarrassed ... upsetting you ... when you've showed me such kindness."

Tazewell, a hawk surveying the unexpected movements of his prey, peered into her face.

"Will you help me up?"

He hesitated but did as she asked.

"Why didn't you tell me what you wanted, Tazewell?"

They were both standing now. Inches apart. Almost exactly the same height, Joanna realized. Only his thick muscular bulk gave him the physical advantage.

"These papers are for your father's property, aren't they?" Joanna asked.

"My property."

"Yes, that's what I meant."

"Not Owen's, not yours."

"You're right, Tazewell. All of this belongs to you."

"You do understand then, what an abomination the will was. An utter falsehood."

"No question."

"He was an old man, not in his right mind. That's why I had to help release him from his misery. He begged me, you know. How could I refuse an act of mercy?"

Joanna betrayed no feeling.

"I'm too soft-hearted."

"I see that."

"You do, don't you?"

"And I want you to have what's yours, Tazewell." Joanna picked up the pen as if she were going to sign then stopped. "Oh dear."

"What's wrong?"

"This needs to be witnessed."

"I'll take care of that later."

"But the transfer of property won't be legal unless it's witnessed when I sign it —"

"Later I said."

"But Tazewell, look right here," she stumbled over the text trying to keep her voice strong and steady. "Section 40 (a) (1) … must be executed, witnessed and acknowledged in compliance with Section 45 …" (b) the failure to comply with any of the requirements of … of — what? — yes, subsection (a) will render the transfer on death instrument void and ineffective … See?"

Disbelieving, he began to pace.

"Let's call your friend. The one you told me about who works at Mr. Hornbeck's office. She'll tell you I'm right. Where's the phone?"

"Disconnected."

"What?"

"Disconnected!" he barked, sweat drenching his upper lip.

"All right then. Why don't we go back to town and take care of it together right now —"

"No."

"Why not?"

"What if you're trying to trick me?"

"I wouldn't do that, Tazewell. We're family."

He stopped for a moment. Weighing her words. Suddenly he grabbed her hand, pulling her out the kitchen into the hallway where they entered. Joanna did not resist. She'd convinced him, thank God. Tazewell threw the front door open with such force it ripped the rusty screen off its hinges. As he raced down the porch stairs with Joanna in tow she stumbled on a broken step, her foot twisting.

"Please —"

"Don't be weak, Joanna." His eyes bore into hers. "Our fathers would not want us to be weak."

"You're right. I'm fine." She lied, her ankle burning. And then she saw where they were headed. Not to the car but around the porch, to the garden of roped vines and dead undergrowth.

"Tazewell, where are we going?"

"You'll have to wait here at the house."

"For what?"

"I'm bringing the notary like you said."

"Oh no. It's better if we go together right now."

"It's Sunday. The darned office is closed."

"Oh," Joanna almost collapsed with relief. "We'll go tomorrow then."

"No, you have to stay. It's safer."

"But Charlie will worry about me," she protested, her breath quickening, "when I don't come back for my car —"

"I already told him you wanted me to drive that piece of junk back to the motel, Joanna. That's why I kept the key."

"You kept …"

"Of course. Do you think I'm a fool?"

"No, Tazewell," Joanna answered as they ricocheted through a dry bed of skeleton-stemmed asters to his destination.

The storm cellar, its iron-latch double doors built to withstand all threatening elements, awaited. Ready to be of use again.

26

The Cellar

The abyss beckoned.

"Please let me wait in the house." Joanna hovered at the top of the cellar stairwell.

"We've already been over this," Tazewell huffed. "It's cooler down here. You'll be more comfortable."

"There might be rats —"

"They won't hurt you."

"How do you know?"

"Do I look injured, Joanna? Worse for the wear in any way? No. I spent many a night down here learning the rules of my father's house and am living proof that deprivation builds character. Toughen up, cousin."

He pushed her forward onto the first step. Joanna's ankle, bruised and swollen, endured the indignity in silence. Clutching the wall for balance, she struggled to acclimate her eyes to the darkness.

"It'll only be for a day or two. Maybe three."

He pushed her again, forcing her to stumble down the next step. She caught herself and reared back, the dank putrid air pushing into her lungs until she could barely breathe. A black hole was opening wider with each step.

"I can't see, Tazewell."

"Oh for heaven's sake," he snorted. "Just a minute then."

Tazewell reached for a rusted kerosene lamp hanging above his head just below the entrance. Scratching a match against the stone wall, he illuminated the descent that waited. A dozen steps, no more than a dozen, before they reached the bowels of the family home.

"Let there be light," he giggled.

An old furnace dominated the cavernous space. The stone floor, rough and uneven, looked like a drunken mason had lost his way. Windows were boarded with plywood to insure privacy from prying eyes. One single pane of filthy glass escaped cover. It revealed the overgrown thicket smothering the garden path above.

"A place for you to rest." He lifted the lantern higher so that she might see the narrow cot covered with a crocheted afghan, his mother's finest handiwork. "And there's a laundry sink with running water. No privy, I'm sorry to say, so you'll have to make do with the slop jar in the corner."

Delicate sensibilities offended by the awkward subject, Tazewell quickly directed her attention to a pail of fruit at the bottom of the stairwell. "Fresh apricots from the orchard, a bumper crop this year. Crab apples coming in a few weeks."

Joanna stared at him. In a few weeks?

"Do you like homemade applesauce?"

She did not answer.

Unnerved by her silence, Tazewell turned peevish. "Don't be rude, cousin. I asked you a question."

And still her silent stare resisted. Mocked. Condemned.

"I had no time to lay in proper provisions, all this coming up so unexpectedly, but whose fault is that?" The kerosene flame quivered as his voice rose. "Not mine. Yours. Yours and your damned father's! I hope he's gone to hell where he belongs —"

Joanna's arm moved so fast Tazewell had no chance to shield himself. One moment he held the lantern, the next it had been knocked from his fat, trembling fingers. A projectile launched through space, smashing against the boarded-up window. The glass globe shattered and the tiny flame flew free, catching on the debris beneath the window. Old newspapers, rags, a box of mummified pomegranates from a long-ago harvest.

Tazewell pushed Joanna aside as he lunged down the stairwell. Grabbing the pail, he spilled the fruit across the floor and flipped the faucet on full force.

"Help me, cousin, help me!"

Joanna watched the river of fire flow toward the afghan, the cot, the plump golden apricots. She was moving now, step by step, out of the cellar.

"Get back here!" Tazewell staggered like a madman, dumping ineffectual pails of water on the consuming fire.

Half limping, half crawling up the final steps, she saw cracks of daylight. But just as she managed to climb out, she heard Tazewell clambering up behind her.

"You can't leave ..." he gasped. "You can't ..."

The sky burned bright blue. Birds twittered. Her eyes fluttered against the sun's glare as her lungs expanded with air. She strained to secure the cellar doors, slamming them against his advance — but where was the damned lock? Where was it!? She heard him swearing, begging, choking from the smoking inferno below.

She threw her full weight against the doors, gripping the edges of splintery wood until her fingertips bled. But he was too strong. One door lifted an inch, then the other. He was pushing harder and harder. Rolling off, she hobbled a few feet to the garden and took shelter in the grape arbor's tangled thicket. Belly to belly with dirt and slugs and burrowing earthworms.

The cellar doors burst open. She cowered as he leapt out with horrifying force. The back of his shirt and trousers were blue-black with flames.

"Help me! Goddammit ... please, please ... where are you?"

Joanna shut out his groans and epithets, her shallow breath quickening with every second. And then all was quiet. Except for the ravenous crackling of fire. Escaping pockets of flame from the cellar lapped at the clapboard exterior of the farmhouse. Red-orange fingers yearning to come together ...

As she crept through the verdant overgrowth, she could see him lying on his back a dozen yards from the blackened cellar entrance. Still. Utterly still. Her heart pounding, she inched closer and then froze.

Smoke stinging her eyes, she stumbled to her feet and limped away from the burning house. Toward the car in the driveway. The door was unlocked but there were no keys in the ignition. Yes, she remembered that now. When Tazewell—

"Joanna …"

She froze in horror as her cousin struggled to his feet.

"Save the house," he rasped, lurching over to a weathered garden hose coiled next to the front steps. Falling on the faucet, he unleashed the water from the well.

Joanna blanched at the sight of the raw seared flesh across his back and legs. He appeared numb to pain, to sensation, to anything beyond a singular obsession to save the melting structure in front of him.

"Get the hoses behind the tractor barn!" he yelled, spraying the water in wild frantic circles.

"Throw me the car keys, Tazewell."

"What? I can't hear you!"

She moved closer. "I'll go for the fire trucks."

"There's no time! The hoses are behind the barn!"

The leaves of the sugar maples shuddered as a hot prairie wind swept across the flat lands. The fire blazed brighter, catching its branches.

"It's too big. We need help, Tazewell." But she was talking to a deaf man. Deaf, dumb, and blind to anything but his own will.

"For Christ's sake, I'll get 'em myself. Hold this, damnit!"

"Please, Tazewell, throw me the keys before it's too late—"

The crash came with a roar that dazed both of them. A majestic maple, its trunk ablaze, wrenched from its roots and toppled onto the shale roof. Within seconds the family homestead was being eaten alive by giant tongues of flame. Tazewell collapsed to his knees, an unrepentant Job railing against Nature and her injustice.

His howls of fury echoing in her ears, Joanna hobbled down the country lane to the blacktop. Step by step, minute by minute. Five passed. Maybe ten. Now on the hard road, she only had a mile to go — she could make it. Somebody would stop to give her a lift. A half dozen cars had passed Tazewell's Ford only an hour before. Or was it two hours? Three?

She looked up to see the sun riding lower in the sky and lost her balance, the injured ankle twisting again. Joanna gasped and doubled over, the pain shooting through her calf. A circle of Holsteins lowed in the nearby pasture under a cluster of sycamores. Stamina eroding with each halting step, she leaned against the roadside fence to catch her breath and watched the animals drink from a concrete trough green with algae. Her body ached for water. Water and food and rest ...

A car engine sounded in the distance. She jerked her neck toward Tazewell's place. The fire still burned, blackening the landscape with ember and ash. And then she saw it. The blue Ford emerged from the black cloud like an avenging angel.

"My God." Joanna spun around, searching for a place to hide. Behind the trees, the trough ...

A cow lifted her head, ears twitching, eyes luminous. Hank Williams's melodious voice filled the air, sailing out the open windows of a beat-up pickup as it turned onto the blacktop. The same pickup they had passed hours before. Joanna waved her arms like a crazed marionette but the farmer, shielding his eyes from the glare of the western sun, did not notice.

"You'll cry and cry," the old-timer warbled along with his buddy on the radio airwaves. "Lord, that man could sing."

Joanna limped into the middle of the road to flag him down.

The farmer, his hearing and eyesight not as sharp as they used to be, squinted at the blurry image down the way but did not slow.

"What the heck ... not another stupid deer?" he groused.

"STOP, please stop!"

The farmer tooted his horn.

Joanna stood her ground. She could hear the motor of Tazewell's Ford speeding closer by the second.

"Darned doe!" The farmer laid on his horn again.

"Help me!" Joanna screamed at the top of her lungs, so loud a flock of crows scattered from the highest branch of the sycamore. Loud enough for the old farmer to hear and discern the doe actually had two legs instead of four. As he slowed to a crawl to get a better look, Joanna hobbled to the passenger side, swung open the door and clambered inside.

"Just a minute here lady, I don't know who you think —"

"Drive!" she ordered. "Back to the highway!"

His aged reflexes stalled. By the time he realized Tazewell's Ford was headed straight toward him it was too late to turn. Too late to do anything.

Bearing down at full speed, the Ford was close enough that Joanna could see Tazewell's face. The desperate man in the driver's seat had nothing left to lose.

Joanna stabbed the heel of her good foot down onto the accelerator. Hard.

"You cracked my toe, lady! Stop!"

She pushed the pedal to its limit. The pickup jolted forward and Joanna grabbed the wheel to steer into Tazewell's path.

"Jesus, save us!" The farmer wailed, eighty-one years flashing before his eyes.

And then she swerved.

Tazewell skidded, smashing through the pasture fence into the concrete trough under the cluster of Kentucky sycamores. His beloved Ford rolled over onto its roof, low tread Firestones spinning out of control. The Holsteins trotted away, cowbells clanging into the distance until all sound disappeared.

27

Rectified

By the time Joanna climbed back into consciousness the old farmer had already hightailed down the road to the Gibsons and called for help. The paramedic at her side when she awoke, a handsome, dark-haired young man who bore an uncanny resemblance to her father in his wedding photograph, told her she was one lucky lady. Not a mark on her. Later, after the CAT scan, MRI, and a good tight ice wrap for her twisted ankle, the ER physician confirmed no serious damage. A minor concussion most likely, considering her blackout, the prefrontal cortex a little shaken. Rest. That's all she could do really. Rest. The brain's normal filters might be sensitive to noise and light for a few days, but she'd be back to herself in no time.

"Herself." Which self?

The stable self she used to be with her family and clients in Pasadena? The troubled self she became after she and her father returned to Pontiac? Or the alien self that floated at liberty in her shaken body ever since the accident? For better or for worse, an unfamiliar detachment now embedded itself in every cell of her being.

About to check out of the hospital, Joanna decided to visit her cousin's room.

Candied violets punched into a sagging vanilla frosted cake — that's what Tazewell's black-eyed pasty face looked like. He'd hit the steering wheel hard. A punctured lung, four broken ribs, fractured collarbone, shattered spine. All because he had been too cheap to trade in an old clunker for a new model with 1996 airbags. Like father, like son. His swollen eyelids cracked open. Pain at half-mast.

"You?" he rasped.

His voice was barely a whisper but it echoed through the room like a foghorn, assaulting Joanna's ears along with the rest of the hospital cacophony. The fluorescent light above his bed buzzed. In the corridor wheeled carts creaked by. Words ricocheted back and forth from nurse to orderly to visitor in a white-walled world of slamming doors. Muzak seeped through the airways. And somewhere a TV tuned to *All My Children* blared forth Erica's latest act of betrayal.

"You ..." he repeated, the second-degree burns festering underneath bandages strapped across his back.

Chicken giblet gravy. A nurse had told her that the hospital kitchen never served gravy. Bad for patients' cholesterol. Yet the unmistakable aroma of blended fat and flesh and floured milk teased Joanna's nostrils. Perhaps a special delivery from Colonel Sanders? She breathed deeply. Far better to ingest Kentucky Fried than the sensory overload of medicinal sanitation and putrid air freshener.

"Yes," Joanna answered.

Tazewell squeezed his eyes shut to erase the apparition at his bedside. "I'm still here ..."

~

Joanna's pony did not give a damn if her parents found their little girl dead. The chestnut gelding reared, kicked, and bucked to high heaven until his eight-year-old rider lay discarded in the dust while he galloped off into lush cornfields to take his fill. Her mother ran screaming to check Joanna for broken bones, while her father raced off to wrangle the runaway pony.

Bruised, breathless, backside aching in shame, the child awaited her father's return. As soon as he tethered the pony, he dismissed his wife's distress and his daughter's tears. A doctor? To heck with a doctor. The only thing his kid needed was to get back on the pony.

"What did I teach you?" Her dad's fierce eyes embraced her.

She hesitated too long.

"Show the animal who's boss," he bellowed. "Say it."

"Show the animal ..."

"What?"

"I'm not afraid."

He lifted her back into the saddle.

~~~~

Even as Joanna waited for the elevator and realized that Tazewell occupied the same hospital room where her father had died three days before — even at this moment she felt nothing. The elevator doors opened.

Before Joanna could step in, a nervous middle-aged woman barreled out, blocking her escape. The elevator door closed.

"Mrs. Giordano," the woman startled. "What a surprise! My goodness gracious."

Joanna did not respond.

"You remember ... Miss Lidcombe? From Mr. Hornbeck's office?"

"Of course." Joanna was staring at the white roses bunched in her arms.

"How are you?" Miss Lidcombe waxed solicitous and did not wait for an answer. "Your poor father, what a shame."

"Yes, it is —"

"All we have is family. And friends. That's it, isn't it? Family and friends."

Joanna managed a cool nod. "What a lovely bouquet."

"Yes, Tazewell's favorite," Miss Lidcombe blurted, her eyes welling.

"My cousin Tazewell?"

"Excuse my manners. Your cousin, of course. Have the doctors said — well, I don't mean to pry, but I'm not a blood relative and they won't tell me a thing." Miss Lidcombe sniffled.

"You're friends?"

"The dearest but —"

"Yes?"

"Since that terrible crash, he won't talk to me. The nurses said he won't speak to anyone. Did he talk to you?"

"No."

Joanna moved to the elevator and palmed the down button.

~~~~~

Marcus Washington grunted then put down the front page of the morning paper. Aldine Younger — through her descendants now — was still making headlines:

"Car Crash Survivors on Alden Road"

Parallel lines of concern creased his brow. He recalled that Aldine's niece and the odd duck librarian had inherited common blood, but the two seemed as different from one another as opposite sides of the moon. Curious that they were out together at that rambling wreck of a farmhouse before the accident. He saw the property once, when Aldine's half-brother Horatio insisted he come out to foment a lawsuit against some hapless neighbor whose cows crossed over his property line. A lawsuit totally without merit, even if the miserly Horatio had been willing to pay a fair fee to a "colored shylock" he thought he could lowball. The owner and his sad sack of a structure should have both been condemned then.

The old man peered through his reading glasses at the fine print again:

"Mrs. Giordano reported she and her cousin were both racing to the nearest phone to call the fire department in the hope a raging fire that threatened to consume the family farmhouse could be contained ..."

So why was she in a neighbor's pickup going south and he in his car going north? Something was amiss. Marcus shifted, frowning at the pruned bushes in his rose garden. A couple months, three at the most, before the snow would cover them all. He'd warned her to be careful.

Pushing himself out of the comfortable Lincoln rocker crafted by his own hands, he stood, steadied his balance and walked toward the back bedroom, as he had every morning since Aldine Younger's niece knocked on his door.

The treasured diary lay under a magnifying glass on the scarred desk of the Victorian secretary. The private place his mother used to pen proper thank-you notes and heartfelt letters to folks in need of sustenance. Now the sturdy wood bore another woman's joy and grief. He felt Aldine afresh these past days. The girl he once thought he understood but never really knew. Through a veil of years he saw now that her spirit needed to be carried forward by a man of faith. He would not fail her again.

~~~

"I'm sorry to have kept you waiting," Hornbeck announced, steering Joanna into his office. A flicker of distaste clouded his countenance as he glanced toward the empty chair behind his receptionist's desk. "Miss Lidcombe has been under the weather these past few days."

Yes, smashed illusions can do that to a woman in love, Joanna thought. She fell back into the chair her father had sat in a week before.

"My condolences on Mr. Morse's passing. Such a surprise and so sudden ..."

As the lawyer droned on about the unpredictability of this mortal coil, Joanna shifted in her seat to avoid the glare from Hornbeck's desk lamp. She refocused on the antique clock resting on the top shelf of his bookcase. Though appearing to do its job with quiet unobtrusive regularity, all she heard was cacophony. The subtle "tick, tick, tick," loomed large. Annoying. Intolerable —

"... and how is your cousin?"

"Excuse me?"

"The car accident. Such a difficult week for your family. Have the doctors shared the prognosis?"

"No."

"Apparently he lost consciousness behind the wheel?" Hornbeck leaned closer.

"Apparently."

"My, my, and you'd been visiting the family home together just before the fire?"

Impatient with morbid curiosity disguised as concern, Joanna cut him off. "How much do you think the land is worth?"

"Well, the agriculture market has declined a bit but we're still getting at least $5000 per acre." He sighed, calculating the lost real estate. "Too bad the house is gone."

"So, 320 acres at $5000. About $160,000?"

"Approximately."

"Good." Joanna's voice grew husky, her father's presence looming large. "Land has a long life if it's valued."

Hornbeck nodded. "Can't argue with you there. Always a good investment if the numbers don't lie."

The antique clock ticked louder. Joanna's spine stiffened by the second.

"People lie, Mr. Hornbeck. Numbers you can trust."

"Yes, of course. Well, should I draw up the deed in your name then? Let the market deliver when the time comes?"

"I'm not interested in keeping the property."

"No?" Hornbeck looked confused. "Perhaps I misunderstood —"

"I want the property deeded to my daughters and then sold. The proceeds will go to them."

"Oh." He leaned back in his chair. "I see. That's a bit more complicated. If your girls have not reached their majority —"

"They turned eighteen in February. Young women need investment property of their own."

"Well, that's very generous indeed." And then he added, more a question than a statement, "I hope they appreciate your generosity?"

"A family bequest, Mr. Hornbeck. That's your business, is it not?"

"At your service," he demurred.

"I need to return to my family in California. How soon can we get this done?"

The clock kept ticking.

"Sometime next week I think I can have —"

"I'll be here tomorrow morning to sign the papers." Joanna stood, ready to leave.

Hornbeck scurried to escort her to the door. "I'm sure you've given this careful thought, Mrs. Giordano, though I can't help but inquire —"

"Yes?"

The damned clock still ticked.

"Is this what your father would want?" For as long as Joanna could remember that question had driven her life.

She walked out without answering.

28

Godspeed

Marcus tipped the taxi driver fifty cents and moved with as much deliberate speed as his 88-year-old legs could manage toward the law offices of J.W. Hornbeck & Sons. When he reached the entrance, a collision of bodies tumbled him off balance.

Joanna grabbed the old man's arm to prevent his fall then reacted in surprise. "Mr. Washington?"

Shaken more by her caring touch than his own frailty, he jerked away. "We meet again."

"I hope you're all right." An awkward smile flashed across her face, the memory of their last meeting still discomforting.

"I'll recover," he replied. His crisp pride sustained him as always. "And you?"

"Oh, I'm fine."

"The car accident, I meant. The paper said —"

"Not a scratch. I'm fine," she insisted again.

"A blessing then. Considering —"

"So," Joanna interrupted, "Mr. Hornbeck is your attorney too?"

He didn't answer. Instead, he blurted, "Will you have tea with me?"

"I ... that's very kind, but I don't want to delay your business."

He looked at her, perplexed.

"No need for that now. There's a café just around the corner," Marcus said. "I find the Buttercup to be decent enough."

"Yes, I've been there," she said without enthusiasm.

"Charming in its gentrified way, isn't it?" He chattered on. "Used to be a butcher shop but I suppose your father has been keeping you up on all the hometown lore —"

"My father died two days ago, Mr. Washington."

Marcus looked stricken. "I didn't know."

"I have to get back and start packing."

"You're returning to California already?"

"Tomorrow."

"So soon?"

"Yes," Joanna half-swallowed the word. Not nearly soon enough.

"I wish I could persuade you to stay a day or two longer —"

"That's impossible. My husband is arriving later today so we can fly home together."

"Of course, of course," Marcus demurred. "He must have been concerned when he heard about your accident …"

Joanna had revealed nothing to Peter about the circumstances that preceded the collision on Alden Road. All she told him was that an old farmer with bad eyesight had a bumper cruncher giving her a lift during an emergency at the family homestead. That, and news of a slight concussion his wife may have sustained, were enough. You're not getting on that plane without me, he'd admonished, you've handled too much alone as it is. And for once, when Joanna heard the fear in his voice, she did not argue.

"… I'm glad we have the chance to say goodbye."

"I must be going, Mr. Washington."

"Well then," he rasped, "May I escort you to your vehicle?"

"It's really not necessary —"

"Please. Allow me to be a gentleman."

"All right then," she acquiesced. "I'm only a couple blocks away in the city parking lot."

The odd couple strolled at a slow pace in unquiet contemplation.

"Do you …" Joanna broke the silence then hesitated, "I was wondering if …"

"Yes?"

"A local lady named Lottie McKeown, would you happen to know her?"

"Why do you ask?"

"Her name came up in conversation with my father."

"We met on several occasions. She was quite attached to your aunt as a child."

"Can you tell me where she lives?"

"I'm afraid Mrs. McKeown passed on some years ago."

Joanna escalated her pace. "My car is around the corner."

As they turned down the next street and neared parting, Marcus asked, "Did you go to the courthouse? Were you able to read the files of your aunt's legal history? Examine the transcripts and depositions yourself?"

Joanna closed her eyes for an instant, trying to shut out the images. Dusty dockets in the back room ... an eighteen-year-old girl's will ... the petition for conservatorship ... the swimming text of the *Pontiac Daily Leader* on the library microfilm ... Tazewell's awful recitations of the trial testimony as he hovered over her shoulder —

"I saw enough."

"You know how innocent she was then?"

Marcus's companion maintained her focus on the car down the street, fifty yards at most. They were almost there.

"Bentley was drunk but not Miss Younger. The coroner's report said she barely had any alcohol in her body." His words spilled hard and fast. "She was in the middle of the highway trying to flag down help. Three separate witnesses corroborated that fact alone."

Joanna stretched her neck. Was the red flag up on the parking meter? Her step accelerated. Thirty-five yards, twenty ...

"The Sheriff's evidence proved Bentley ran over her ..."

The sun flashed off the chrome frame of the windshield of Joanna's car. She blinked against the unrelenting light.

"... all that speculation from Bentley's defense about another mystery car hitting her and crossing the Iowa state line to change license plates —"

"She should never have been with him!" Joanna spat. "Never gotten in the damned car."

"She was young —"

"Old enough to know better."

"Perhaps. But she was in such a state at the time —"

"Why do you keep defending her?"

"Why do you judge her so harshly?"

"My father loved her, not me," Joanna fumbled inside her bag for the key as they arrived at her car. "She was no angel."

"Ah, well, she was human after all."

"You were a loyal friend."

"Then why didn't I see her desperation in those last days?" His fading eyes searched hers.

The keychain slipped from Joanna's perspiring fingers. As Marcus bent forward, she blocked his reach.

"I wish I could talk longer." Her face twisted in a sad smile. "I really do need to get back."

Regret, urgent and profound, washed over his face. "Blood runs deep. Deeper than we sometimes understand."

"Goodbye, Mr. Washington. I appreciate your kindness."

He said nothing, simply reached into his pocket to offer his card, then challenged her to reciprocate the favor. "And yours?"

Too weary to deny his request, she fished out a crumpled business card from the inside of her wallet and placed it in his waiting hand.

"Yes." Marcus tucked it inside the tattered lining of his left breast pocket. He cleared his throat. "Godspeed then."

"Yes, you too."

"May I?" He extended his hand.

As she placed her hand in his, Joanna felt the warmth of his touch and, for a moment, imagined hearing the gentle flow of a river current in the distance ...

"Are you leaving now?"

A driver leaned out his car window, angling for a free space.

Joanna pushed the key into the car door and turned away from the old man. Without another word she sped off.

Marcus shielded his eyes from the sun and followed her until all sight was lost.

29

Rooks Creek Bridge

One mile passed. Another. Then another after that. For the first time in these past four decades on earth there appeared to be no immediate destination prompting Joanna Giordano forward. No clients calling for expertise, no place she had to be, no obligation she needed to meet. All the years — truly a lifetime — of pushing, pushing, pushing ... to where? For what? Whipping herself from morning to night to deliver up a humble altar of performance art — always inadequate — to faceless masters who showed no mercy for her spent body or weary spirit. Insanity, thy name is ... insanity.

Joanna laughed out loud. The experience, so unfamiliar for so long, startled her. Then, intrigued by the melody of sound, she laughed again. More mirth spilled forth. Centuries of giddiness released from captivity. The prisoner was escaping, climbing the parapet to freedom. Her eyelids lifted, her breath quickened. Cracking a window for fresh air, she felt a flurry of raindrops. Joanna's foot pressed down on the accelerator. The car seemed to surge forward with a power beyond her control.

In the distance someone walked between the shoulder of the road and a barbed wire fence enclosing a cornfield. Empty now, except for flat colorless husks littering acres of used-up soil. Joanna recalled her mother's warning to avoid hitchhiking strangers at all costs. Rain pelted the windshield in a sudden burst. A vehicle approaching in the opposite direction flashed its headlights. Up ahead the hitchhiker bundled against the elements. A woman? Yes, a woman wearing red shoes.

Lottie.

Joanna reached over to lower the passenger window and called her name. The woman responded with a raised arm, pointing to a diamond-shaped caution marker in front of the wooden bridge just ahead:

DANGEROUS CROSSING

The woman winked, a hooded, yellow-eyed owl wink from a dark forest. Joanna skidded to a stop, spinning into the loose gravel on the flooded embankment. The windshield wipers whooshed and withered, helpless against the downpour as the windows steamed over with Joanna's panting breath. Then, another sound emerged. Something knocking in the wind …

A gate? Yes, surely a gate. Through the passenger window Joanna made out the blurry outlines of a two-story farmhouse dumped at the end of a country lane. At the edge of the property an iron gate swung to and fro. Tappity tap, tappity tap, tappity tap. A woman's knuckles skittered across the driver's window like a playful squirrel on his last chase before a long winter's nap, teasing her to follow.

"Lottie?" Joanna pushed open her car door and got out.

The woman, her back turned, did not reply. She strode toward an old, rusted sign on the other side of the highway. As quickly as the rain dance appeared, it slowed to a tender patter. Only the wind stayed strong. The gate — or something — was still knocking. Joanna followed the red-shoed woman onto the road until she came close enough to decipher the sign's black letters:

ROOKS CREEK BRIDGE

The last raindrops disappeared as the clouds darkened. Night fell fast and with it came a change of seasons. Prairie summer switched places with a brutal winter. Ancient stars peeked through the midnight sky, exposing iced snow drifts on the side of the road.

Joanna blinked, trying to awaken from a hallucinatory dream. Her teeth chattered and her shoulders crunched, helpless to ward off a chill that seared beyond any cold she had ever known.

"Joanna …"

She turned at the sound of a voice she had not heard before.

"Come to me, I will keep you warm." The beautiful girl from an old newspaper photo moved toward her. She wore a grey fox coat and opened her arms to her niece.

Joanna slipped into the embrace. A blood flush surged through her veins. The animal skin enveloped them both.

"I've wanted to meet you forever, did you know that?"

Joanna shook her head.

"It's true," Aldine Younger said with a solemn smile. "Everything I tell you is true. You're my witness, beloved."

Then she pressed her soft dead lips to Joanna's and breathed memory into being …

"Get back into the goddamned car." A bald-headed man stumbled out of the backseat of a 1928 Packard.

"No," the woman wearing the fur coat spat. "You don't own me."

And she kept on walking down the frozen road.

He grabbed her arm from behind and spun her around to face him.

"Who the hell do you think you are?" His speech slurred, his words thick and guttural.

"Get your hands off me."

"That's not the way you used to talk."

"You're drunk."

She pulled away trying to escape. His grip tightened and twisted.

"You made a fool of me in front of my friends."

"You're hurting my wrist."

"That Holloway kid is done with you."

"Hap loves me! He is more of a man than you will ever be —"

His response was quick and sure. His fist slammed against her lovely cheekbone and knocked her to the ground.

"Now look what you made me do. Get the hell up."

She did not answer.

"Stop playing possum, you hear me?"

She did not answer.

He kicked her arm — a drunken half-hearted jab — but she did not answer.

He looked at the crumpled girl in her grey fox coat and swayed on unsteady feet in the silent night. He did not kneel at her side. He did not go for help. He did nothing for a long moment. Then he stared down the empty road and saw no car in sight but his own. He wove a crooked path back to the driver's seat and climbed in, paying no mind to the urine soiling his pants. The key turned at his bidding and the Packard lunged forward …

Joanna, still in her aunt's embrace, watched the car veering toward the spot where they stood. She struggled to cover Aldine, cradling her body with her own, but the form that was once a woman began to dissolve beyond her touch. The face that had been human re-aligned in and out of recognition, finally revealing a portrait of a wistful, cat-eyed child with no mouth. But she must have a mouth because Joanna heard her screaming. Joanna did not realize it was her own voice. Screaming until no sound remained.

~

An unseasonably cold wind chilled Peter's neck as the automatic double doors of the Comfort Inn lobby swung open. Waiting at the check-in counter for the night clerk, his travel valise still in hand, he turned around.

"My God." The sight of the disheveled woman stunned him. "Joanna?"

She stood silent, her eyes expressionless.

He rushed over and clasped her close to his chest, both hearts beating in a fierce new rhythm.

"Darling. I'm here, I'm here. What happened to you?"

He heard her whisper but the words were muffled, their meaning unclear.

"What did you say?"

Joanna clutched him tighter. Her throat still throbbed, raw with grief for the girl who had been lost. Another day, another time, she hoped she could tell him.

Second sight comes with a price. Sometimes the toll road home leads through hell.

Pasadena 1997

A hummingbird dive-bombed into a bed of red abutilon, just missing the head of the gardener turning over soil in anticipation of spring. Joanna, although not the intended target, tensed and ducked. A natural instinct ever since the collision in Illinois. Yet another of the concussion's unanticipated after-affects, according to several doctors that Joanna consulted at her husband's insistence. There were other complications as well. Malaise drifted through her days like a low-grade virus she could not shake. Her once prodigious energy tanked. Joanna's clients were informed that their CPA was cutting back hours for health reasons and referred to other reputable practitioners in the area. Peter counseled the twins not to expect as much from their mother when they came home from college at Thanksgiving. Rest, that's what the family GP ordered, rest and time.

Joanna moved back into the family bedroom after their return from Illinois.

"Thank God the bad dreams are gone," Peter smiled during their first night together in the same bed. "You haven't had any since you came back, have you?"

"No more dreams," Joanna reassured him, spooning closer.

At night she sought solace in her husband's arms. When morning came she found comfort collecting flowers from the family garden. Instead of bunching them together in a vase she arranged individual stems in asymmetrical patterns inspired by an autumn display of Ikebana at the Huntington. Folded leaves, polished stones, beach driftwood cradled in a circle of lemons and thorned roses, tall amaryllis side by side next to a midget maidenhair fern. The family home bloomed with whimsy, providing an invisible order she craved but could not yet access.

There were occasional signs of progress that buoyed hopes for a brighter future. The anniversary dinner when they made plans for next year's getaway to Europe … Joanna's unexpected announcement in the produce aisle at Gelson's that it was time to merge with another CPA firm to share the workload … the news that Sarah earned a spot on the water polo team and Elisabeth won a summer internship in New York … But whenever Peter broached tentative questions about the days before and after her father's death, Joanna became defensive.

If her husband pressed for more details about how the family homestead fire started or where she'd been the night he arrived from the airport, Joanna made her usual swift detour. Her head was hurting again. She needed to go rest. Later she agonized over why she wasn't able to give Peter the answers he deserved. Was it because he might not believe what she experienced? Or that she did not believe it herself?

After Christmas he gently suggested a visit to a psychologist might help ease her headaches and soothe the grief over her father's passing. Joanna kept the first appointment but refused to return for a second. When Peter wanted to know why, his wife quoted the psychologist: "Trauma is a complicated neurological event." Then Joanna kissed her husband, pulled on her gardening gloves and went outside to dig in the dirt. For months she'd been trying to right herself, a boat capsized by a terrible undertow more powerful than her own meager controls. But the only survival was on dry land. She needed the earth beneath her feet.

Birds of paradise were flying and roses exploding in glorious pastel rainbows. Joanna nurtured them all, doting on the baby hibiscus just outside the sunroom. The budded bush was delivered to her doorstep on Valentine's Day, a precious remembrance from her twins. Attached to a small green leafed stalk, the nurseryman's label introduced a new beauty on the block: "Cosmic Dancer." She planted her gift between the fifty-year old fig tree and a waxy giant gardenia that perfumed the summer air come rain or shine. The baby hibiscus took root and produced its second bloom within a few weeks. Trying to coax a third, Joanna was on her knees fertilizing one fine day in early March, when Peter stepped out of the sunroom door carrying a large package wrapped in brown paper.

"It's a package from Illinois."

Joanna stopped digging.

The package sat in his palms, waiting to be received.

"I'll leave it here," Peter placed the package on the sunroom porch and turned to go back inside.

"Peter, wait."

"Yes?"

She hesitated, her throat dry and tight. "Would you bring me a glass of water?"

"Sure thing."

"Thank you." Such a good man, her husband. When there is trust enough, love can be a wondrous thing.

The sun's rays slanted closer as teardrops of sweat seeped into her eyes. Joanna wiped her forehead with the back of her forearm and stood up. Her knees trembled. She turned to face the package. A brood of parrots flew overhead. The Pasadena parrots, they were called by locals, descendants of refugee birds that escaped a pet store generations before. Once caged on display in a Colorado Boulevard storefront, now wild and free. They squawked and screeched and flapped against the spring sky, their native voices no longer accommodating human vanity. Natural law ruled their universe, the rest be damned.

Joanna walked across the stepping stones on the graveled path to the sunroom porch. She picked up the Illinois delivery and carried it inside. Sinking back into the cushions of an old wicker love seat, she held the package a long moment then snipped the corded string with her garden clippers. The brown paper fell away, revealing a double thick cardboard carton, the kind used to mail ruby red Texas grapefruits during the holidays. When she lifted the lid, a different harvest awaited. Underneath the crumple of old newspaper packed to protect the contents, a sealed envelope sat atop a weathered leather journal. The ink-stained scribble, written in a shaky hand, was addressed to Joanna. She stripped off her gardening gloves and pulled out the sheet of ecru stationery:

March 1, 1997

Dear Mrs. Giordano:

It is my great hope that this letter finds you well. Allow me to express my appreciation for our crossed paths during your recent visit.

As I am currently dependent on my caretaker since an unfortunate fall, I thought it best to transfer the enclosed while I am still of sound mind and body.

Shortly before your aunt's untimely death, she gave me her private diary included within for safekeeping. I honored her wish through these many years but now, with my own transition within sight, I must pass the torch so to speak. Miss Younger would take comfort knowing her valued property is in trustworthy hands.

You will find also enclosed a velvet box containing a memento that once belonged to Mrs. Lottie McKeown, the lady mentioned the day of your departure. Just before her sudden passing some years back, Mrs. McKeown dropped by to reminisce about old times and asked that I find a proper home for her keepsake.

These belong to you.

Sincerely,
Marcus Washington, Esq.

Her hand reached for the velvet box first. A gold pendant lay coiled on a satin bed, its violet stone as vibrant as the night Lottie wore it at the Log Cabin. She fingered its delicate clasp.

"Little Lottie," she murmured, returning the pendant to its box and setting it on the table next to her.

As Joanna lifted the cover of the diary and leafed through its pages, a dizzying assortment of words spilled out. The lapis blue ink was fading and the penmanship was a riot of style. Small and precise on one page, a loose uneven scrawl on the next. A journal entry here, a snippet of verse there. Her breath quickened at the sight of the elegant business card clipped to a folded drawing of a young girl's profile. Both were attached to the entry dated April 4, 1928.

THORNTON HERR
Architect

1111 East Green Street	409 Euclid Ave.,
Pasadena, California	Oak Park, Illinois

Thornton Herr. According to the historic preservation office at Pasadena City Hall, that was the name of the architect who designed their home ...

Half-buried beneath blank diary pages still waiting to be used, she saw the corner of an old, faded black-and-white snapshot. Joanna pulled out the photo and stared at the family portrait. A fat-cheeked infant, a prize ribbon attached to his baby gown, was held by a beaming little girl with long curls and pale eyes. Behind her a handsome man with a thick swatch of silvery hair rested his hand on the girl's shoulder. A soft moan of recognition slipped through Joanna's lips.

Her hand shaking, she flipped over the photograph and read the inscription written in a child's hand:

"Junior Morse, the Most Beautiful Baby in Livingston County, me and Papa M. August 8, 1920."

The white-haired man from her dreams was her dad's lost father ...

Outside the sunroom window a drizzle of scarlet-gold leaves drifted from a high branch in the old camphor tree, molting in its perennial rite of spring. Joanna tucked the picture back between the blank pages that had secured it from prying eyes. She was still cradling the portfolio in her lap when Peter entered with a glass of chilled water.

"More papers from your father's lawyer?"

"No. A gift."

"From whom?"

"A girl who died."

As Joanna pulled the amethyst pendant free to fasten around her throat, a wisp of paper hidden beneath the satin lining slipped to the floor. Peter set down the glass and leaned forward to retrieve what had fallen.

"Joanna, you lost something here. It looks like —"

"A poem?"

"I'm not sure."

"Read it to me."

"The handwriting's so small —"

"Please?"

Struck by the urgency in his wife's voice, Peter squinted at the pale ink and began: "The Lady of the River … binds us … together … near and dear as … newborns … embraced … by —"

Peter stopped, unable to decipher the last word.

"Grace," Joanna finished, soft and certain.

"Yes," he looked up in surprise. "How did you know?"

Joanna beckoned her husband closer, making room for Peter on the wicker love seat. Then Joanna handed him the card of Mr. Thornton Herr, the man who built their house.

Now they will both know what came before.

Family Photos

My Aunt Aldine
Age 14

My father, Owen Junior
Age 6

THURSDAY, MARCH 2, 1933.

eiress Found Slain

BODY FOUND IN ROAD AFTER DRINKING PARTY

Suspect Admits Being With Pontiac Belle Before Killing.

Special Dispatch to The Chicago American.

PONTIAC, March 1.— Aldine Yonger, beautiful town belle and clerk in the Pontiac Candy Shoppe, was found dead early this morning on a gravel road two miles outside of here. Her skull was fractured.

Within an hour after the finding of the body, Sheriff George Heckman arrested Amere Earl Bentley, member of one of the oldest families in this community.

Bentley, 26, and married to one of the younger social leaders of the city, admitted to Sheriff Heckman that he had been with the girl, but claimed that he did not remember any of the events that transpired during the evening.

HAD SEVERAL DRINKS.

Bentley told officials that he had taken Miss Yonger to a road house and had several drinks and that some time after midnight they had gone to the Log Cabin barbecue stand for a sandwich.

Attendants at the barbecue stand told the sheriff that the couple had left there about 1 o'clock this morning.

At 1:30 this morning John Smith, Cletus Wildhaber and his sister, Bessie, were returning from a

C HEIRESS FOUND SLAIN ON ROADSIDE.

Younger, 20, found with fractured skull near ... Earle Bentley, son of former mayor, is

A coroner's inquest will be held tonight at 8 o'clock, and officials here have sent for Dr. William D. McNally of Chicago to perform the autopsy...

Aldine Younger

CHICAGO-AMERICAN
March 2, 1933

Obituaries

Asher Bentley, age 62 years, died of mesenteric thrombosis on July 13, 1956. His 1952 Ford sedan was valued at $1400 by his widow, his only surviving family.

Herbert Powell, age 77 years, was killed in an auto collision on September 18, 1940. According to public records his family listed "farm management" under occupation on the death certificate. He died in debt with $2300 owed on an advance of his life insurance policy. His body was interred in Graceland cemetery near the resting place of Aldine Younger.

Frederick Heinemann, age 87, died of complications from old age and hardening of the arteries on March 27, 1963. The estate was valued in excess of $107,000. In 1972 his property, originally owned by his father-in-law, William Younger, and later partially owned by his niece, Aldine Younger, was awarded a Centennial Farm certificate of honor by the Governor of Illinois for the distinction of being under one family's control for over a hundred years. His descendants continue to own the farm and work the land to this day. The share of acreage bequeathed to Aldine Younger as a child is estimated to be worth over $1,000,000.

Family Trees

DESCENDANT CHART FOR
WILLIAM P. YOUNGER

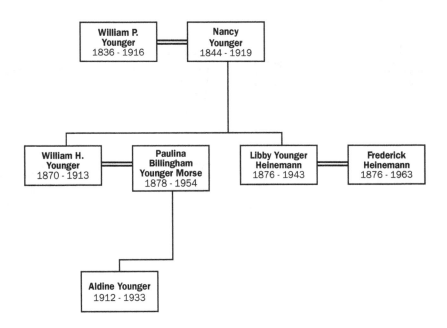

DESCENDANT CHART FOR
WILLIAM PHILLIP HEINEMANN

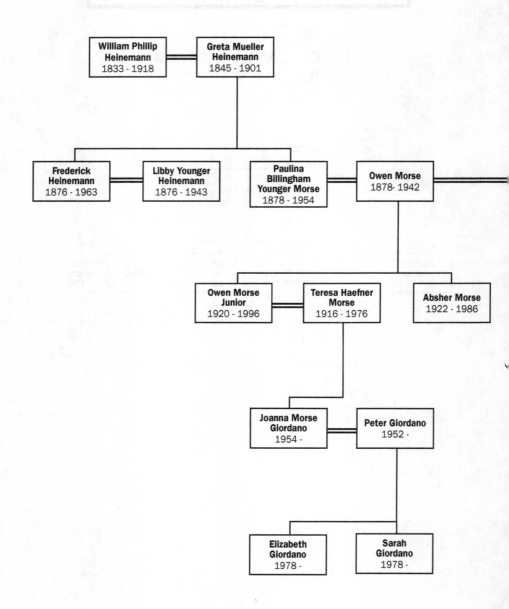

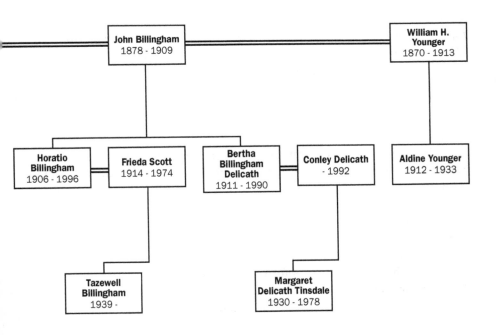

Author's Statement

My aunt, Aldine Younger, bequeathed a tragic legacy that has left its mark on three generations of our family.

This book was inspired by oral histories, clarified through personal interviews and documented with extensive research. The central characters are based on real people. Certain names are taken from historical public records. Others have been changed to protect the privacy of those who assisted in my mission to understand the circumstances that led to my aunt's killing.

My resources included the newspapers that covered the arrest and trial of Asher Bentley: the *Chicago-American*, the *Chicago Daily Times*, the *Pontiac Daily Leader*, and the *Fairbury Blade*, as well as the 1933–1935 trial transcripts from the Illinois Supreme Court overturning the manslaughter conviction of Asher Bentley and the embezzlement conviction of Herbert Powell. The discovery of family legal documents filed with my grandmother's personal correspondence and accounting ledgers in the law office of her former attorney was invaluable in understanding the labyrinthine court proceedings that dominated my aunt's life from her childhood until her death.

When my father and I returned to Illinois in 1996 to make my first inquiries into my aunt's past, I was astonished to learn that over six decades after her death, her name was known, the "accident" remembered. A number of individuals were happy, even eager, to share their memories. Others, put off by lingering distaste for roadhouse scandal, declined to offer any assistance. Aldine Younger was still stirring up strong public opinion in her hometown.

For all the factual evidence and lively recollections that fueled my journey, I knew that the "true" story of Aldine Younger could only be accessed through the liberating power of fiction. Like all novels this one is a potpourri of experience, metaphor, and hard-earned insight. Characters are composites, relationships embellished, drama heightened, and many scenes entirely the work of this writer's imagination.

Subjects choose us as much as we choose them. The ghosts of my father's tribe dined at our family table every night of my childhood, like it or not. In a sense I grew up with Aunt Aldine. But I believe all ghosts, within and without, long to be released. For any child-woman wrenched from a place of safety and belonging before she is fully grown, there comes a time to transcend the past. To make peace with who they were and what they can now become. I wish that for Aldine.

I wish that for all lost daughters.

Acknowledgments

This book has been a labor of love started, paused and begun again over two decades.

I am grateful to the following for their assistance and encouragement as I completed my story.

FAMILY

Michael, my devoted husband, extraordinary partner, fellow seeker and intrepid co-investigator in uncovering the crimes of the past. His generosity of spirit has blessed me beyond measure.

Brigit and Patrick, our amazing, beautiful children. Their loving faith and pride in my writer's journey keep me on the high path.

My father, Owen, my mother, Teresa, and maternal grandmother, Georgia, whose love, resilience, and courage in the face of hardship continue to inspire me every day of my life.

Uncle Absher and Aunt Betty ~ Cousins Jon and Norma; each one a truthteller that helped shine light on our shared ancestral roots.

Sandi Duncan, spiritual sister, researcher, trusted beta reader.

THE WITNESSES AND RECORD KEEPERS OF LIVINGSTON COUNTY, ILLINOIS

They provided invaluable connections and opened doors of silence that had been locked for six decades.

Wayne Decker, my father's dearest childhood friend ~ Jerry Duffy ~ Laraine Meyers ~ Mary Seloti O'Brien ~ Anna Schlipf ~ Peg Spalding ~ Leona Sutter ~ Thomas Herr Esq. ~ Hubert "Ruby" Boswell

LITERARY PATHFINDERS

At key moments these colleagues gave me the guidance I needed to risk more, dig deeper, and direct my creative vision to a larger canvas.

Sonja Bolle
Jeffrey Deaver
Rachel Howzell Hall
David Isaacs
Janet Leahy
Joanne Leedom-Ackerman
Aimee Liu
Heidi Rose Robbins
Howard Rodman
Cody Sisko
Doug Stanton and Anne Stanton
Jennifer Rudolph Walsh
Matt Wise

MY OUTSTANDING PUBLISHING TEAM

Kim Dower, gifted poet, brilliant publicist, guru-in-action
Maddee James, website maven par excellence

MISSION POINT PRESS STALWARTS

Editor Tanya Muzumdar
Designer Jen Wahi
Copy Editor Hart Cauchy
Proofreader Darlene Short
Marketing: Chris Johns ~ Geoff Affleck ~ Tricia Frey ~ Katryna Deligiannis
And
Doug Weaver, the man who made it happen

About the Author

Georgia Jeffries is a writer of Emmy Award-winning drama and acclaimed noir fiction.

Honored with multiple Writers Guild Awards, Golden Globes, and the Humanitas Prize, her work in film has been praised by the *Los Angeles Times* as "standing ovation television."

Born in the Illinois heartland, she worked as a journalist for *American Film* before writing and producing the groundbreaking female-driven series, *Cagney & Lacey, China Beach*, and *Sisters*. Her screenwriting career has been distinguished by extensive field research, from patrolling the mean streets of Rampart with the LAPD to crashing a Vegas bounty hunters' convention to reporting from a Walter Reed Army Hospital surgical bay. Each investigation was the basis for one of her many docudramas and series pilots for CBS, ABC, NBC, HBO, and Showtime.

Her short stories have appeared in national suspense anthologies, including Mystery Writers of America's *Odd Partners* and Sisters in Crime's *The Last Resort*. She has also written biography and historical profiles for *HuffPost, Los Angeles Review of Books,* and University of California Press.

A cum laude UCLA graduate, Jeffries is a professor at the USC School of Cinematic Arts, where she created the first BFA Television Thesis program at an American university.

You can find Georgia Jeffries online at: georgiajeffries.com

Printed in the USA
CPSIA information can be obtained
at www.ICGtesting.com
LVHW092051101024
793249LV00007B/259/J

9 781961 302600